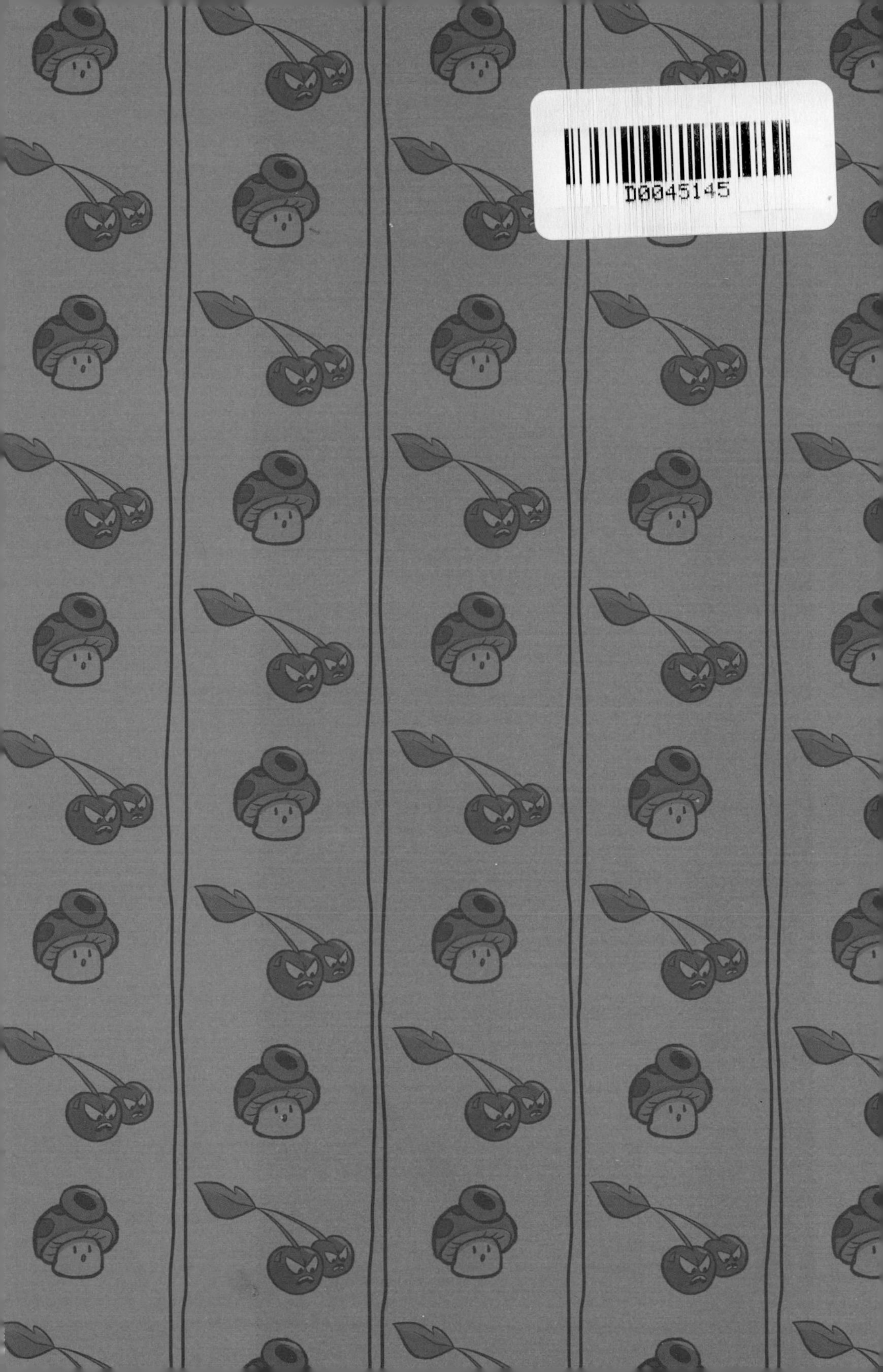

PLANTS VS. ZOMBIES™

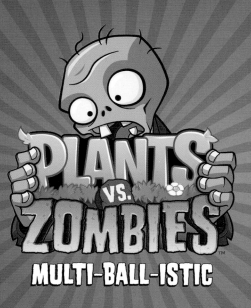

MULTI-BALL-ISTIC

Written by PAUL TOBIN

Art by CHRISTIANNE GILLENARDO-GOUDREAU

Colors by HEATHER BRECKEL

Letters by STEVE DUTRO

Cover by CHRISTIANNE GILLENARDO-GOUDREAU

DARK HORSE BOOKS

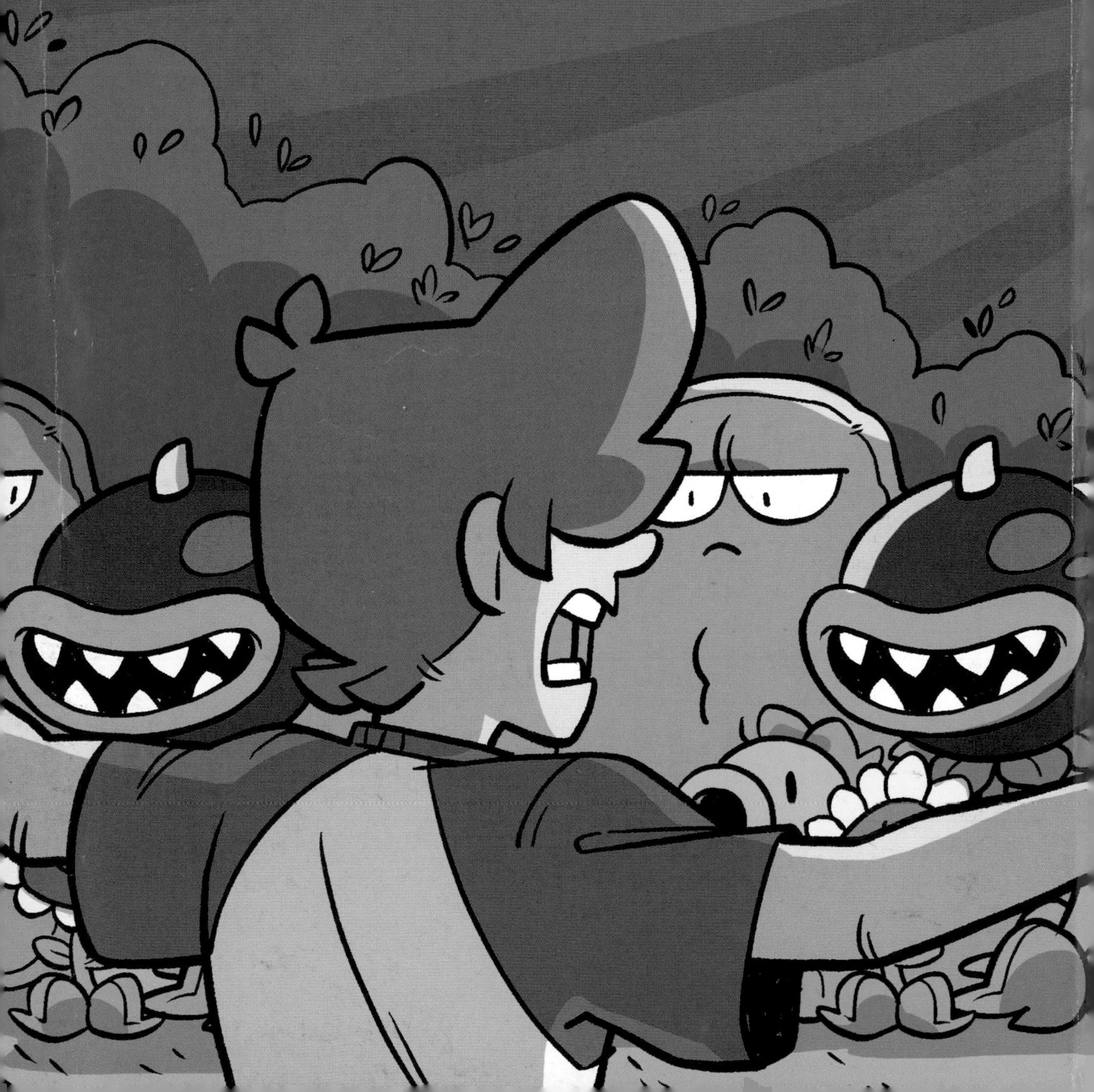

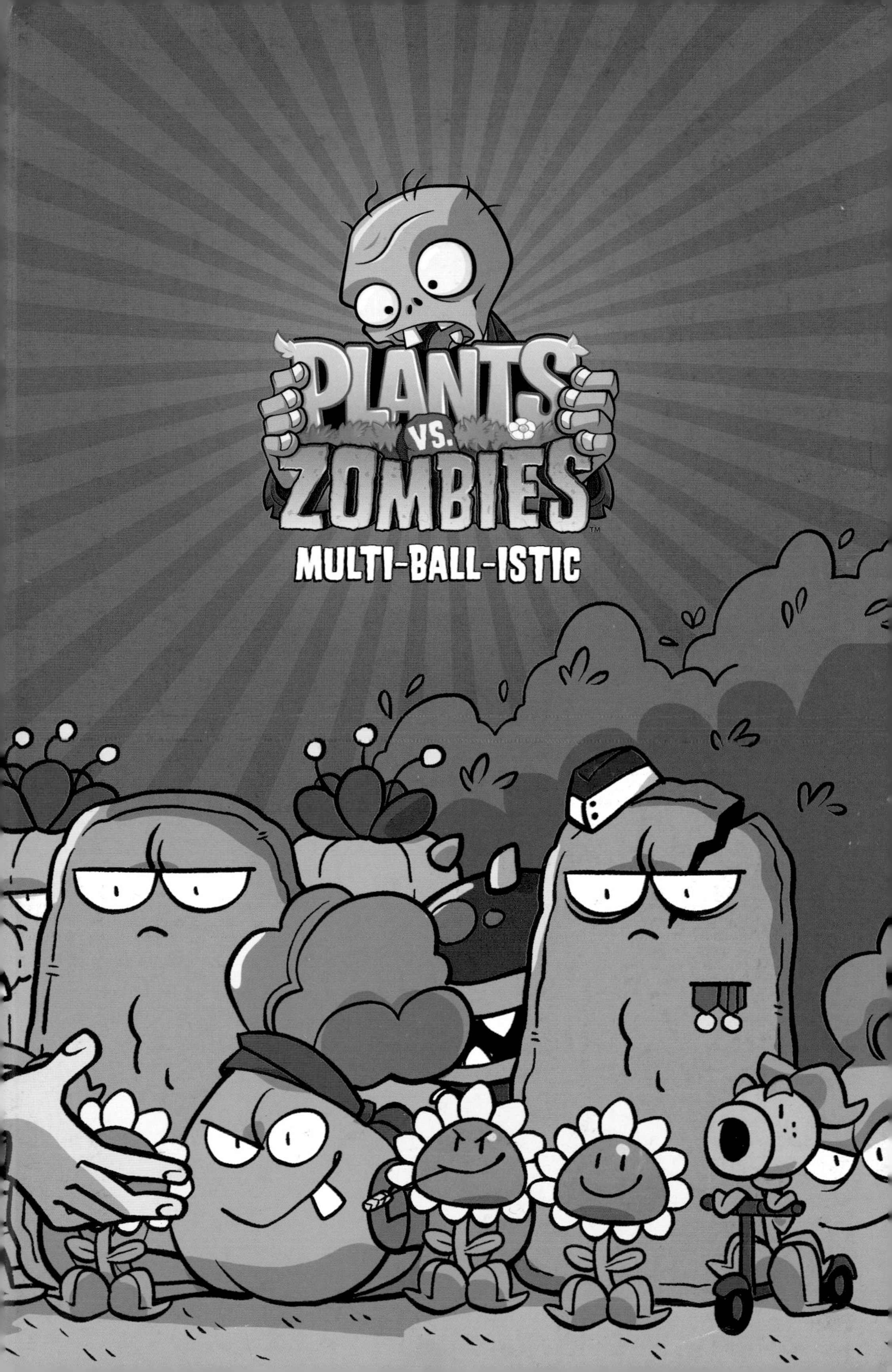
PLANTS VS. ZOMBIES
MULTI-BALL-ISTIC

President and Publisher **MIKE RICHARDSON**
Senior Editor **PHILIP R. SIMON**
Assistant Editor **JOSHUA ENGLEDOW**
Designer **BRENNAN THOME**
Digital Art Technician **ALLYSON HALLER**

Special thanks to Kristen Star, Joshua Franks, Jessica Leung,
and everyone at PopCap Games and EA Games.

First Edition: December 2020
Ebook ISBN 978-1-50671-316-8
Hardcover ISBN 978-1-50671-307-6

1 2 3 4 5 6 7 8 9 10
Printed in China

DarkHorse.com
PopCap.com

▷ No plants were harmed in the making of this graphic novel or the making of our Neighborville-sized test pinball machine.

Library of Congress Cataloging-in-Publication Data

Names: Tobin, Paul, writer. | Gillenardo-Goudreau, Christianne, artist. |
    Breckel, Heather, colourist. | Dutro, Steve, letterer.
Title: Multi-ball-istic / written by Paul Tobin ; art by Christianne
    Gillenardo-Goudreau ; colors by Heather Breckel ; letters by Steve
    Dutro.
Description: Milwaukie, OR : Dark Horse Books, [2020] | Series: Plants vs.
    Zombies vol. 17 | Audience: Ages 8+ | Audience: Grades 4-6 | Summary:

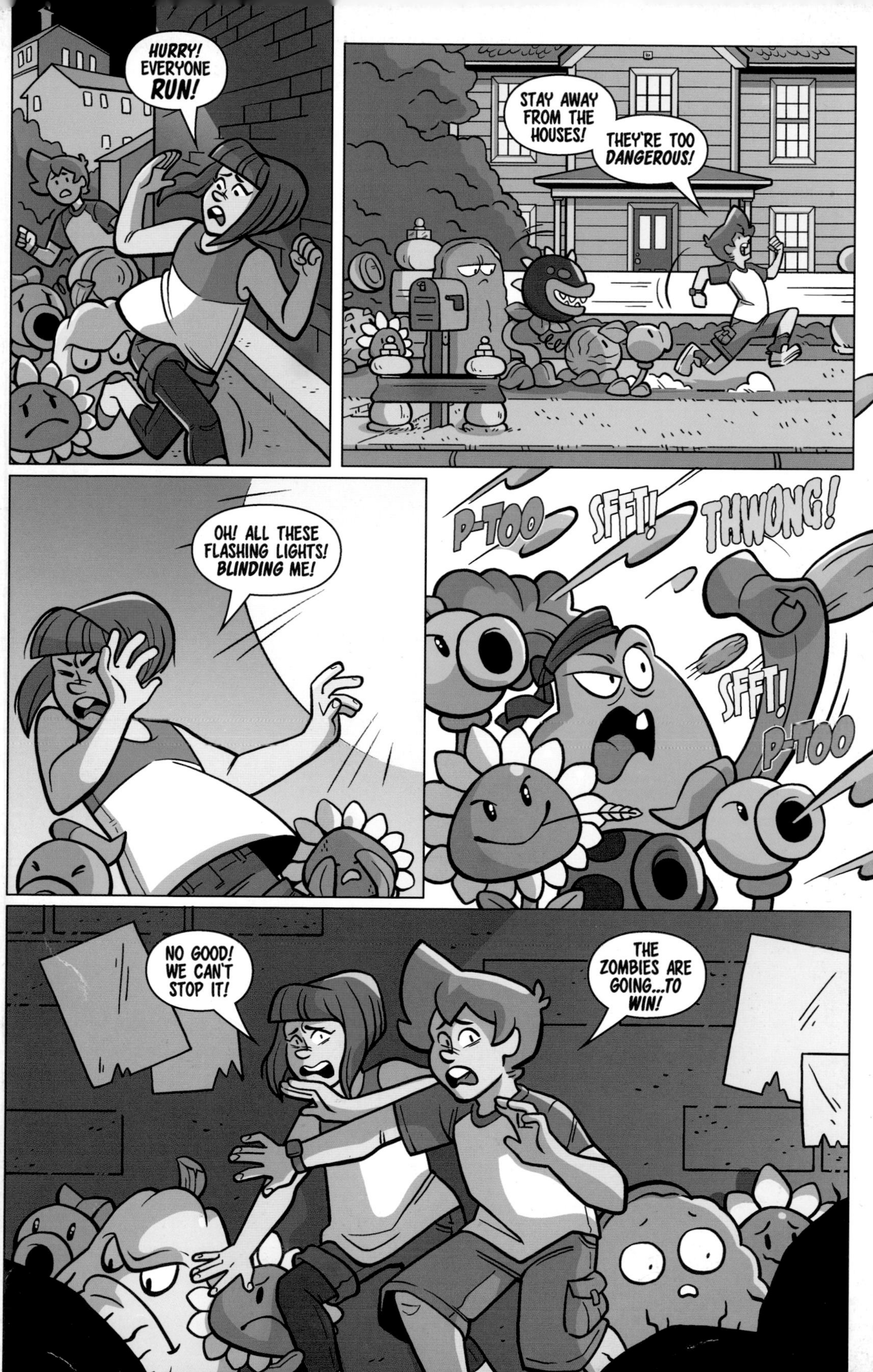
HURRY! EVERYONE RUN!
STAY AWAY FROM THE HOUSES!
THEY'RE TOO DANGEROUS!
OH! ALL THESE FLASHING LIGHTS! BLINDING ME!
P-TOO
SFFT!
THWONG!
SFFT!
P-TOO
NO GOOD! WE CAN'T STOP IT!
THE ZOMBIES ARE GOING...TO WIN!

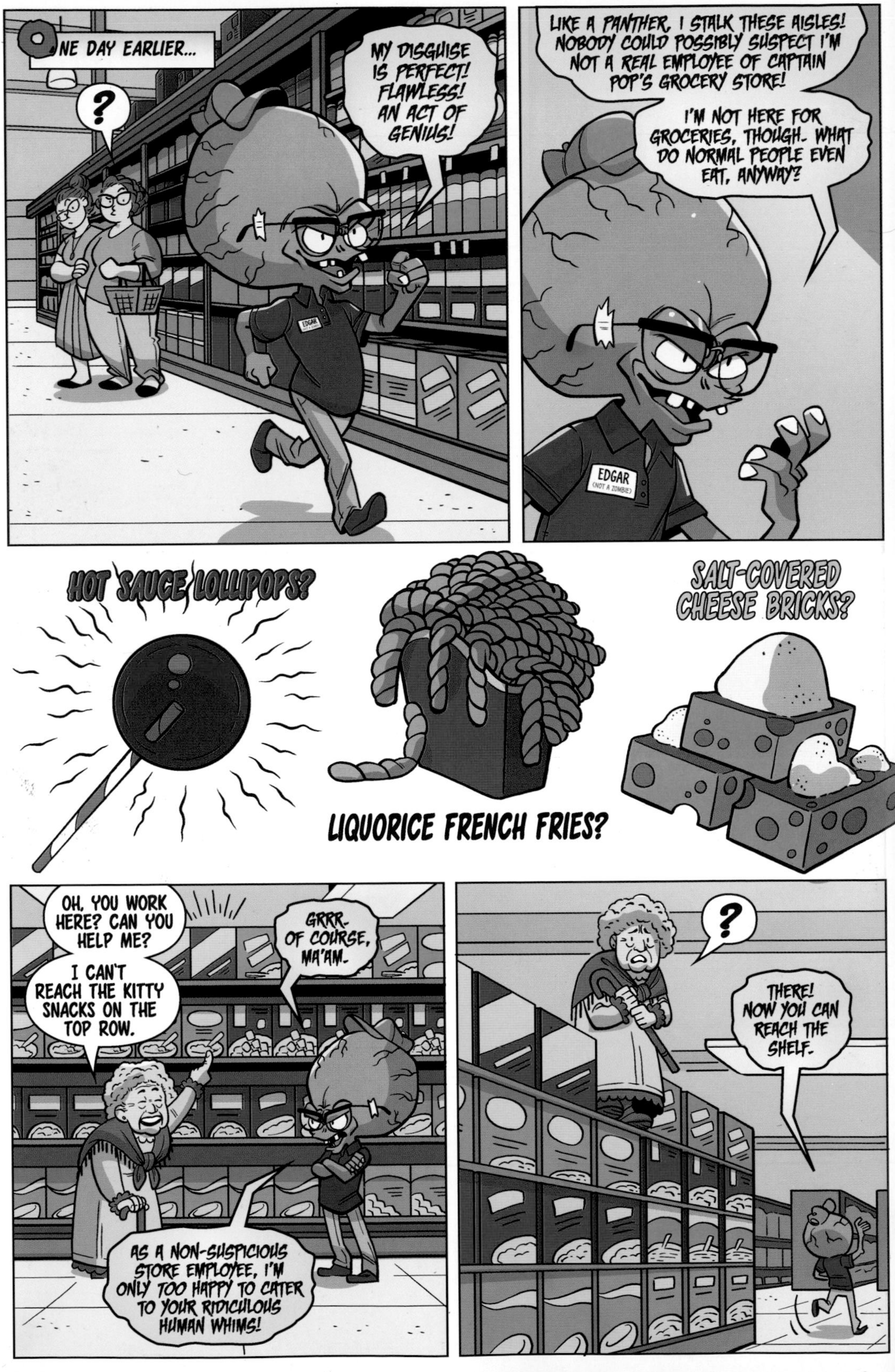
ONE DAY EARLIER...
?
MY DISGUISE IS PERFECT! FLAWLESS! AN ACT OF GENIUS!
EDGAR
LIKE A PANTHER, I STALK THESE AISLES! NOBODY COULD POSSIBLY SUSPECT I'M NOT A REAL EMPLOYEE OF CAPTAIN POP'S GROCERY STORE!
I'M NOT HERE FOR GROCERIES, THOUGH. WHAT DO NORMAL PEOPLE EVEN EAT, ANYWAY?
EDGAR (NOT A ZOMBIE)
HOT SAUCE LOLLIPOPS?
LIQUORICE FRENCH FRIES?
SALT-COVERED CHEESE BRICKS?
OH, YOU WORK HERE? CAN YOU HELP ME?
I CAN'T REACH THE KITTY SNACKS ON THE TOP ROW.
GRRR. OF COURSE, MA'AM.
AS A NON-SUSPICIOUS STORE EMPLOYEE, I'M ONLY TOO HAPPY TO CATER TO YOUR RIDICULOUS HUMAN WHIMS!
?
THERE! NOW YOU CAN REACH THE SHELF.

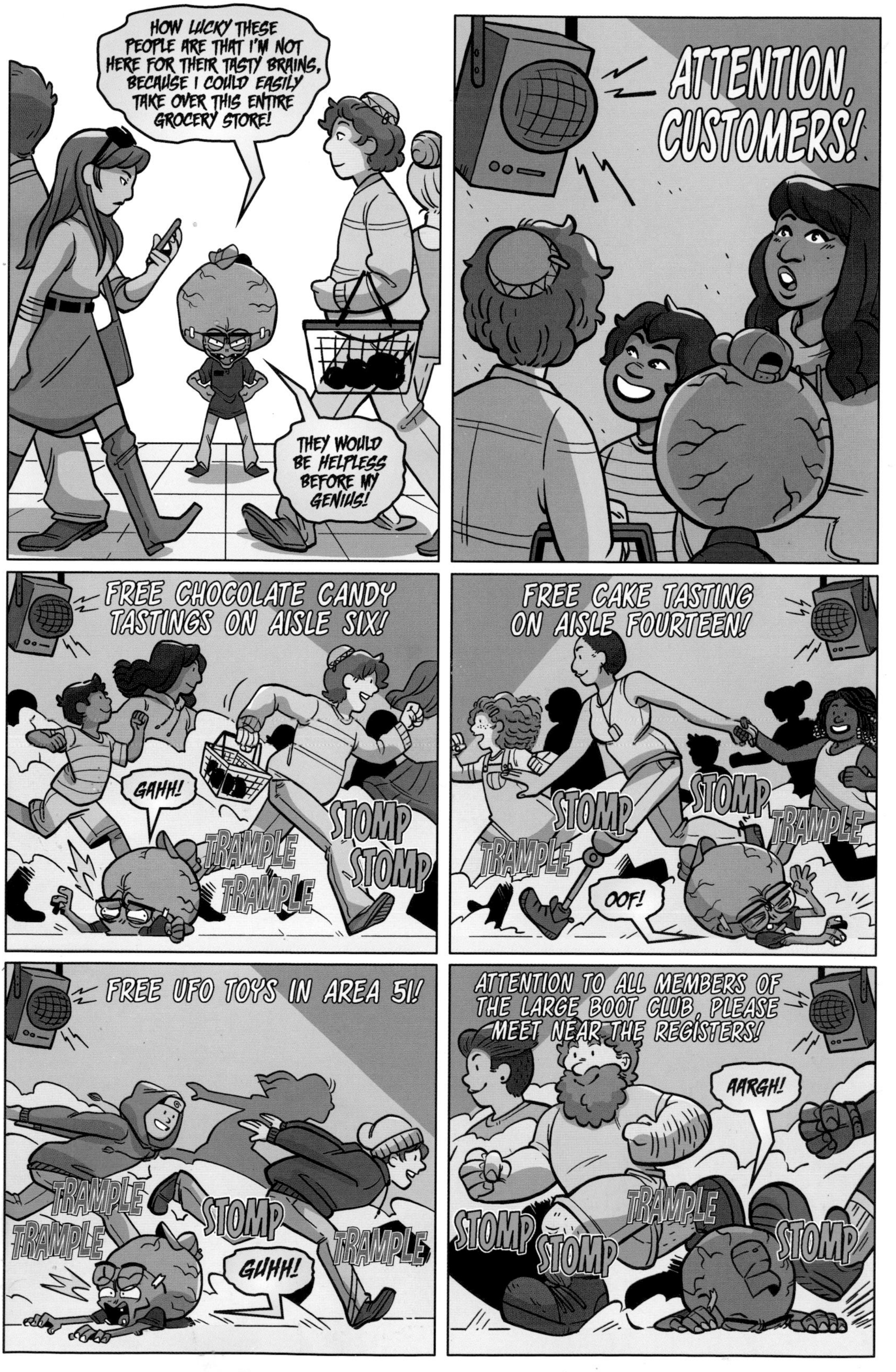
HOW LUCKY THESE PEOPLE ARE THAT I'M NOT HERE FOR THEIR TASTY BRAINS, BECAUSE I COULD EASILY TAKE OVER THIS ENTIRE GROCERY STORE!
THEY WOULD BE HELPLESS BEFORE MY GENIUS!
ATTENTION, CUSTOMERS!
FREE CHOCOLATE CANDY TASTINGS ON AISLE SIX!
GAHH!
STOMP
TRAMPLE
STOMP
TRAMPLE
FREE CAKE TASTING ON AISLE FOURTEEN!
STOMP
STOMP
TRAMPLE
TRAMPLE
OOF!
FREE UFO TOYS IN AREA 51!
TRAMPLE
TRAMPLE
STOMP
TRAMPLE
GUHH!
ATTENTION TO ALL MEMBERS OF THE LARGE BOOT CLUB, PLEASE MEET NEAR THE REGISTERS!
AARGH!
TRAMPLE
STOMP
STOMP
STOMP

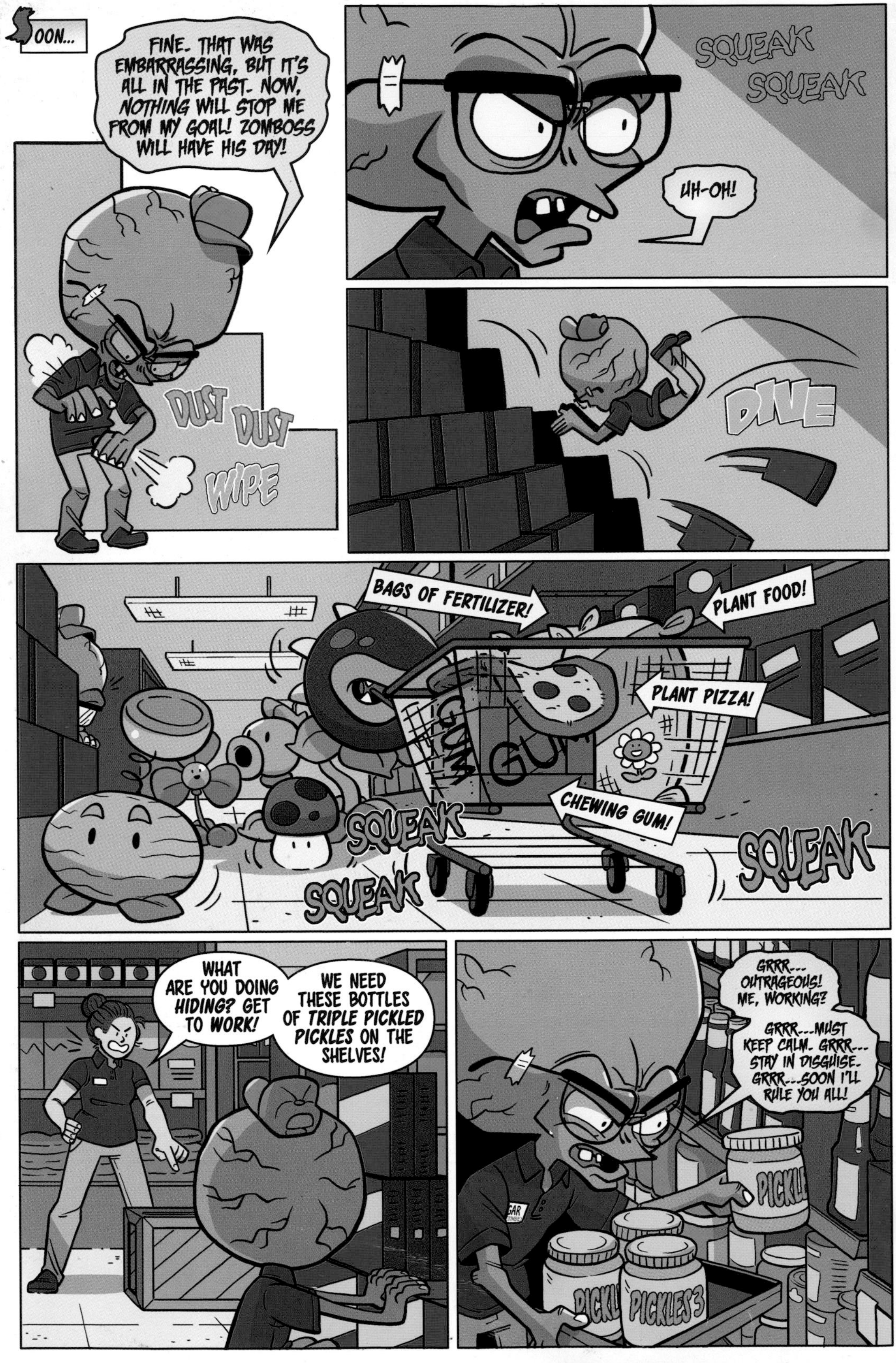
SOON...
FINE. THAT WAS EMBARRASSING, BUT IT'S ALL IN THE PAST. NOW, NOTHING WILL STOP ME FROM MY GOAL! ZOMBOSS WILL HAVE HIS DAY!
DUST DUST
WIPE
SQUEAK SQUEAK
UH-OH!
DIVE
BAGS OF FERTILIZER!
PLANT FOOD!
PLANT PIZZA!
GUM GUM
CHEWING GUM!
SQUEAK
SQUEAK
SQUEAK
WHAT ARE YOU DOING HIDING? GET TO WORK!
WE NEED THESE BOTTLES OF TRIPLE PICKLED PICKLES ON THE SHELVES!
GRRR... OUTRAGEOUS! ME, WORKING?
GRRR...MUST KEEP CALM. GRRR... STAY IN DISGUISE. GRRR...SOON I'LL RULE YOU ALL!
PICKLES3

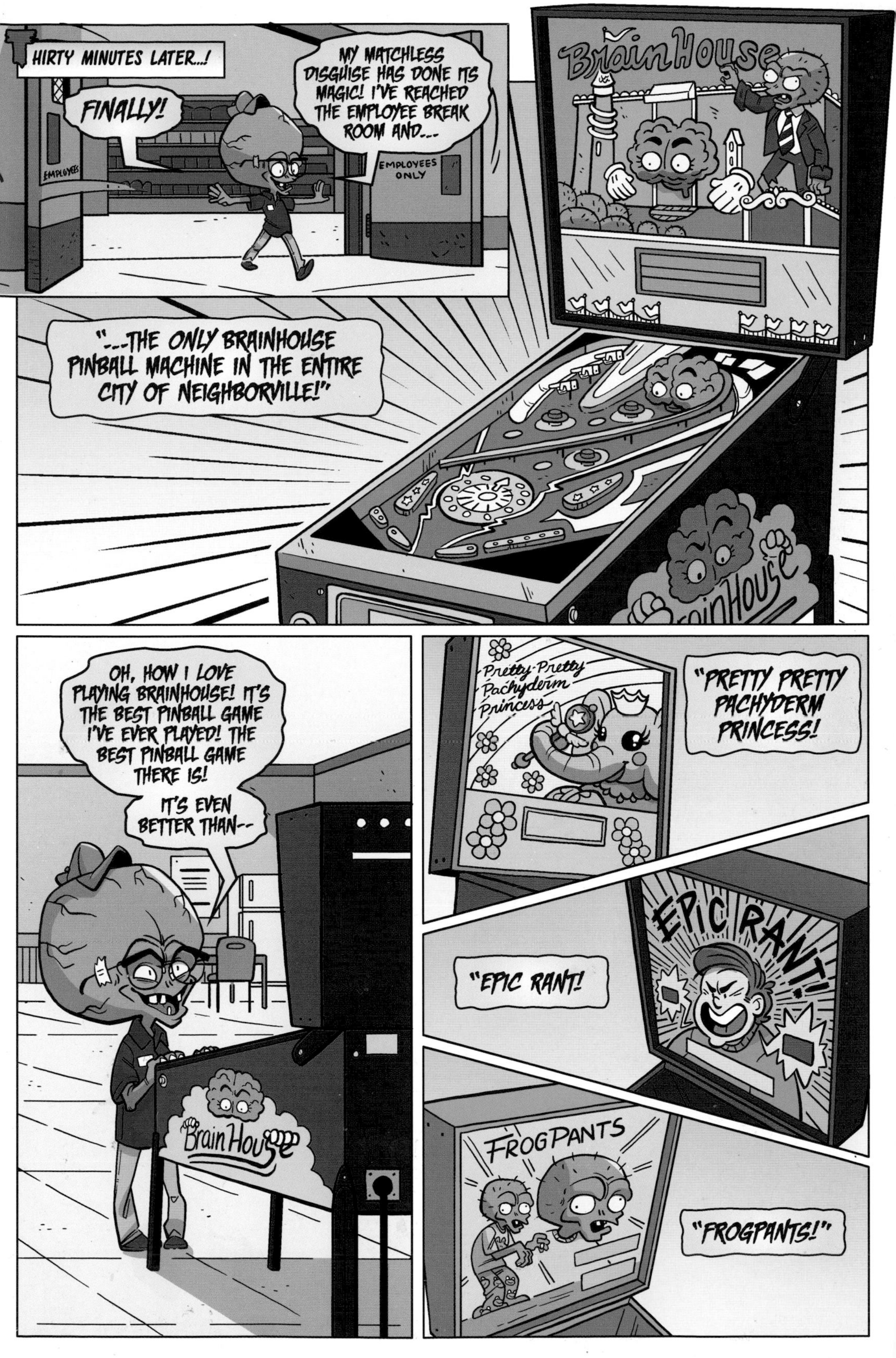
THIRTY MINUTES LATER...!
EMPLOYEES
FINALLY!
MY MATCHLESS DISGUISE HAS DONE ITS MAGIC! I'VE REACHED THE EMPLOYEE BREAK ROOM AND...
EMPLOYEES ONLY
BrainHouse
"...THE ONLY BRAINHOUSE PINBALL MACHINE IN THE ENTIRE CITY OF NEIGHBORVILLE!"
OH, HOW I LOVE PLAYING BRAINHOUSE! IT'S THE BEST PINBALL GAME I'VE EVER PLAYED! THE BEST PINBALL GAME THERE IS!
IT'S EVEN BETTER THAN--
BrainHouse
Pretty Pretty Pachyderm Princess
"PRETTY PRETTY PACHYDERM PRINCESS!
"EPIC RANT!
EPIC RANT!
FROGPANTS
"FROGPANTS!"

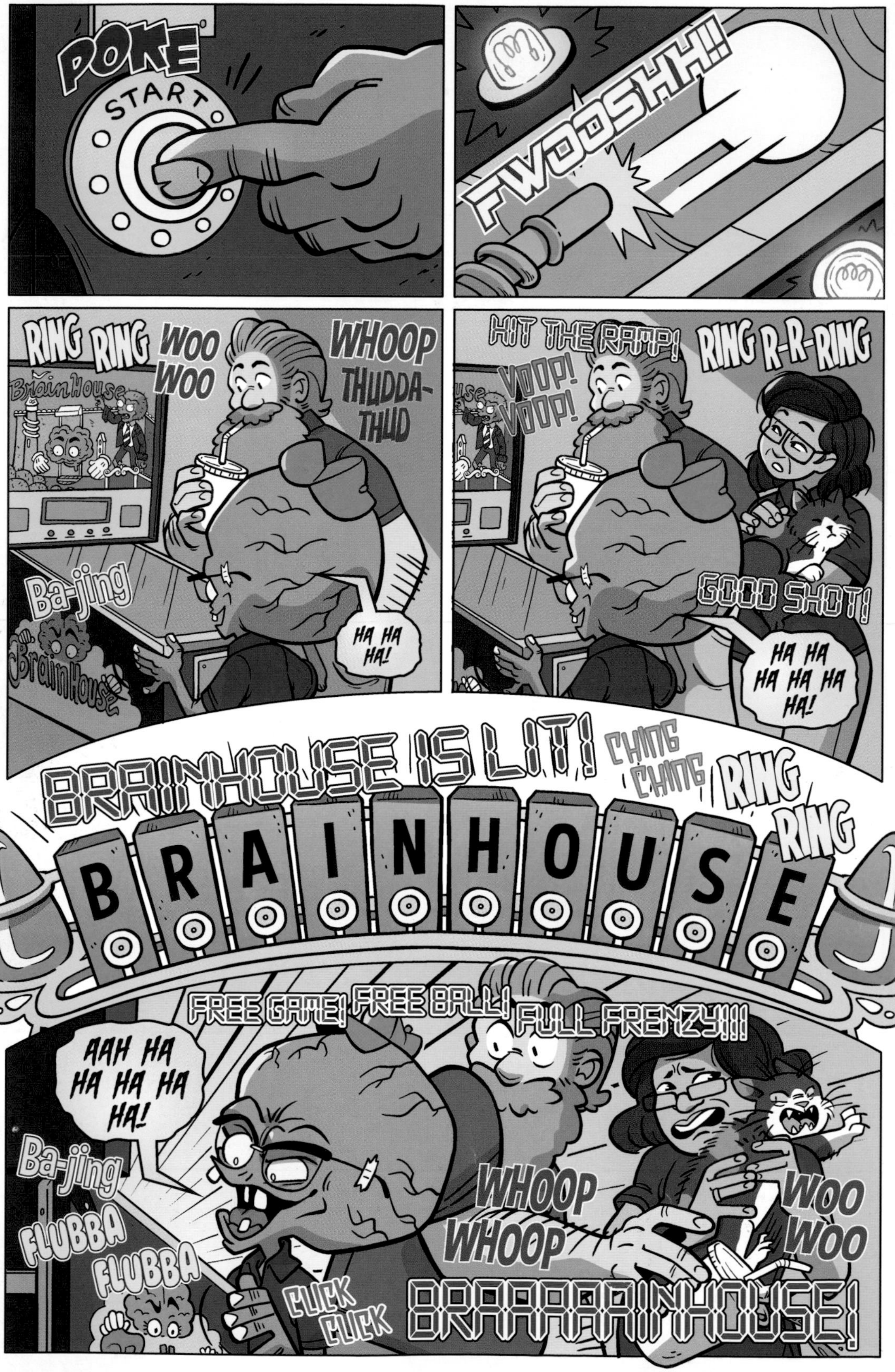
POKE
START
FWOOSHH!!
RING RING
WOO WOO
WHOOP
THUDDA-THUD
BrainHouse
Ba-jing
BrainHouse
HA HA HA!
HIT THE RAMP!
RING R-R-RING
VOOP! VOOP!
GOOD SHOT!
HA HA HA HA HA HA!
BRAINHOUSE IS LIT!
CHING CHING
RING RING
BRAINHOUSE
FREE GAME! FREE BALL! FULL FRENZY!!!
AAH HA HA HA HA HA!
Ba-jing
FLUBBA FLUBBA
WHOOP WHOOP
WOO WOO
CLICK CLICK
BRAAAAAINHOUSE!

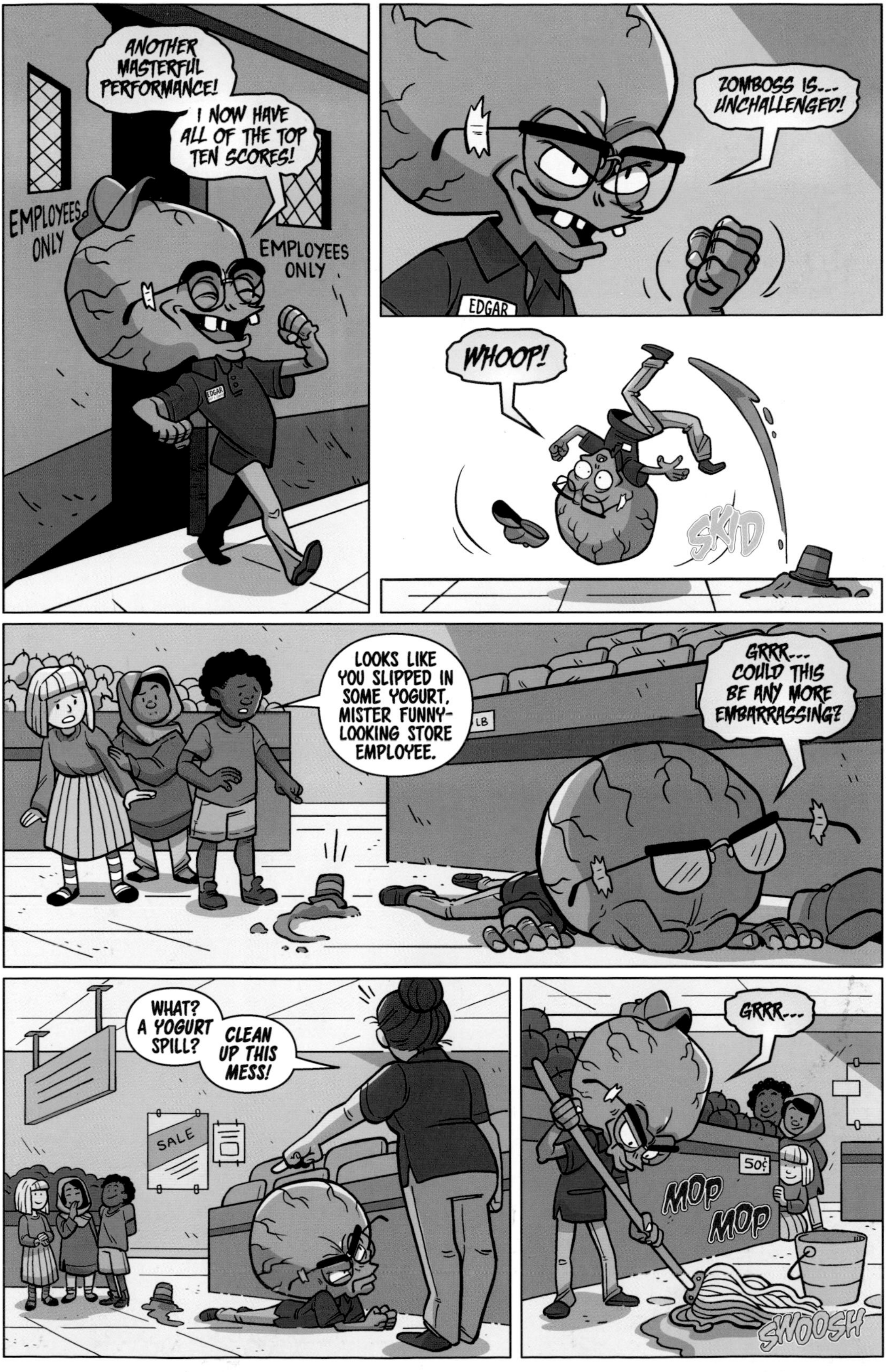
ANOTHER MASTERFUL PERFORMANCE!
I NOW HAVE ALL OF THE TOP TEN SCORES!
EMPLOYEES ONLY
EMPLOYEES ONLY
EDGAR
ZOMBOSS IS... UNCHALLENGED!
EDGAR
WHOOP!
SKID
LOOKS LIKE YOU SLIPPED IN SOME YOGURT, MISTER FUNNY-LOOKING STORE EMPLOYEE.
GRRR... COULD THIS BE ANY MORE EMBARRASSING?
LB
WHAT? A YOGURT SPILL?
CLEAN UP THIS MESS!
SALE
GRRR...
50¢
MOP
MOP
SWOOSH

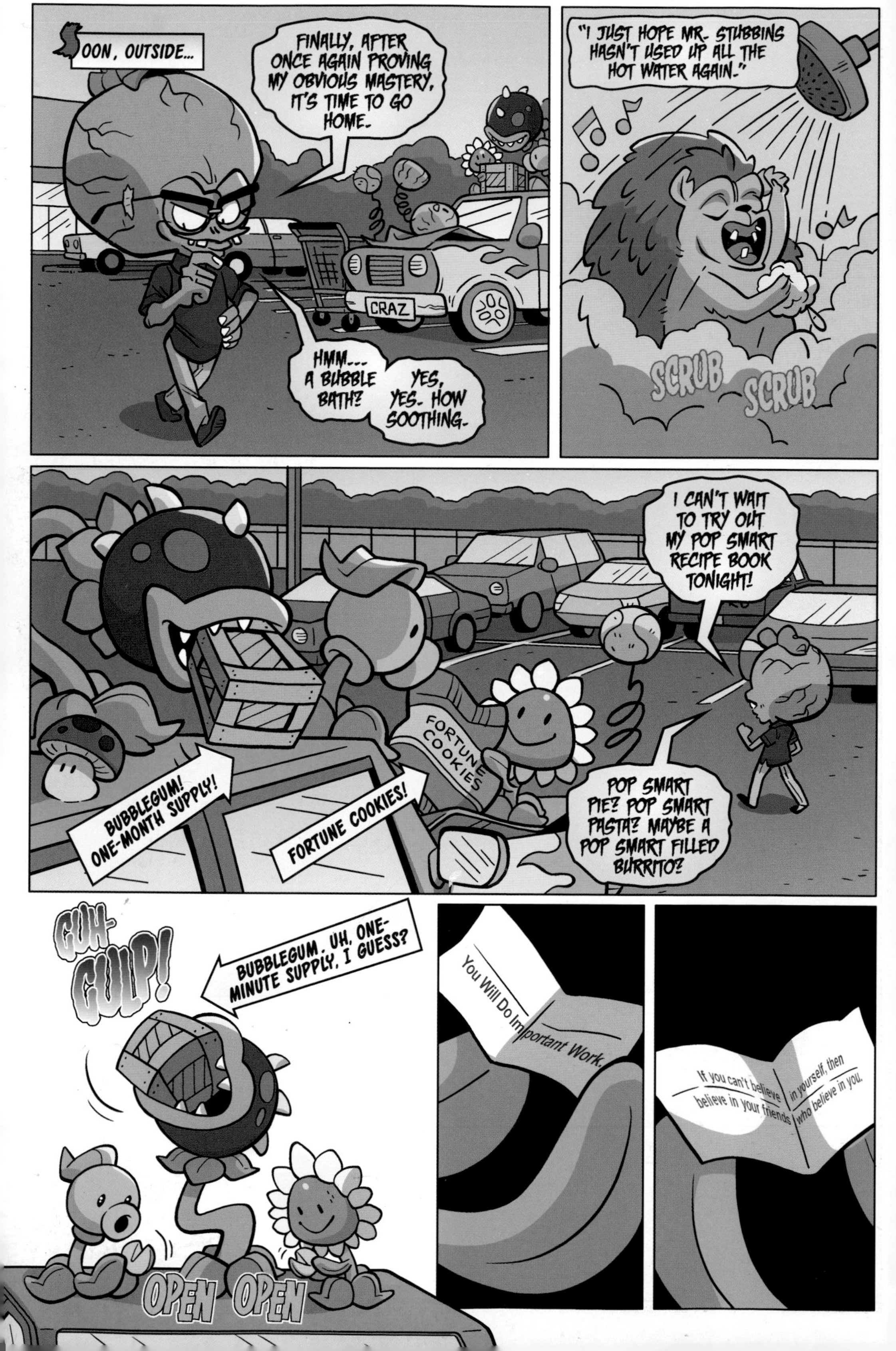
SOON, OUTSIDE...
FINALLY, AFTER ONCE AGAIN PROVING MY OBVIOUS MASTERY, IT'S TIME TO GO HOME.
CRAZ
HMM... A BUBBLE BATH?
YES, YES. HOW SOOTHING.
"I JUST HOPE MR. STUBBINS HASN'T USED UP ALL THE HOT WATER AGAIN."
SCRUB
SCRUB
I CAN'T WAIT TO TRY OUT MY POP SMART RECIPE BOOK TONIGHT!
FORTUNE COOKIES
BUBBLEGUM! ONE-MONTH SUPPLY!
FORTUNE COOKIES!
POP SMART PIE? POP SMART PASTA? MAYBE A POP SMART FILLED BURRITO?
GUH-GULP!
BUBBLEGUM. UH, ONE-MINUTE SUPPLY, I GUESS?
OPEN
OPEN
You Will Do Important Work.
If you can't believe in yourself, then believe in your friends who believe in you.

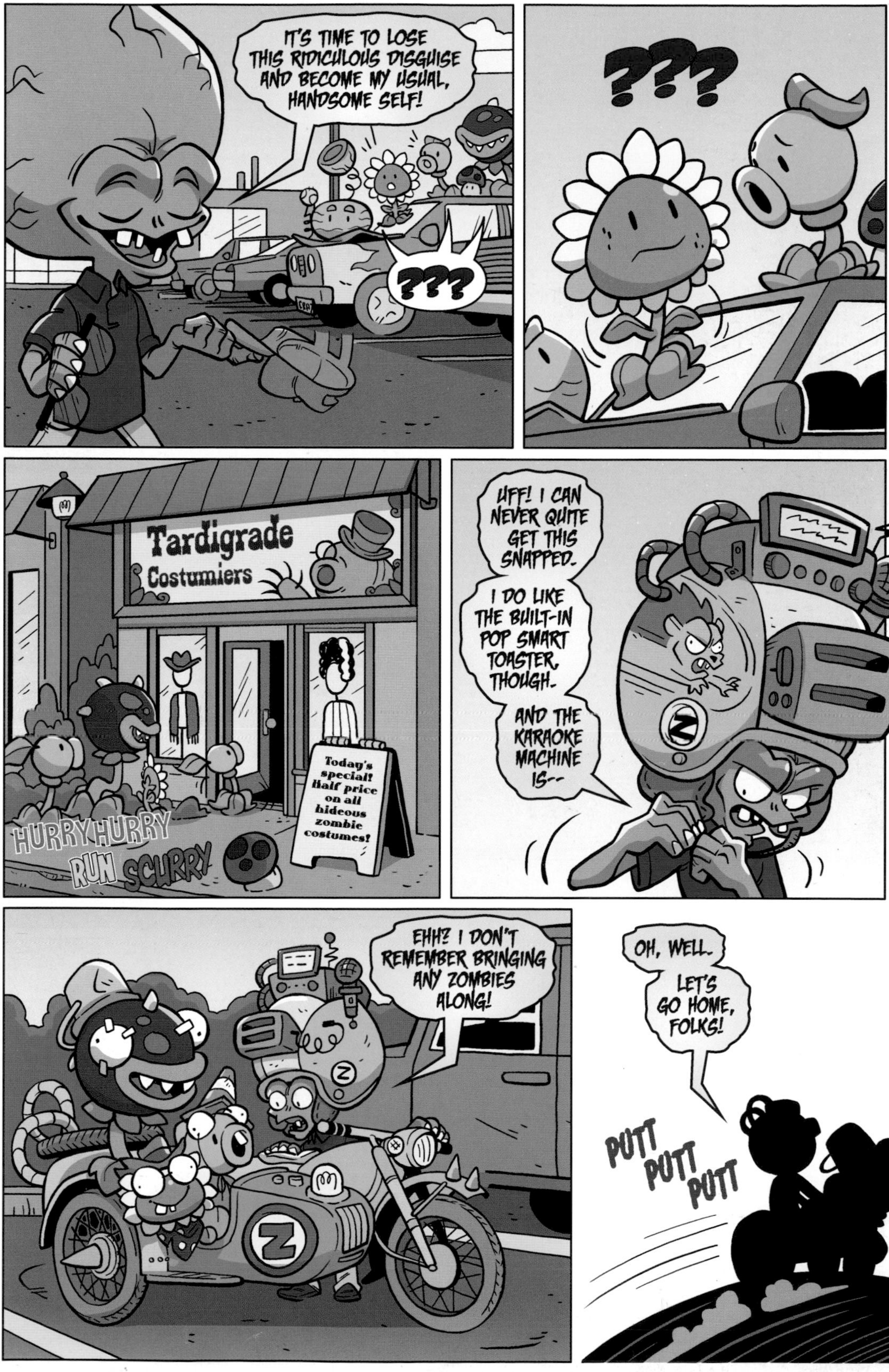

IT'S TIME TO LOSE THIS RIDICULOUS DISGUISE AND BECOME MY USUAL, HANDSOME SELF!
???
???
Tardigrade Costumiers
Today's special! Half price on all hideous zombie costumes!
HURRY HURRY RUN SCURRY
UFF! I CAN NEVER QUITE GET THIS SNAPPED.
I DO LIKE THE BUILT-IN POP SMART TOASTER, THOUGH.
AND THE KARAOKE MACHINE IS--
EHH? I DON'T REMEMBER BRINGING ANY ZOMBIES ALONG!
OH, WELL.
LET'S GO HOME, FOLKS!
PUTT PUTT PUTT

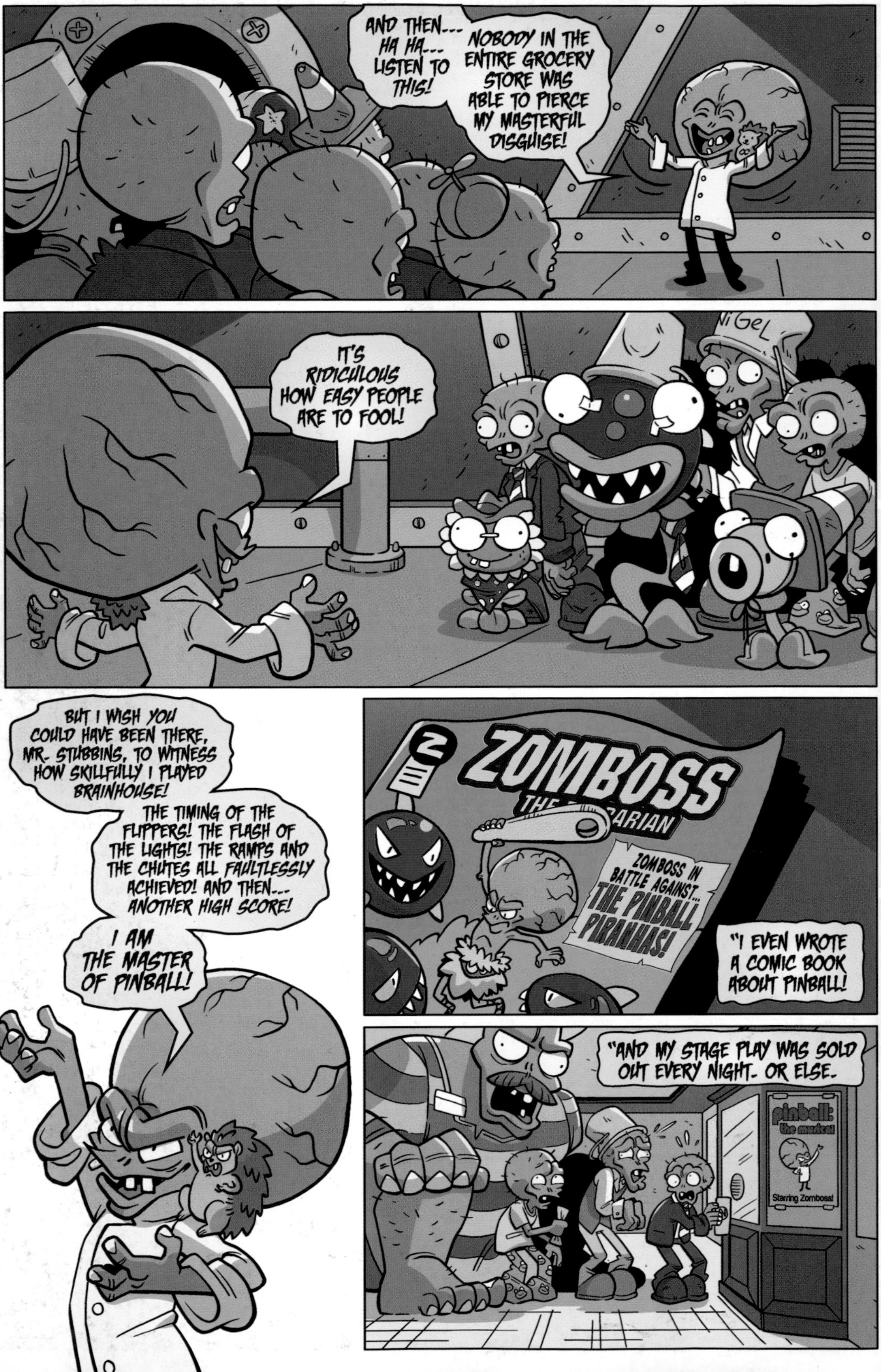
AND THEN... HA HA... LISTEN TO THIS!
NOBODY IN THE ENTIRE GROCERY STORE WAS ABLE TO PIERCE MY MASTERFUL DISGUISE!
NiGeL
IT'S RIDICULOUS HOW EASY PEOPLE ARE TO FOOL!
BUT I WISH YOU COULD HAVE BEEN THERE, MR. STUBBINS, TO WITNESS HOW SKILLFULLY I PLAYED BRAINHOUSE!
THE TIMING OF THE FLIPPERS! THE FLASH OF THE LIGHTS! THE RAMPS AND THE CHUTES ALL FAULTLESSLY ACHIEVED! AND THEN... ANOTHER HIGH SCORE!
I AM THE MASTER OF PINBALL!
2
ZOMBOSS
ZOMBOSS IN BATTLE AGAINST... THE PINBALL PIRANHAS!
"I EVEN WROTE A COMIC BOOK ABOUT PINBALL!
"AND MY STAGE PLAY WAS SOLD OUT EVERY NIGHT. OR ELSE.
pinball: the musical
Starring Zomboss!

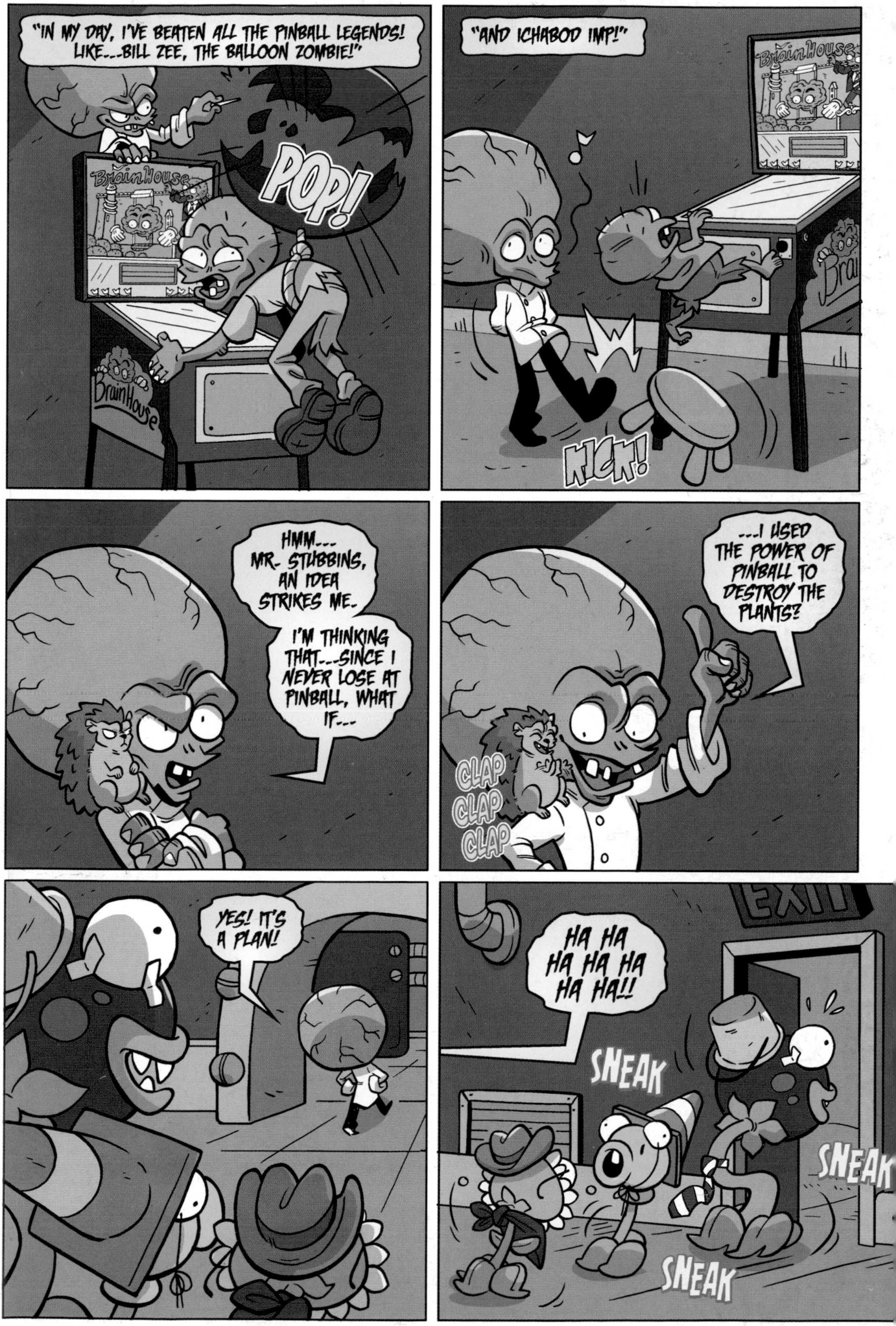
"IN MY DAY, I'VE BEATEN ALL THE PINBALL LEGENDS! LIKE...BILL ZEE, THE BALLOON ZOMBIE!"
POP!
"AND ICHABOD IMP!"
KICK!
HMM... MR. STUBBINS, AN IDEA STRIKES ME.
I'M THINKING THAT...SINCE I NEVER LOSE AT PINBALL, WHAT IF...
...I USED THE POWER OF PINBALL TO DESTROY THE PLANTS?
CLAP CLAP CLAP
YES! IT'S A PLAN!
EXIT
HA HA HA HA HA HA HA!!
SNEAK
SNEAK
SNEAK

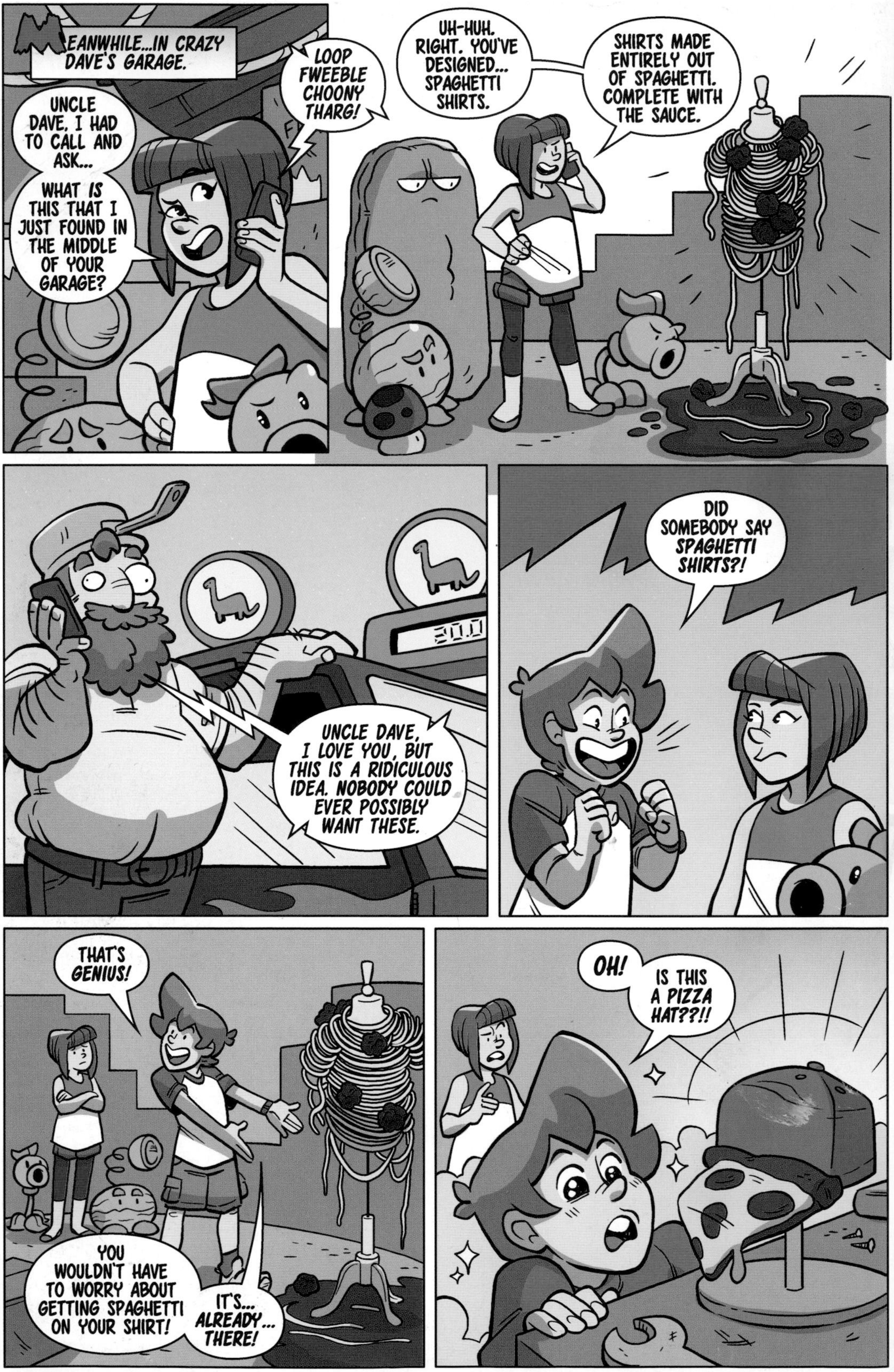
MEANWHILE...IN CRAZY DAVE'S GARAGE.
UNCLE DAVE, I HAD TO CALL AND ASK...
WHAT IS THIS THAT I JUST FOUND IN THE MIDDLE OF YOUR GARAGE?
LOOP FWEEBLE CHOONY THARG!
UH-HUH. RIGHT. YOU'VE DESIGNED... SPAGHETTI SHIRTS.
SHIRTS MADE ENTIRELY OUT OF SPAGHETTI. COMPLETE WITH THE SAUCE.
UNCLE DAVE, I LOVE YOU, BUT THIS IS A RIDICULOUS IDEA. NOBODY COULD EVER POSSIBLY WANT THESE.
DID SOMEBODY SAY SPAGHETTI SHIRTS?!
THAT'S GENIUS!
YOU WOULDN'T HAVE TO WORRY ABOUT GETTING SPAGHETTI ON YOUR SHIRT!
IT'S... ALREADY... THERE!
OH!
IS THIS A PIZZA HAT??!!

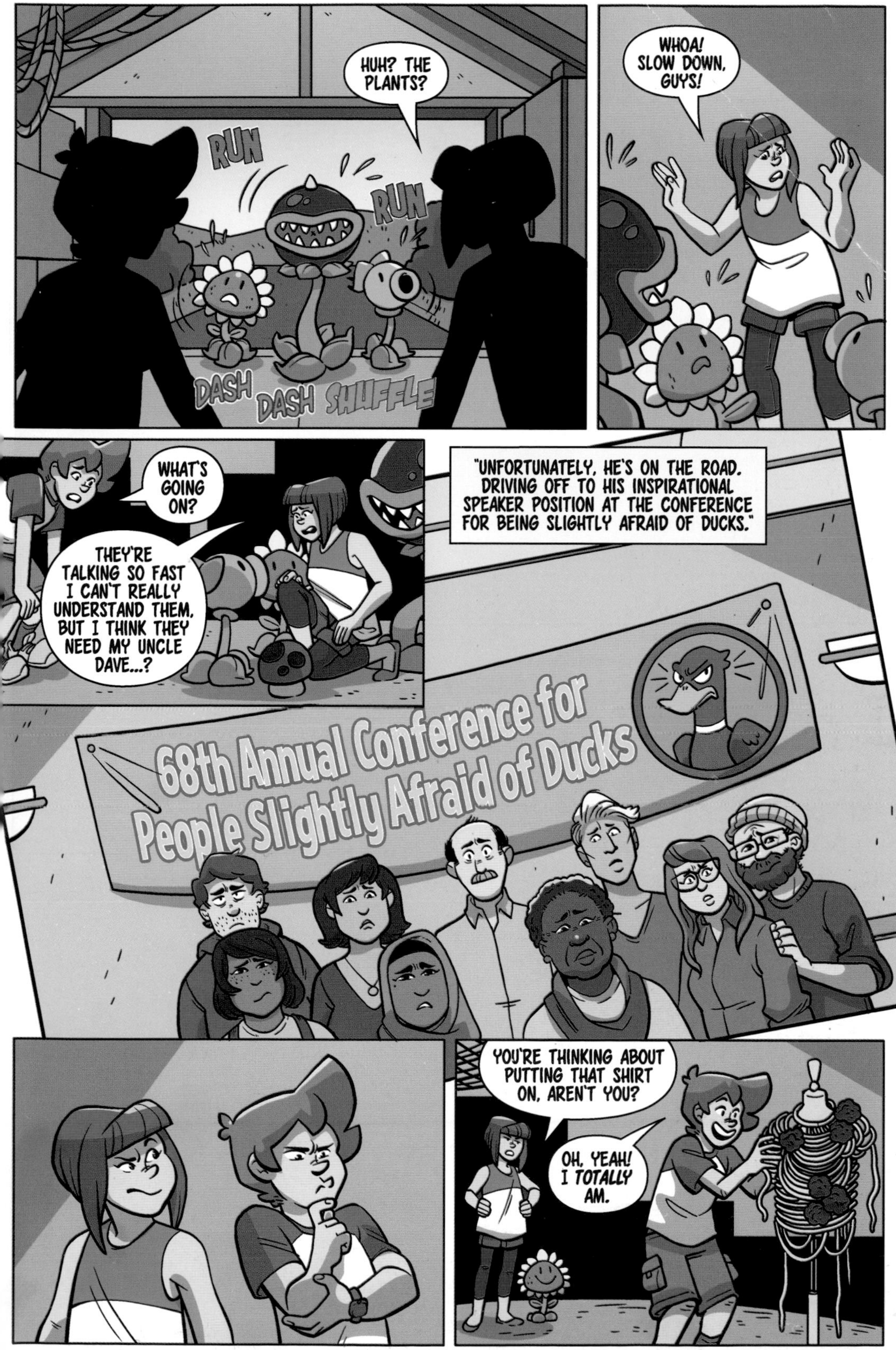
HUH? THE PLANTS?
RUN
RUN
DASH
DASH
SHUFFLE
WHOA! SLOW DOWN, GUYS!
WHAT'S GOING ON?
THEY'RE TALKING SO FAST I CAN'T REALLY UNDERSTAND THEM, BUT I THINK THEY NEED MY UNCLE DAVE...?
"UNFORTUNATELY, HE'S ON THE ROAD. DRIVING OFF TO HIS INSPIRATIONAL SPEAKER POSITION AT THE CONFERENCE FOR BEING SLIGHTLY AFRAID OF DUCKS."
68th Annual Conference for People Slightly Afraid of Ducks
YOU'RE THINKING ABOUT PUTTING THAT SHIRT ON, AREN'T YOU?
OH, YEAH! I *TOTALLY* AM.

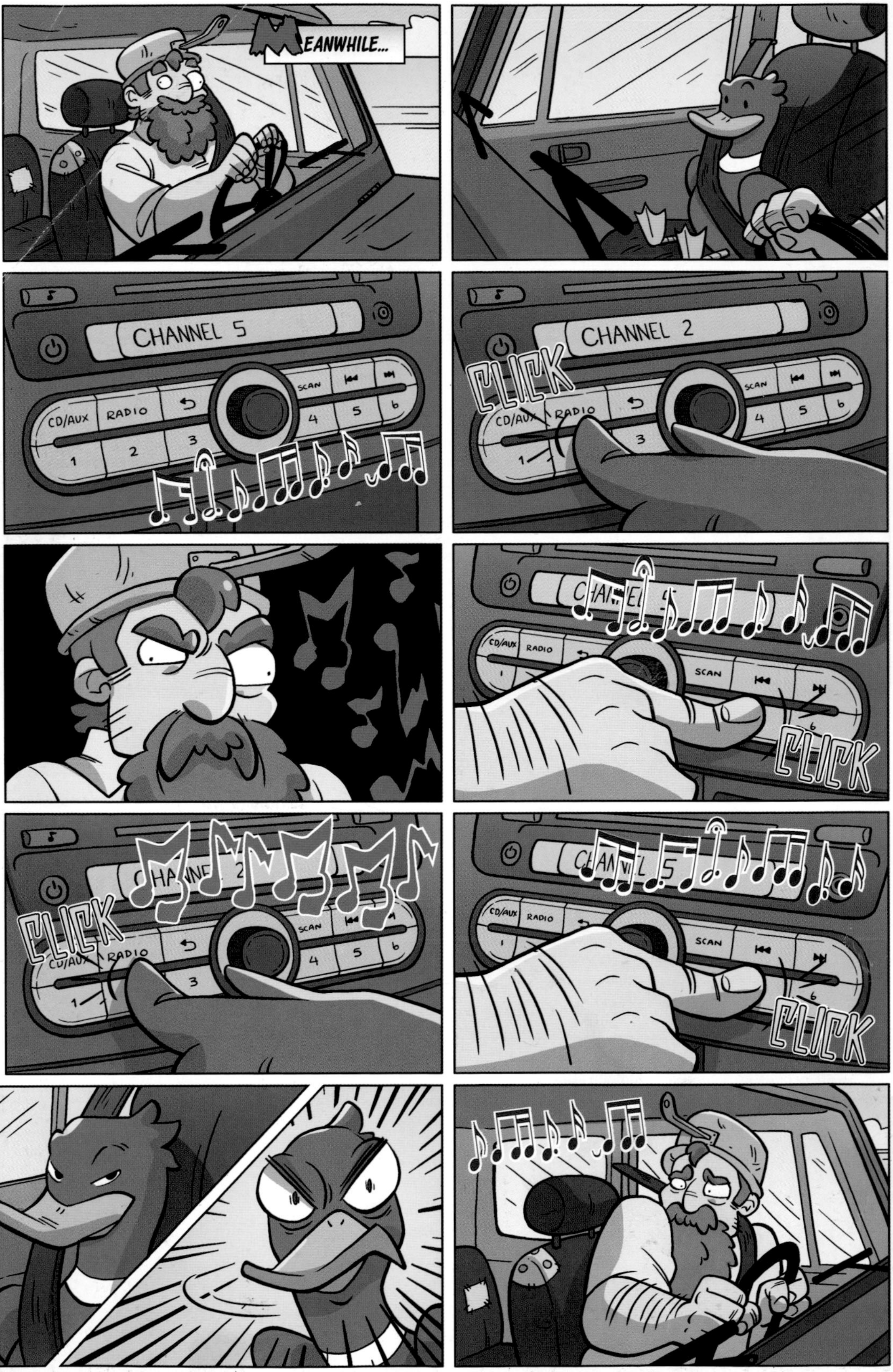

MEANWHILE...
CHANNEL 5
CD/AUX
RADIO
SCAN
CHANNEL 2
CLICK
CLICK
CLICK
CLICK

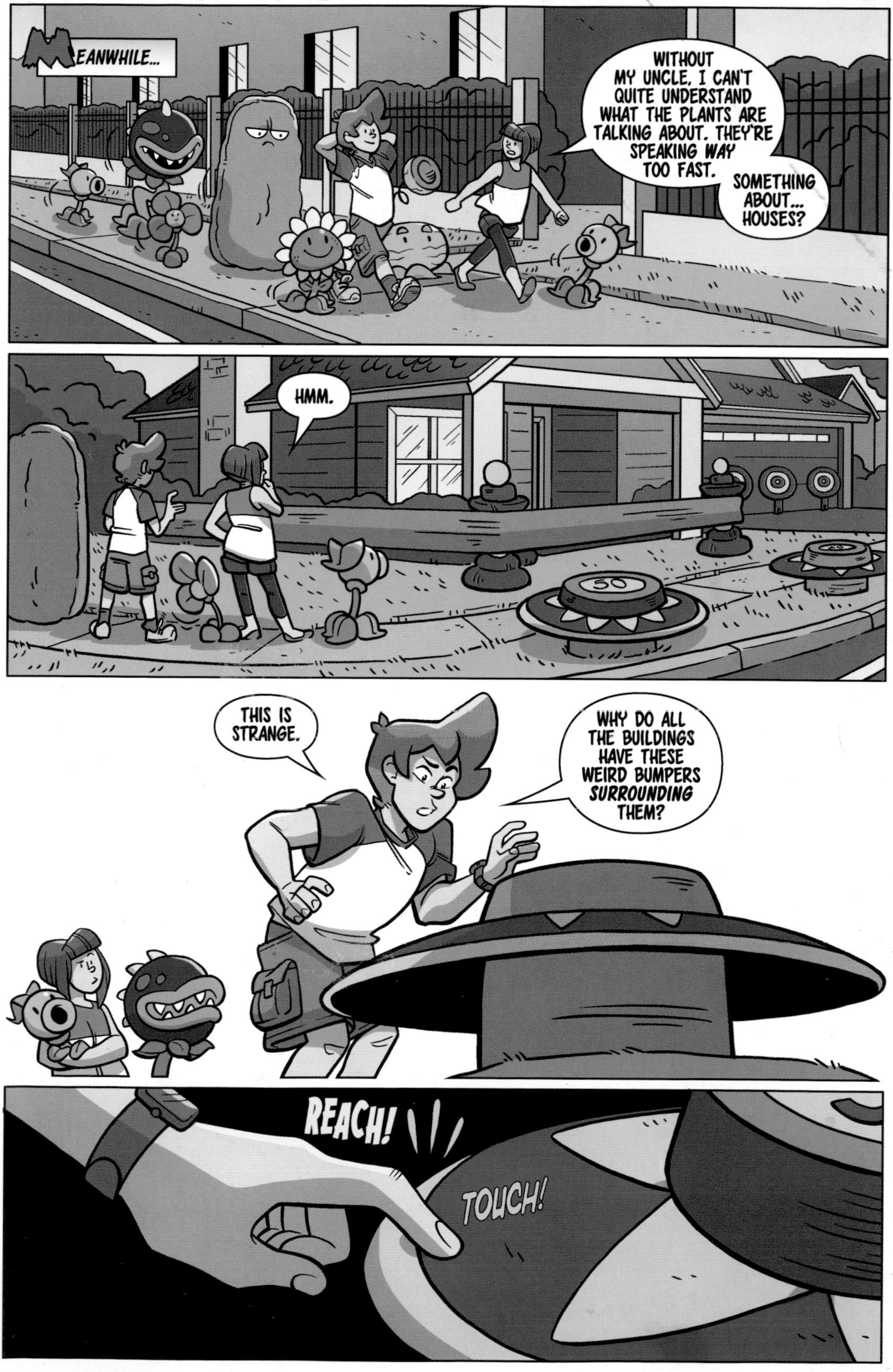
MEANWHILE...
WITHOUT MY UNCLE, I CAN'T QUITE UNDERSTAND WHAT THE PLANTS ARE TALKING ABOUT. THEY'RE SPEAKING WAY TOO FAST.
SOMETHING ABOUT... HOUSES?
HMM.
50
THIS IS STRANGE.
WHY DO ALL THE BUILDINGS HAVE THESE WEIRD BUMPERS SURROUNDING THEM?
REACH!
TOUCH!

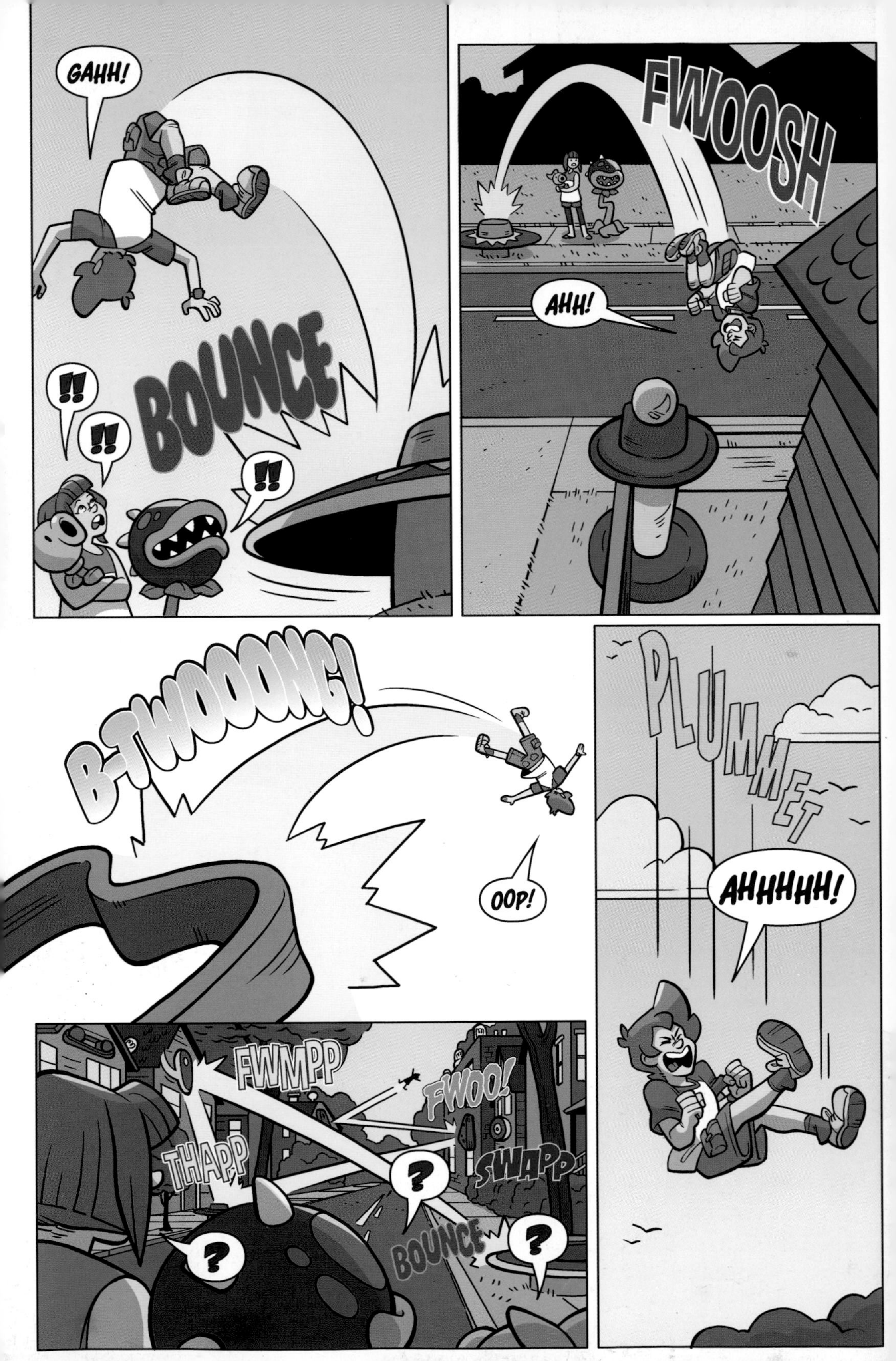
GAHH!
BOUNCE
!!
!!
!!
FWOOSH
AHH!
B-TWOOOONG!
OOP!
PLUMMET
AHHHHH!
FWMPP
FWOO!
THAPP
SWAPP
?
?
BOUNCE
?

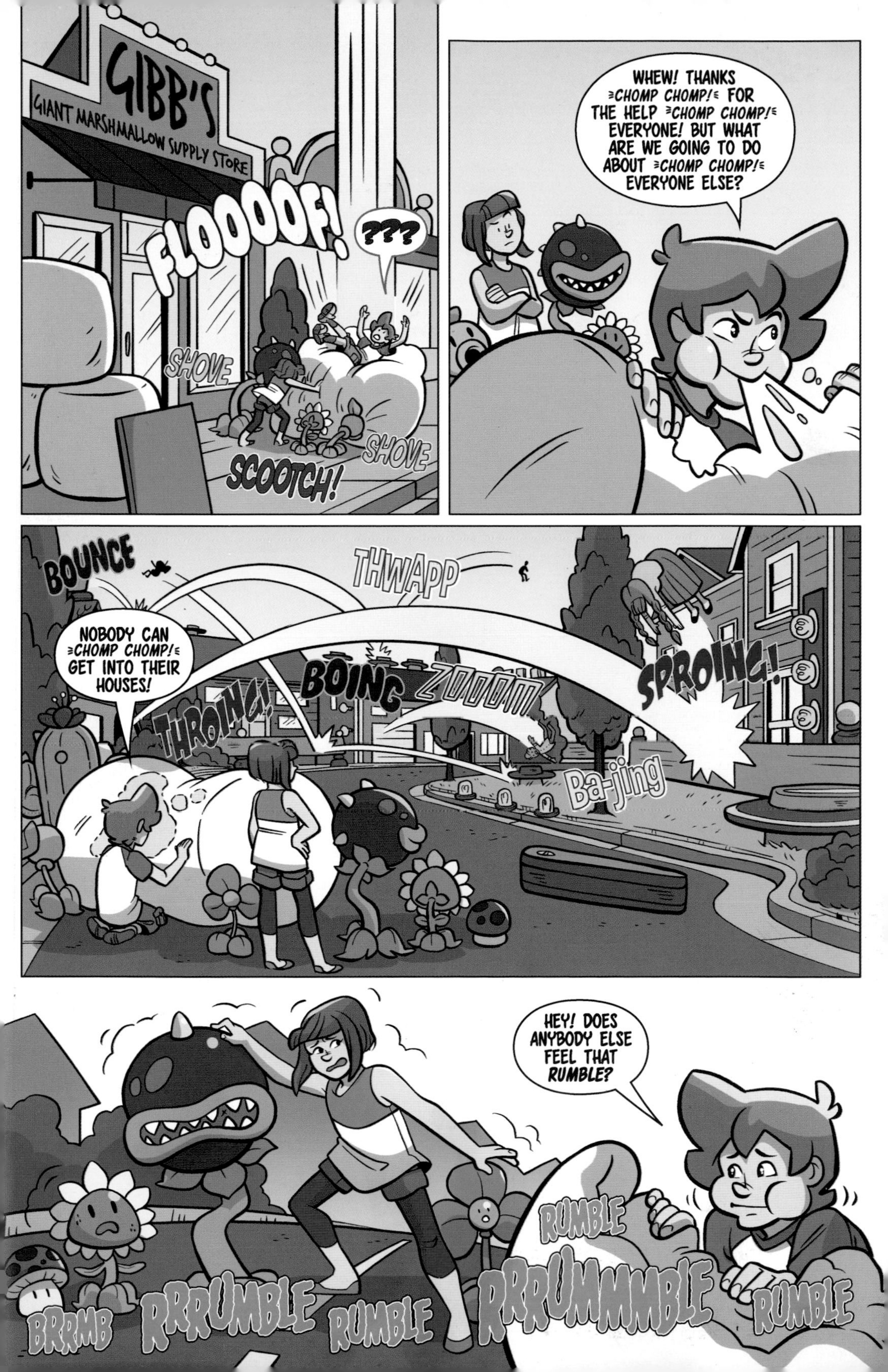
GIBB'S
GIANT MARSHMALLOW SUPPLY STORE
FLOOOOF!
???
SHOVE
SHOVE
SCOOTCH!
WHEW! THANKS ≡CHOMP CHOMP!≡ FOR THE HELP ≡CHOMP CHOMP!≡ EVERYONE! BUT WHAT ARE WE GOING TO DO ABOUT ≡CHOMP CHOMP!≡ EVERYONE ELSE?
BOUNCE
THWAPP
NOBODY CAN ≡CHOMP CHOMP!≡ GET INTO THEIR HOUSES!
THROING!
BOING
ZOOOM
SPROING!
Ba-jing
HEY! DOES ANYBODY ELSE FEEL THAT RUMBLE?
RUMBLE
BRRMB
RRRUMBLE
RUMBLE
RRRUMMMBLE
RUMBLE

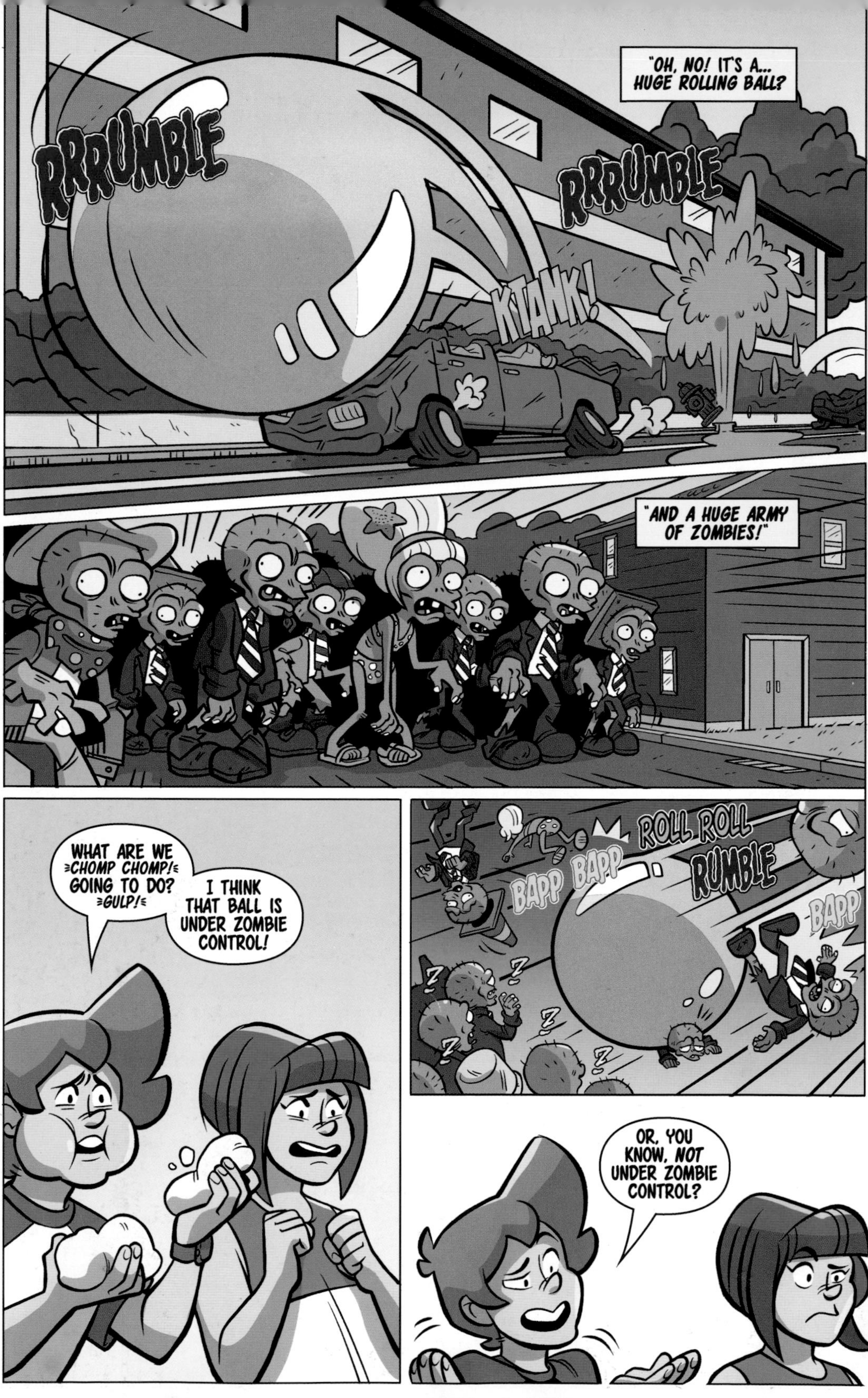

"OH, NO! IT'S A... HUGE ROLLING BALL?
RRRUMBLE
RRRUMBLE
KTANK!
"AND A HUGE ARMY OF ZOMBIES!"
WHAT ARE WE CHOMP CHOMP! GOING TO DO? GULP!
I THINK THAT BALL IS UNDER ZOMBIE CONTROL!
BAPP BAPP
ROLL ROLL
RUMBLE
BAPP
Z
Z
Z
Z
Z
OR, YOU KNOW, NOT UNDER ZOMBIE CONTROL?

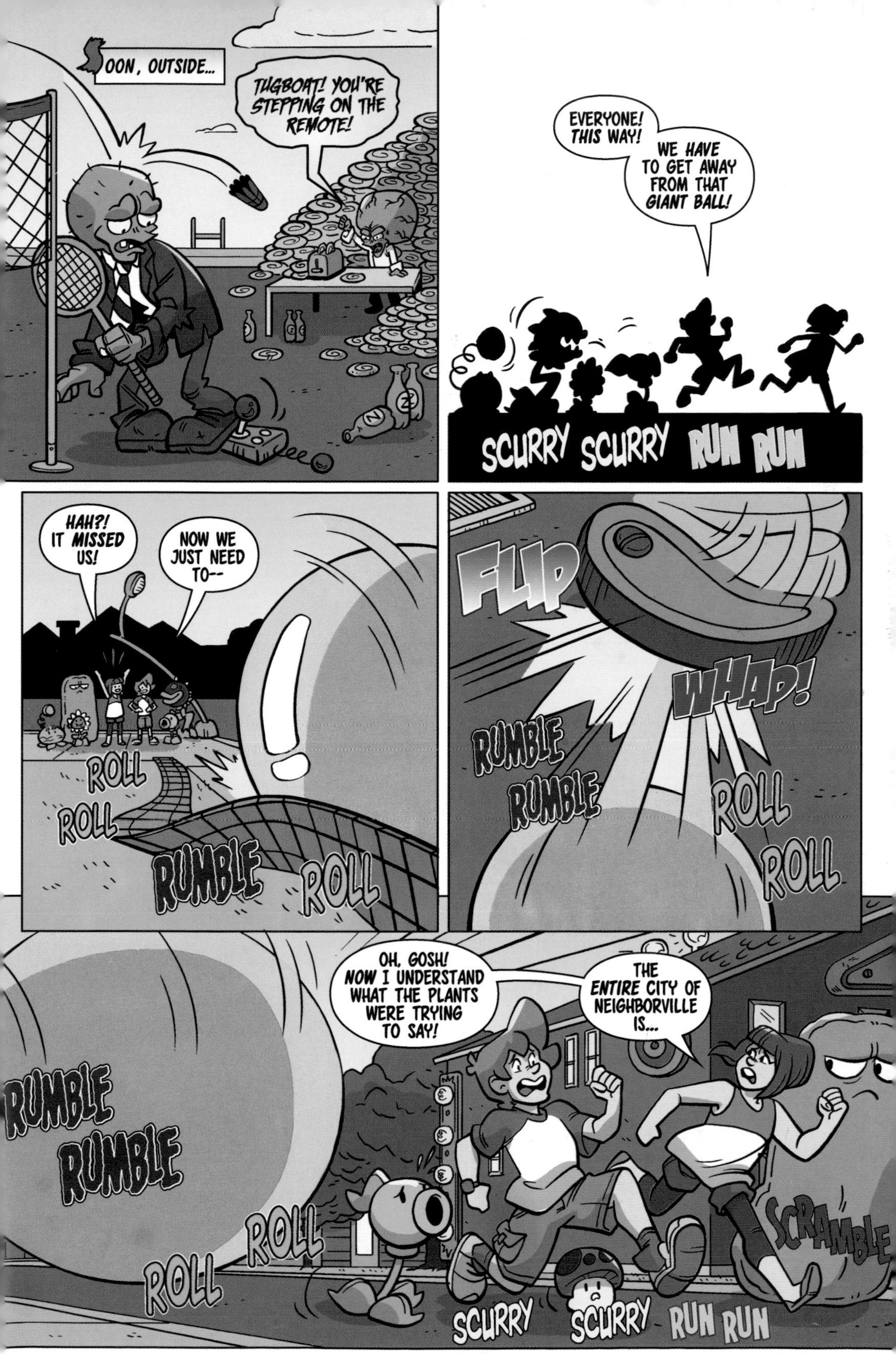
SOON, OUTSIDE...
TUGBOAT! YOU'RE STEPPING ON THE REMOTE!
EVERYONE! THIS WAY!
WE HAVE TO GET AWAY FROM THAT GIANT BALL!
SCURRY SCURRY RUN RUN
HAH?! IT MISSED US!
NOW WE JUST NEED TO--
ROLL
ROLL
RUMBLE
ROLL
FLIP
WHAP!
RUMBLE
RUMBLE
ROLL
ROLL
OH, GOSH! NOW I UNDERSTAND WHAT THE PLANTS WERE TRYING TO SAY!
THE ENTIRE CITY OF NEIGHBORVILLE IS...
RUMBLE
RUMBLE
ROLL
ROLL
SCRAMBLE
SCURRY SCURRY RUN RUN

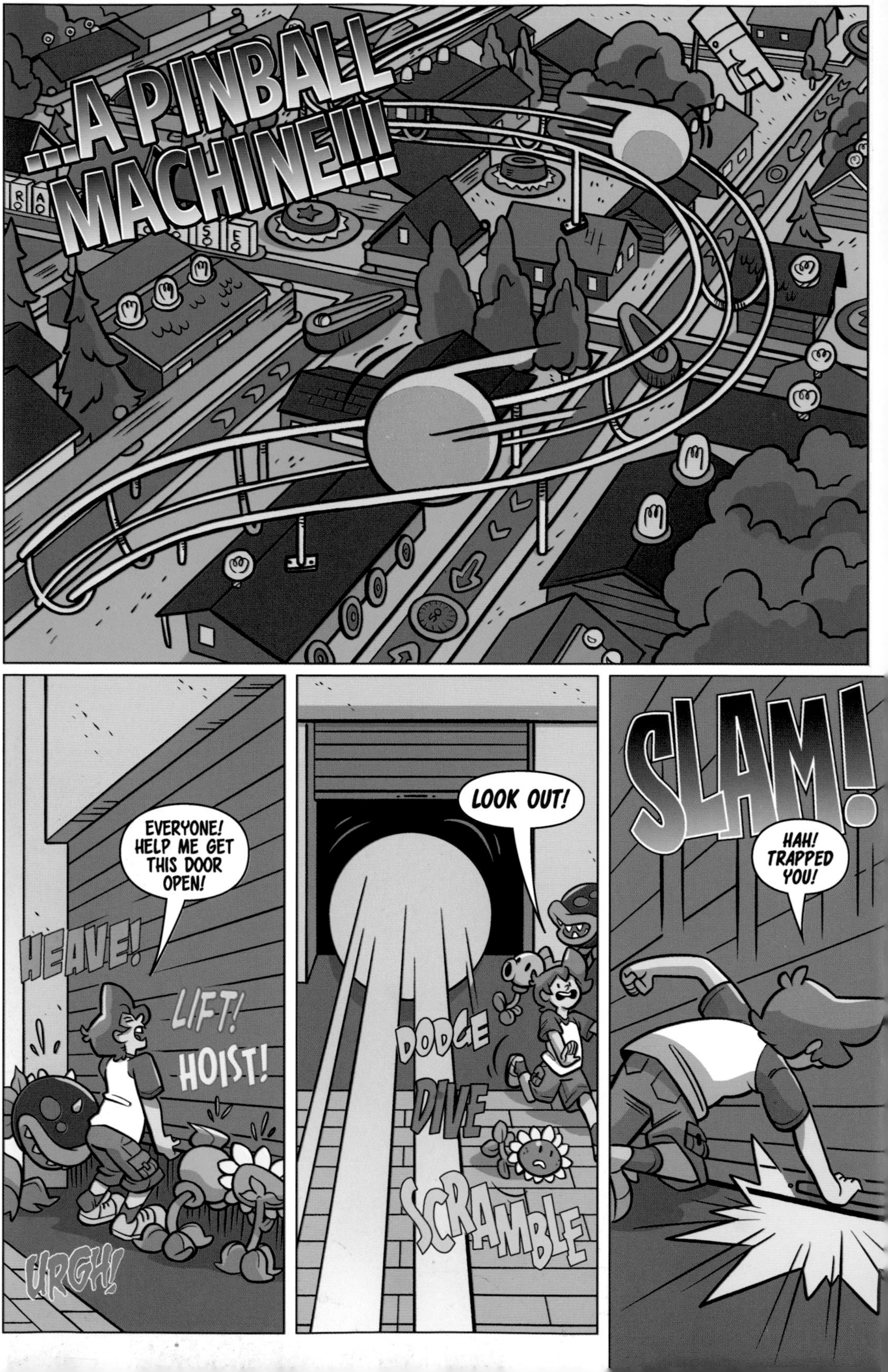
...A PINBALL MACHINE!!!
EVERYONE! HELP ME GET THIS DOOR OPEN!
HEAVE!
LIFT!
HOIST!
URGH!
LOOK OUT!
DODGE
DIVE
SCRAMBLE
SLAM!
HAH! TRAPPED YOU!

GREAT WORK, EVERYONE! BUT ALL WE'RE DOING IS RUNNING AROUND. WE HAVE TO FIND A WAY TO STOP THIS CRAZINESS!

IT'S OBVIOUSLY ONE OF ZOMBOSS' SCHEMES!

BUT, WHERE IS HE? AND WHAT'S HIS PLAN?

GAHH! A FLIPPER?

SOAR!

FLIP

WHOOOOOOSH!

FWOOP!

HEY! LOOK AT THAT!

HA HA HA HA! MR. STUBBINS, IT'S WORKING PERFECTLY!

WEEE-OOO NEIGHBORVILLE

WITH THIS SCALE-MODEL PINBALL MACHINE OF NEIGHBORVILLE WIRED INTO THE ACTUAL CITY, I HAVE CONTROL OF EVERYTHING THAT'S HAPPENING!

FOOMK!

RING

RING

WEEE-OOO

RING

GIBBA GIBBA

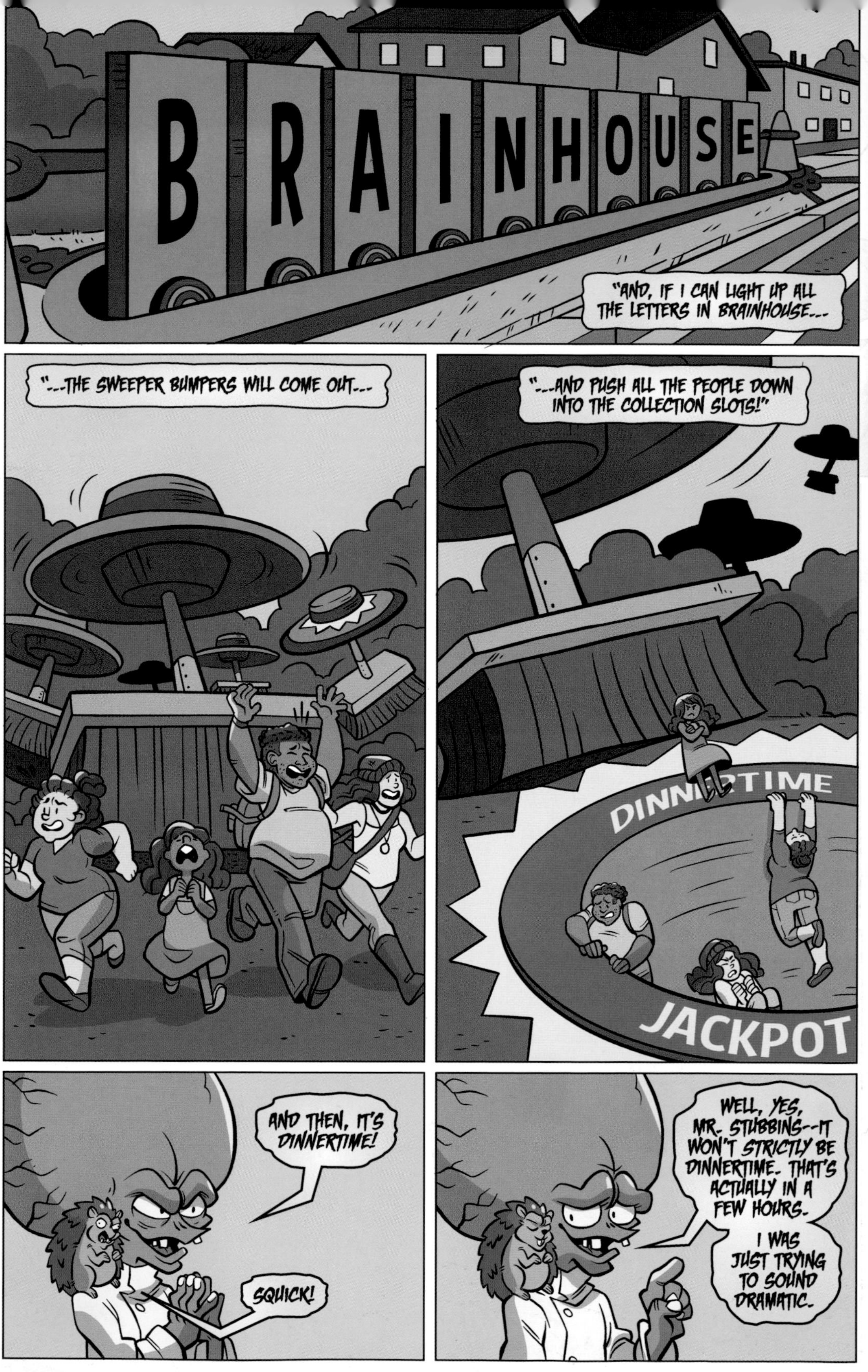
BRAINHOUSE
"AND, IF I CAN LIGHT UP ALL THE LETTERS IN BRAINHOUSE...
"...THE SWEEPER BUMPERS WILL COME OUT...
"...AND PUSH ALL THE PEOPLE DOWN INTO THE COLLECTION SLOTS!"
DINNERTIME
JACKPOT
AND THEN, IT'S DINNERTIME!
SQUICK!
WELL, YES, MR. STUBBINS--IT WON'T STRICTLY BE DINNERTIME. THAT'S ACTUALLY IN A FEW HOURS.
I WAS JUST TRYING TO SOUND DRAMATIC.

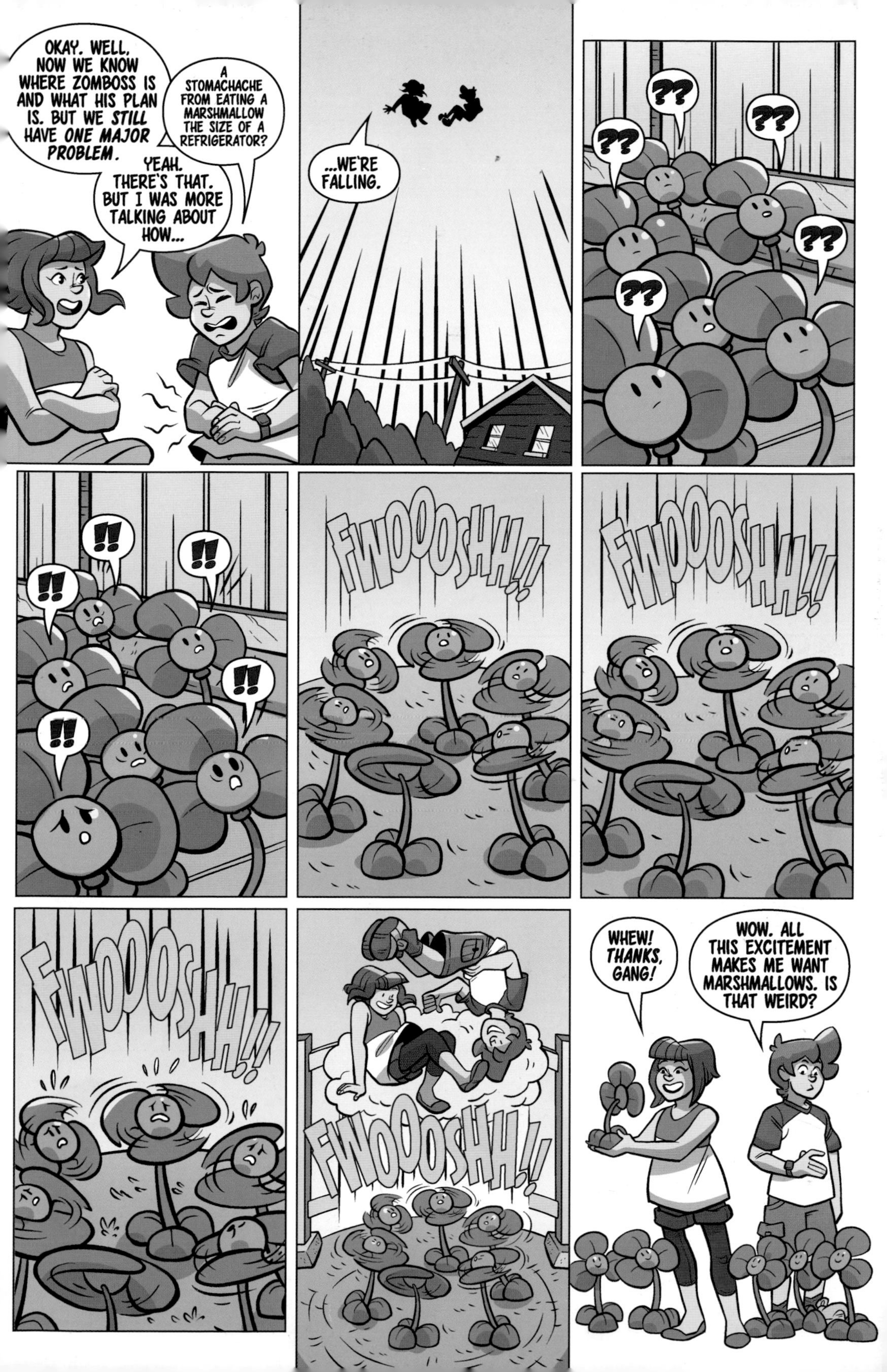
OKAY. WELL, NOW WE KNOW WHERE ZOMBOSS IS AND WHAT HIS PLAN IS. BUT WE STILL HAVE ONE MAJOR PROBLEM.
YEAH. THERE'S THAT. BUT I WAS MORE TALKING ABOUT HOW...
A STOMACHACHE FROM EATING A MARSHMALLOW THE SIZE OF A REFRIGERATOR?
...WE'RE FALLING.
??
??
??
??
??
!!
!!
!!
!!
!!
FWOOOSHH!!
FWOOOSHH!!
FWOOOSHH!!
FWOOOSHH!!
WHEW! THANKS, GANG!
WOW. ALL THIS EXCITEMENT MAKES ME WANT MARSHMALLOWS. IS THAT WEIRD?

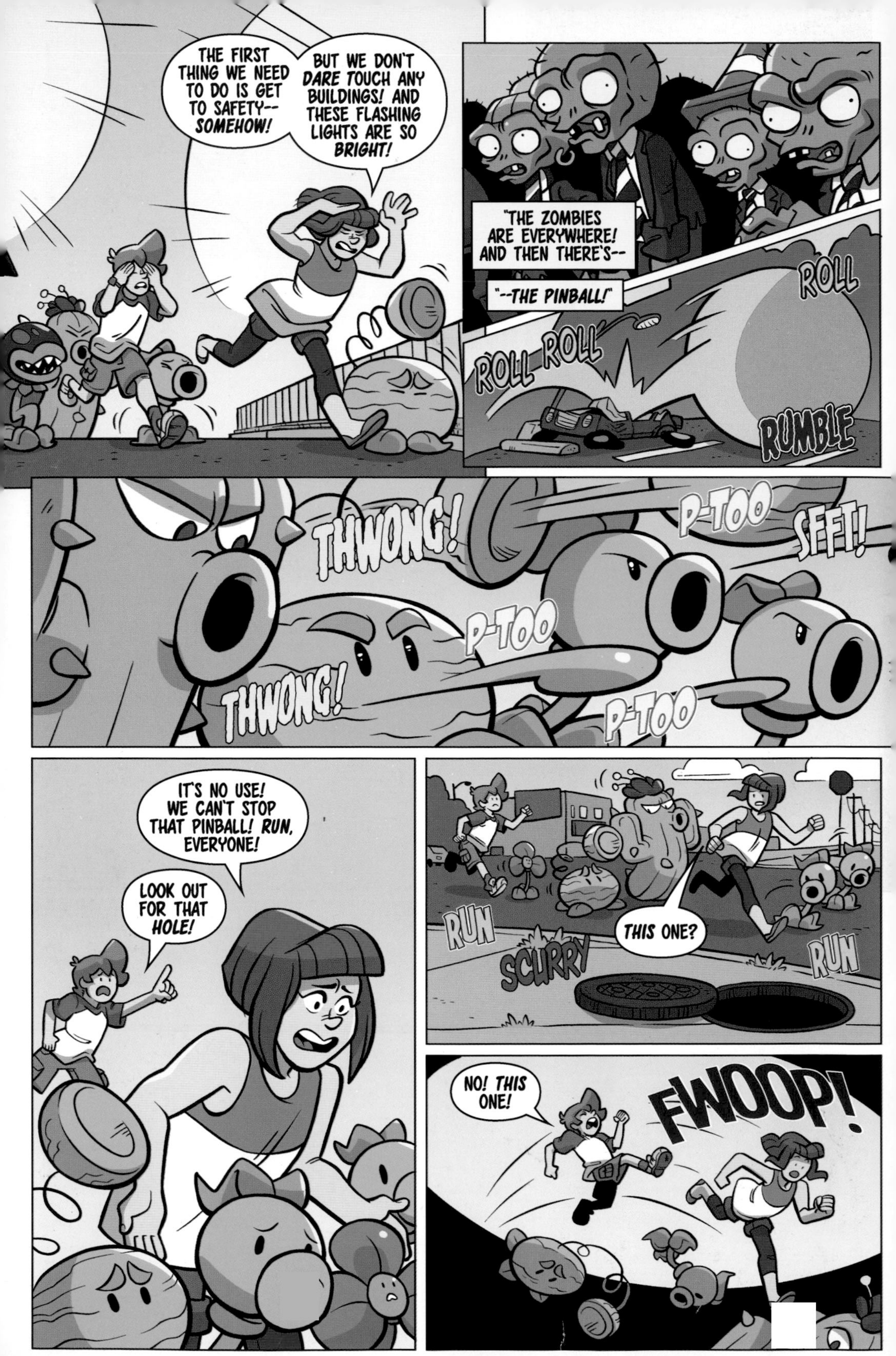
THE FIRST THING WE NEED TO DO IS GET TO SAFETY-- *SOMEHOW!*
BUT WE DON'T *DARE TOUCH* ANY BUILDINGS! AND THESE FLASHING LIGHTS ARE SO *BRIGHT!*
"THE ZOMBIES ARE EVERYWHERE! AND THEN THERE'S--
"--THE PINBALL!"
ROLL
ROLL ROLL
RUMBLE
THWONG!
P-TOO
SFFT!
P-TOO
THWONG!
P-TOO
IT'S NO USE! WE CAN'T STOP THAT PINBALL! *RUN,* EVERYONE!
LOOK OUT FOR THAT *HOLE!*
RUN
SCURRY
THIS ONE?
RUN
NO! THIS ONE!
FWOOP!

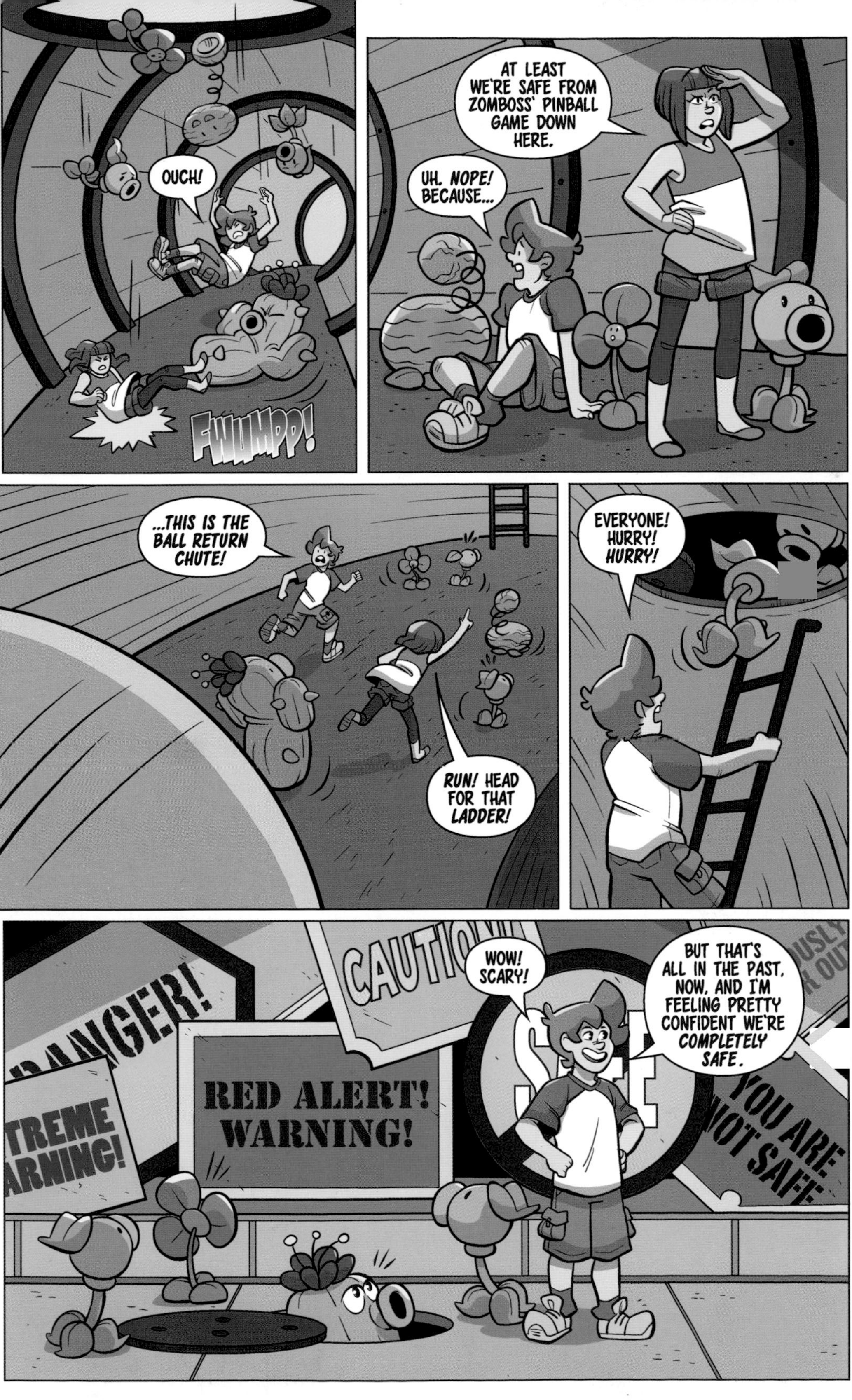
OUCH!
FWUMPP!
AT LEAST WE'RE SAFE FROM ZOMBOSS' PINBALL GAME DOWN HERE.
UH. NOPE! BECAUSE...
...THIS IS THE BALL RETURN CHUTE!
RUN! HEAD FOR THAT LADDER!
EVERYONE! HURRY! HURRY!
CAUTION
DANGER!
TREME WARNING!
RED ALERT! WARNING!
YOU ARE NOT SAFE
WOW! SCARY!
BUT THAT'S ALL IN THE PAST, NOW, AND I'M FEELING PRETTY CONFIDENT WE'RE COMPLETELY SAFE.

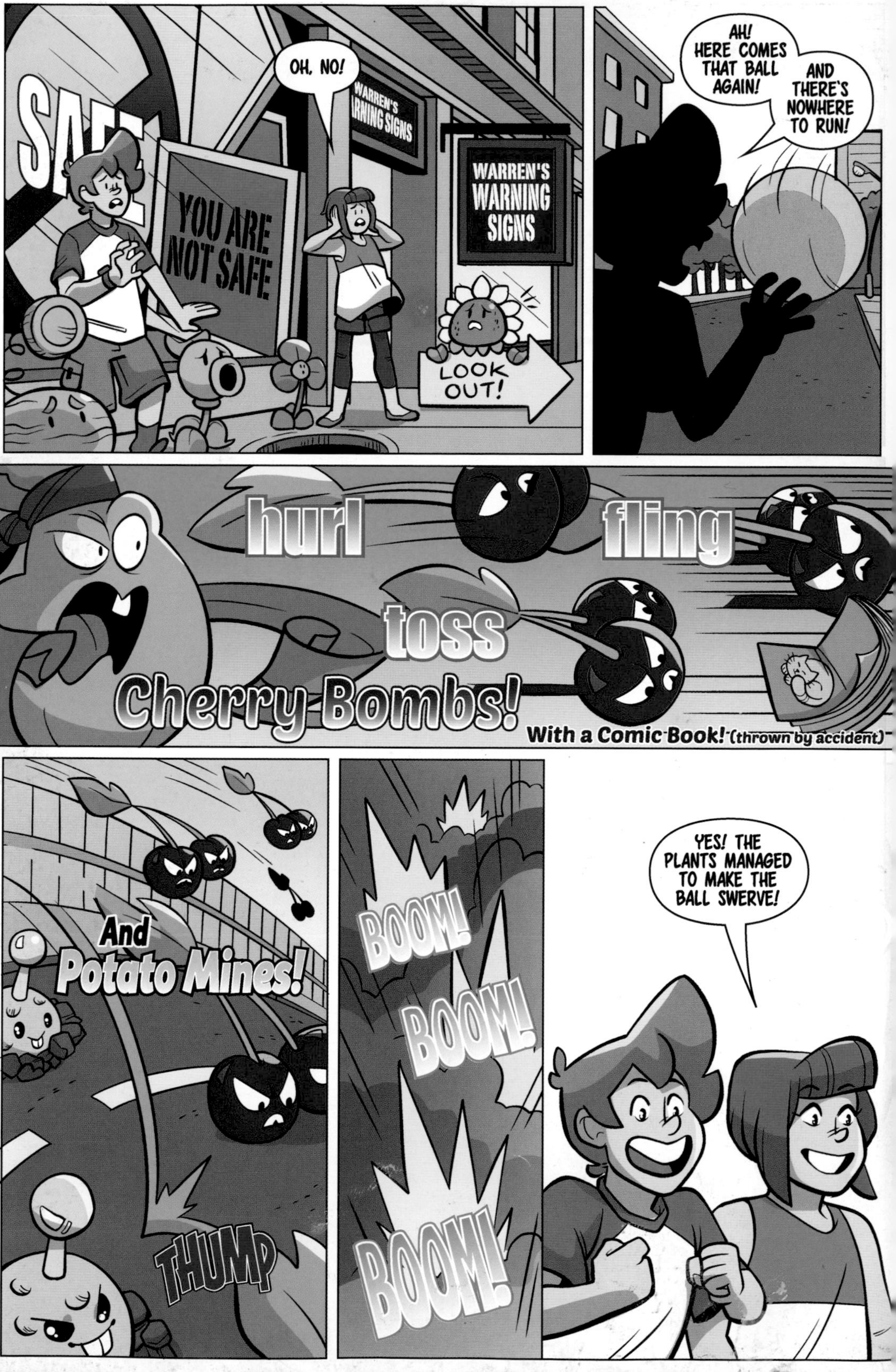
SAFE
YOU ARE NOT SAFE
OH, NO!
WARREN'S WARNING SIGNS
WARREN'S WARNING SIGNS
LOOK OUT!
AH! HERE COMES THAT BALL AGAIN!
AND THERE'S NOWHERE TO RUN!
hurl
fling
toss
Cherry Bombs!
With a Comic Book! (thrown by accident)
And Potato Mines!
THUMP
BOOM!
BOOM!
BOOM!
YES! THE PLANTS MANAGED TO MAKE THE BALL SWERVE!

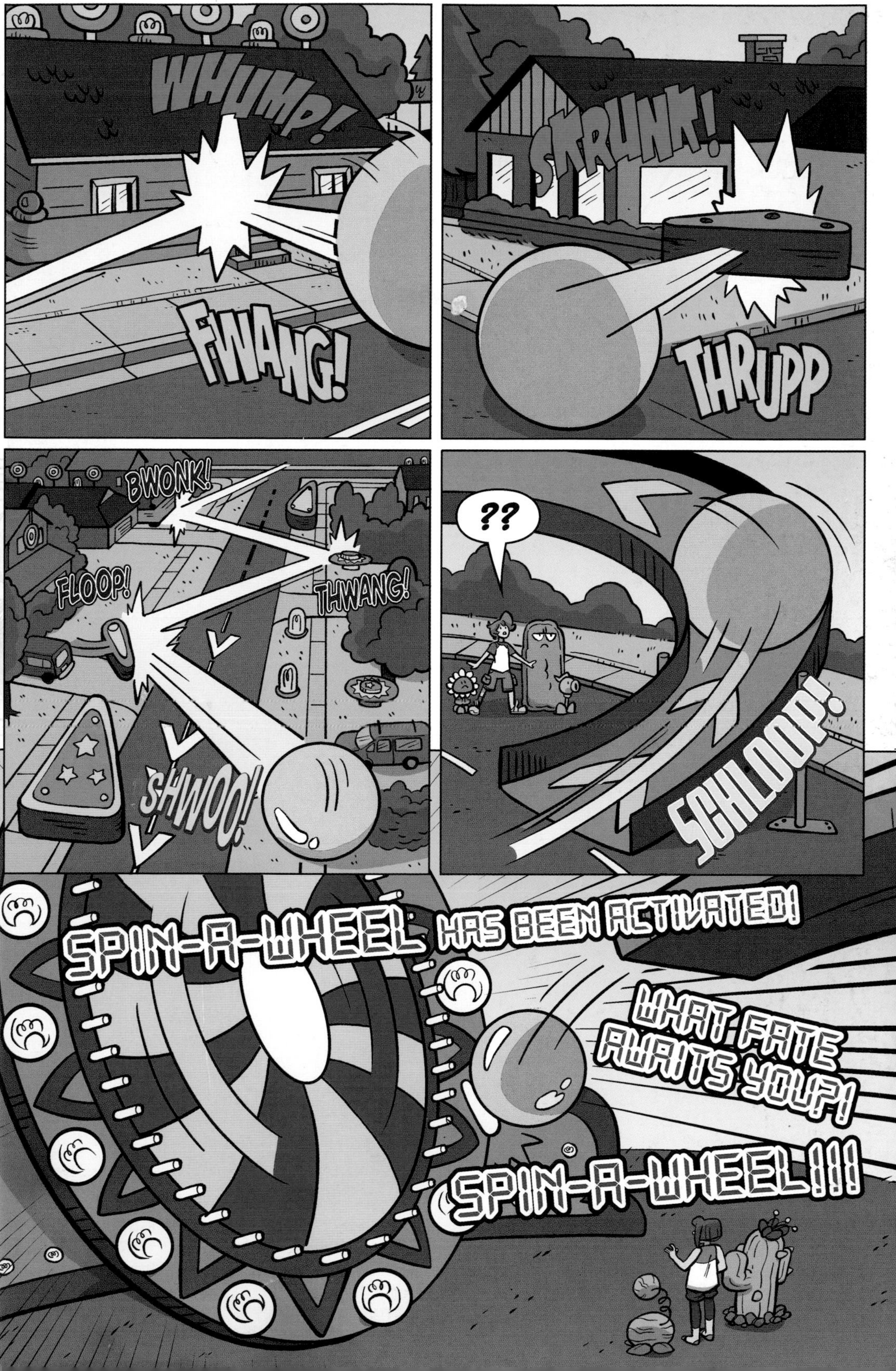
WHUMP!
FWANG!
SKRUNK!
THRUPP
BWONK!
THWANG!
FLOOP!
SHWOO!
??
SCHLOOP!
SPIN-A-WHEEL HAS BEEN ACTIVATED!
WHAT FATE AWAITS YOU?!
SPIN-A-WHEEL!!!

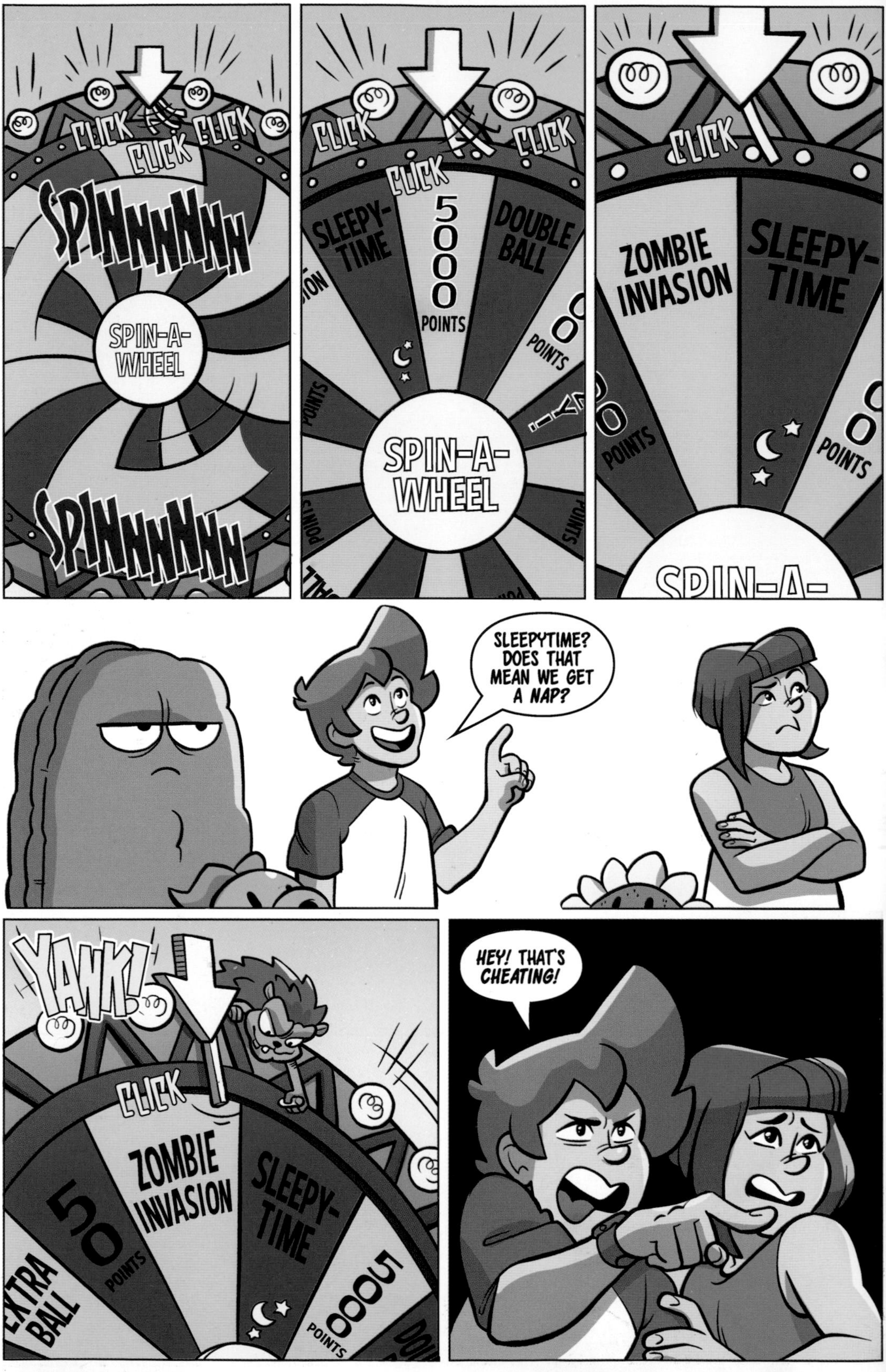
CLICK
CLICK
CLICK
SPINNNNNN
SPIN-A-WHEEL
SPINNNNNNN
CLICK
CLICK
CLICK
SLEEPY-TIME
5000 POINTS
DOUBLE BALL
SPIN-A-WHEEL
CLICK
ZOMBIE INVASION
SLEEPY-TIME
SLEEPYTIME? DOES THAT MEAN WE GET A NAP?
YANK!
CLICK
EXTRA BALL
50 POINTS
ZOMBIE INVASION
SLEEPY-TIME
HEY! THAT'S CHEATING!

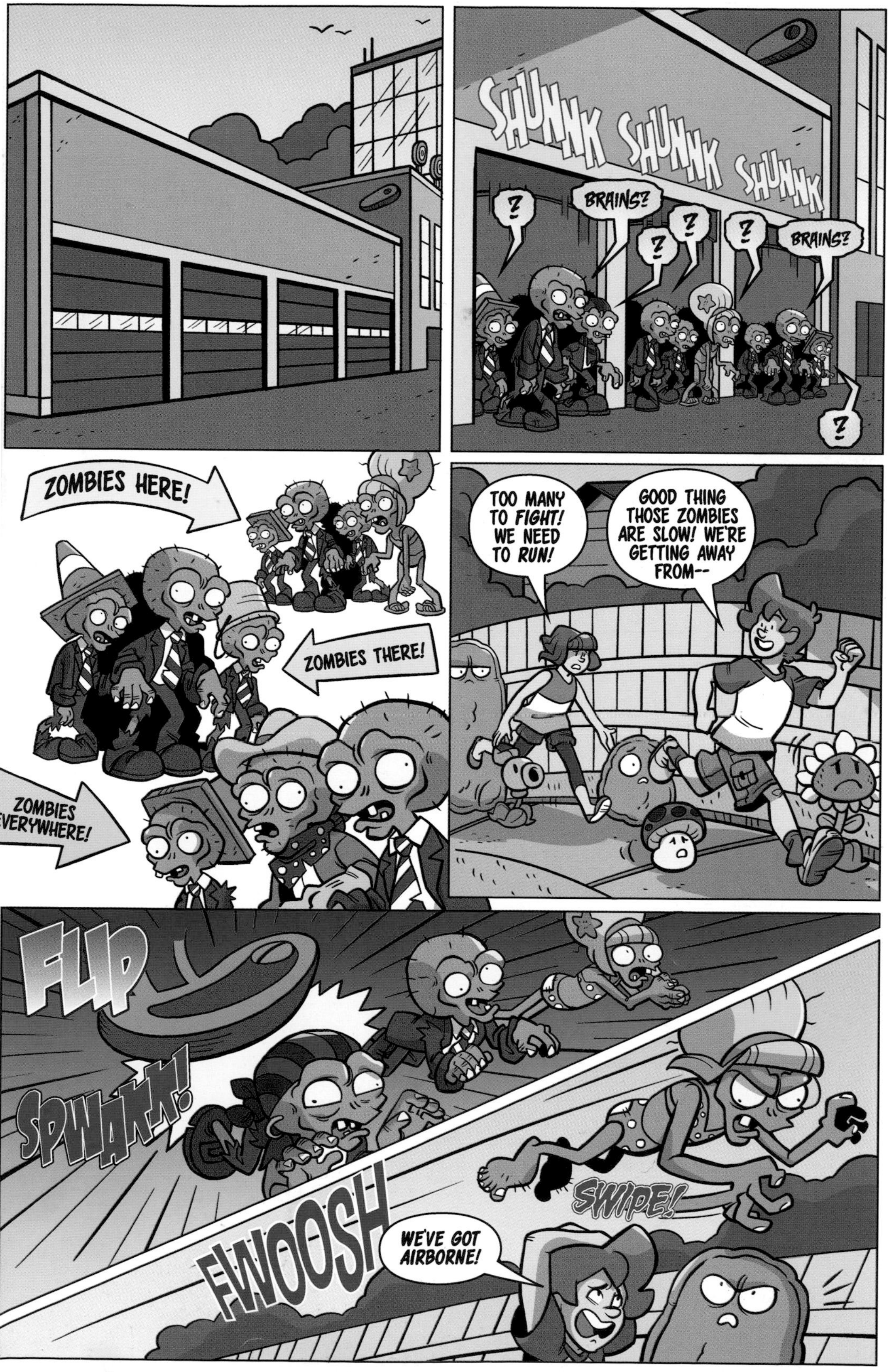

SHUNNK SHUNNK SHUNNK
?
BRAINS?
?
?
?
BRAINS?
?
ZOMBIES HERE!
ZOMBIES THERE!
ZOMBIES EVERYWHERE!
TOO MANY TO FIGHT! WE NEED TO RUN!
GOOD THING THOSE ZOMBIES ARE SLOW! WE'RE GETTING AWAY FROM--
FLIP
SPWANK!
SWIPE!
FWOOSH
WE'VE GOT AIRBORNE!

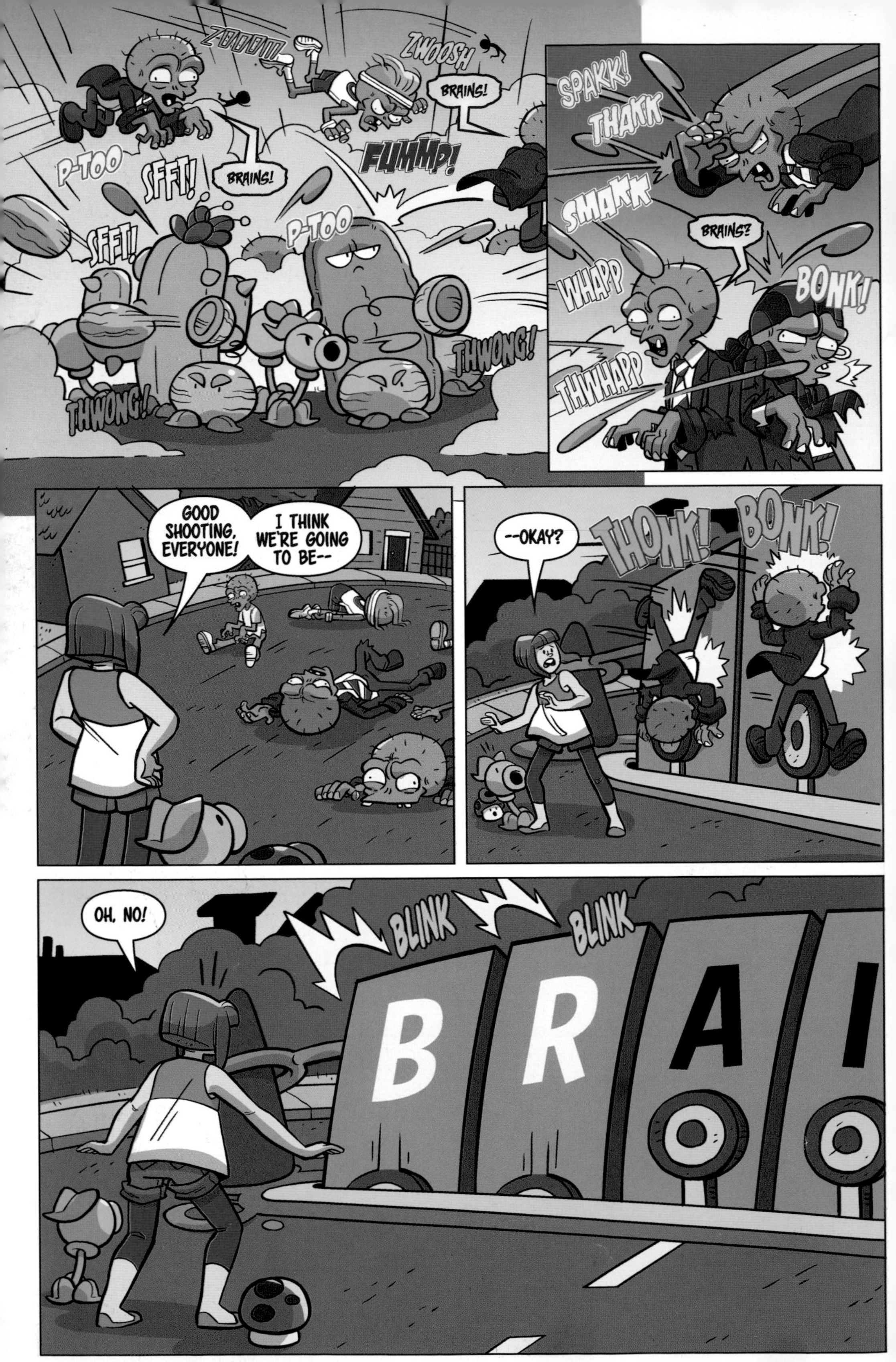
ZOOOM
ZWOOSH
BRAINS!
P-TOO
SFFT!
BRAINS!
FUMMP!
SFFT!
P-TOO
THWONG!
THWONG!
SPAKK!
THAKK
SMAKK
BRAINS?
WHAPP
BONK!
THWHAPP
GOOD SHOOTING, EVERYONE!
I THINK WE'RE GOING TO BE--
--OKAY?
THONK!
BONK!
OH, NO!
BLINK
BLINK
B
R
A
I

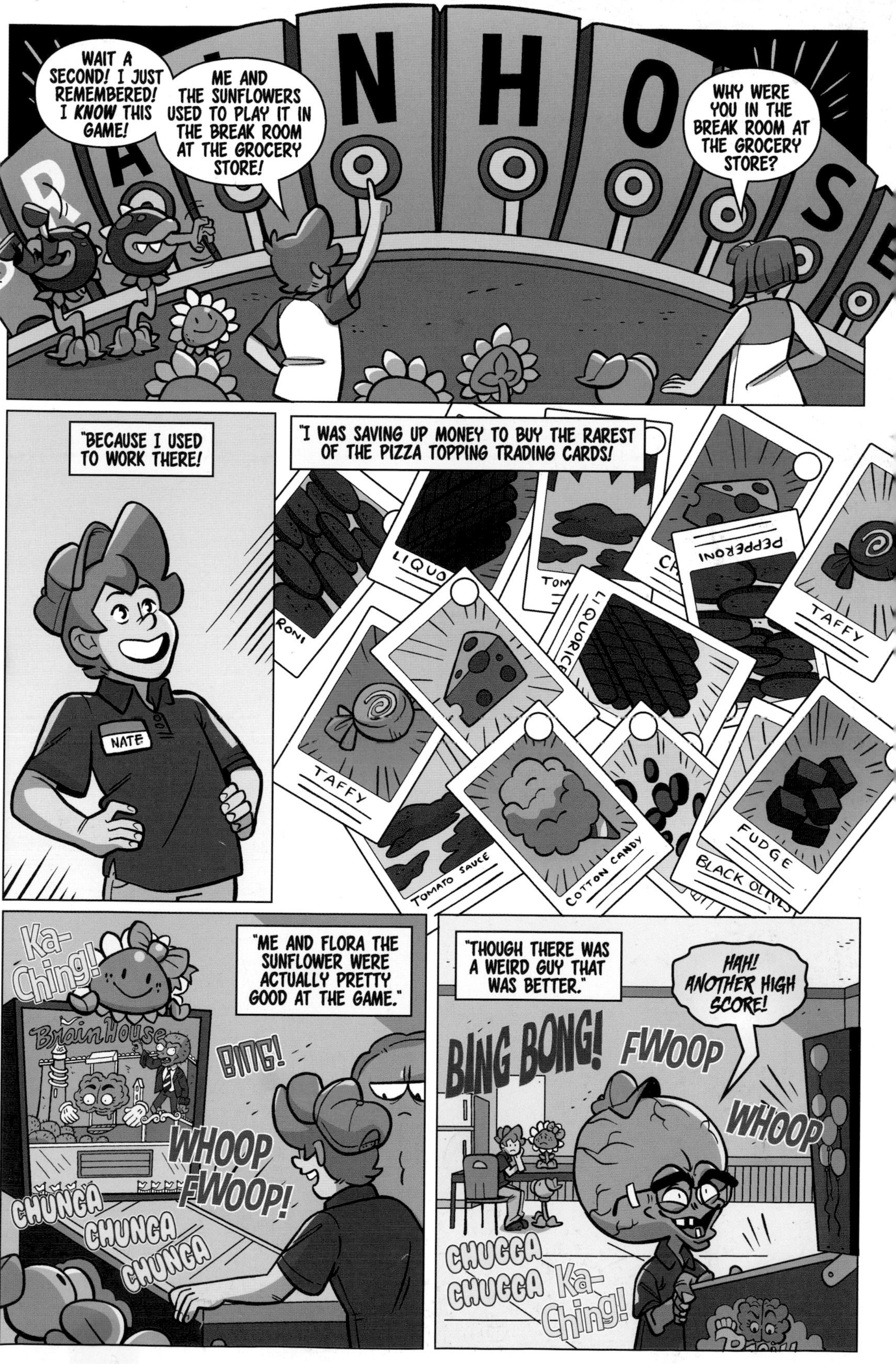
WAIT A SECOND! I JUST REMEMBERED! I KNOW THIS GAME!
ME AND THE SUNFLOWERS USED TO PLAY IT IN THE BREAK ROOM AT THE GROCERY STORE!
WHY WERE YOU IN THE BREAK ROOM AT THE GROCERY STORE?
"BECAUSE I USED TO WORK THERE!
NATE
"I WAS SAVING UP MONEY TO BUY THE RAREST OF THE PIZZA TOPPING TRADING CARDS!
PEPPERONI
TAFFY
LIQUORICE
TAFFY
FUDGE
BLACK OLIVES
COTTON CANDY
TOMATO SAUCE
KA-CHING!
"ME AND FLORA THE SUNFLOWER WERE ACTUALLY PRETTY GOOD AT THE GAME."
BrainHouse
BING!
WHOOP FWOOP!
CHUNGA CHUNGA CHUNGA
"THOUGH THERE WAS A WEIRD GUY THAT WAS BETTER."
HAH! ANOTHER HIGH SCORE!
BING BONG!
FWOOP
WHOOP
CHUGGA CHUGGA
KA-CHING!

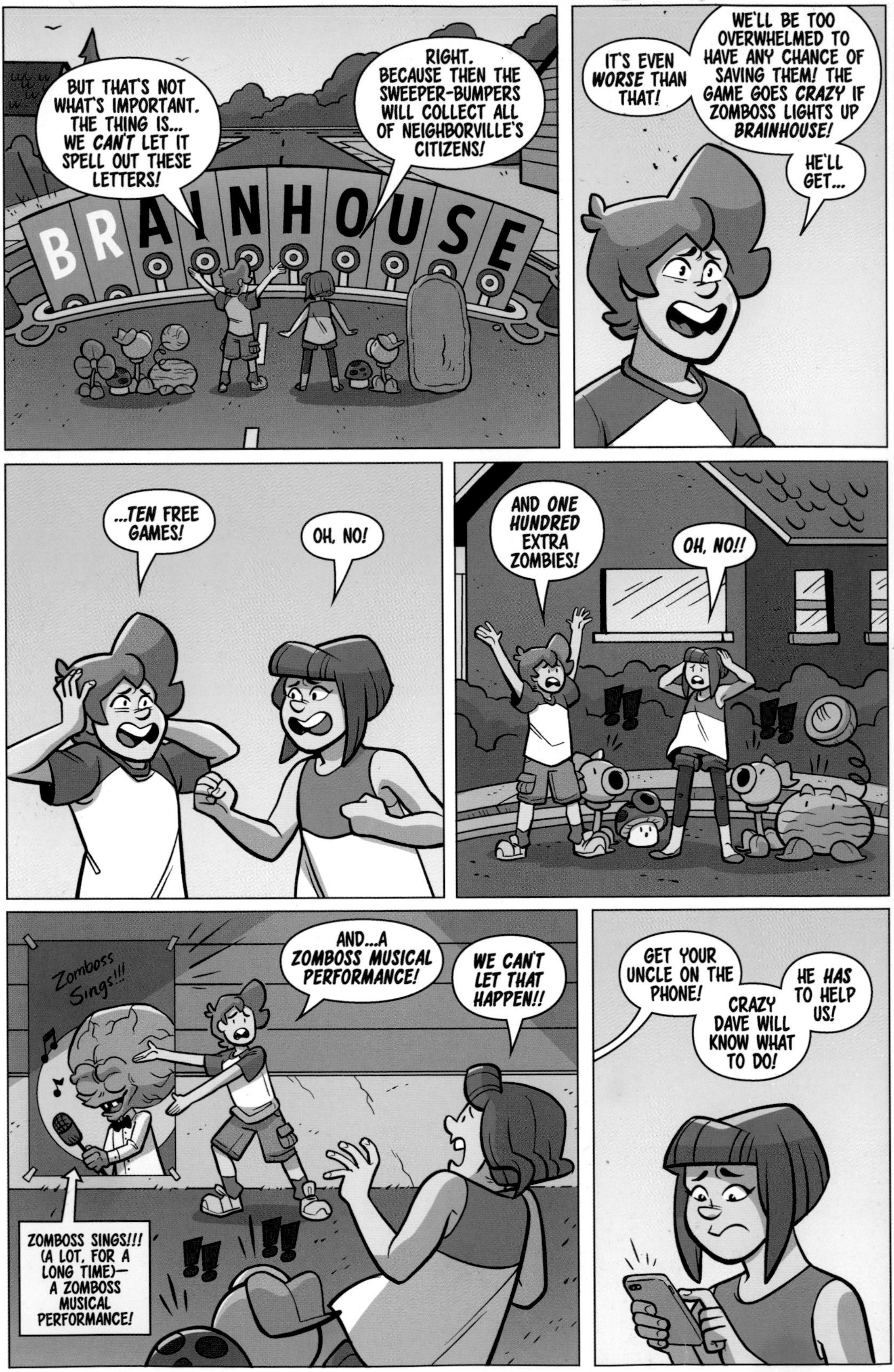

BUT THAT'S NOT WHAT'S IMPORTANT. THE THING IS... WE *CAN'T* LET IT SPELL OUT THESE LETTERS!
RIGHT. BECAUSE THEN THE SWEEPER-BUMPERS WILL COLLECT ALL OF NEIGHBORVILLE'S CITIZENS!
BRAINHOUSE
IT'S EVEN *WORSE* THAN THAT!
WE'LL BE TOO OVERWHELMED TO HAVE ANY CHANCE OF SAVING THEM! THE GAME GOES *CRAZY* IF ZOMBOSS LIGHTS UP *BRAINHOUSE!*
HE'LL GET...
...*TEN FREE* GAMES!
OH, NO!
AND *ONE HUNDRED* EXTRA ZOMBIES!
OH, NO!!
Zomboss Sings!!!
AND...A *ZOMBOSS MUSICAL PERFORMANCE!*
WE CAN'T LET THAT HAPPEN!!
ZOMBOSS SINGS!!! (A LOT, FOR A LONG TIME)— A ZOMBOSS MUSICAL PERFORMANCE!
GET YOUR UNCLE ON THE PHONE!
CRAZY DAVE WILL KNOW WHAT TO DO!
HE *HAS* TO HELP US!

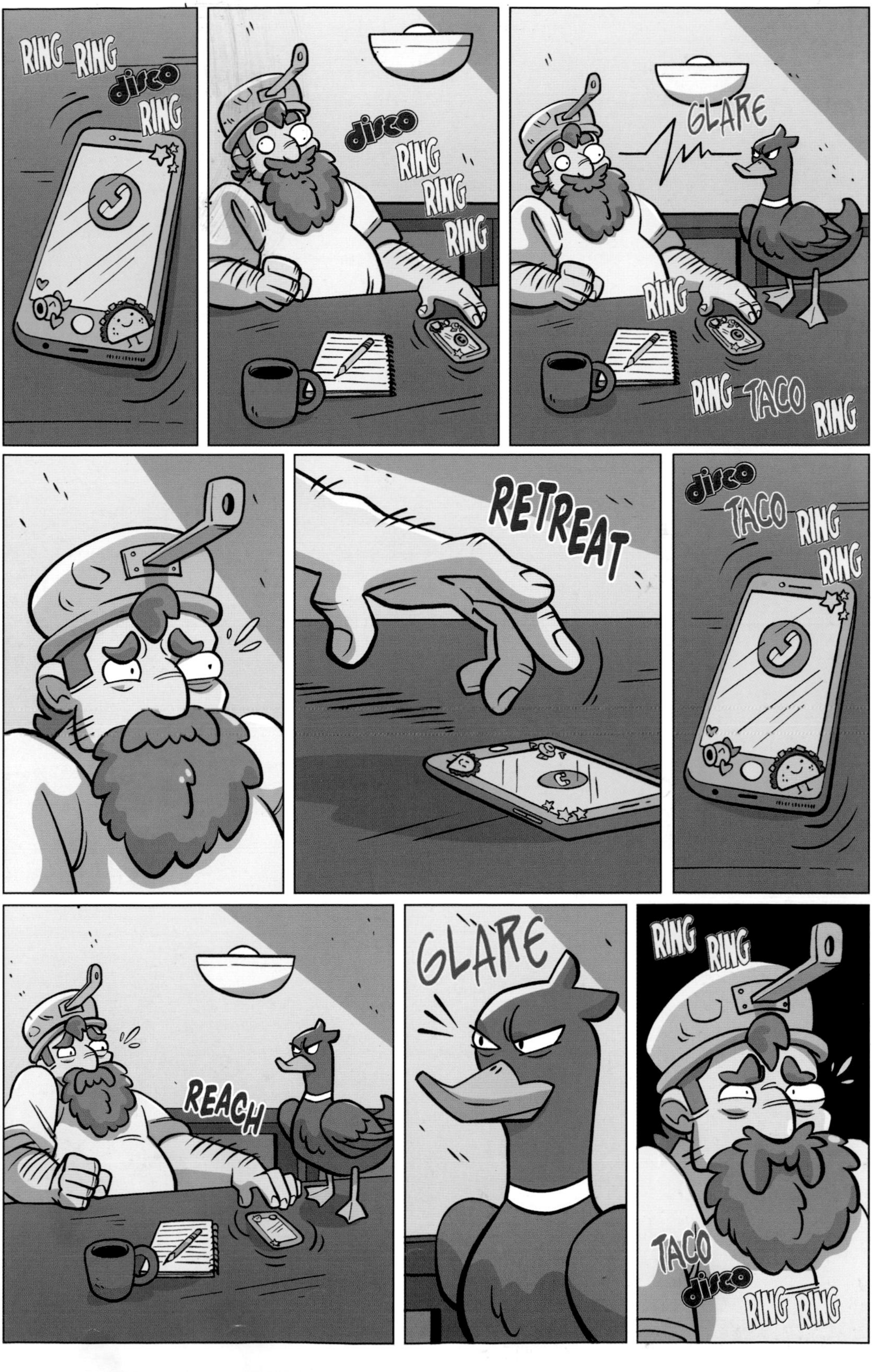
RING RING
disco
RING
disco
RING
RING
RING
GLARE
RING
RING TACO RING
RETREAT
disco
TACO RING
RING
REACH
GLARE
RING RING
TACO
disco
RING RING

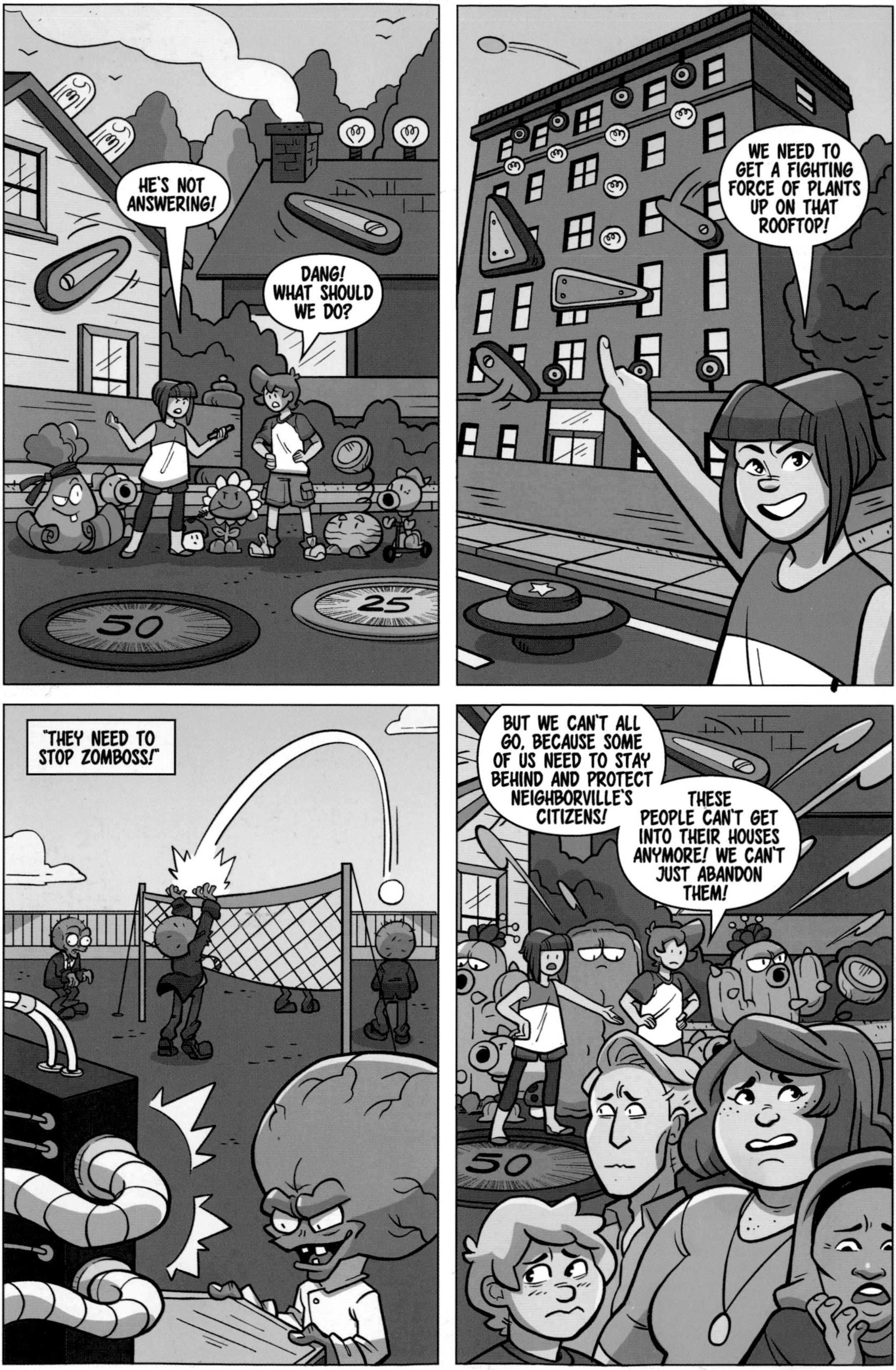
HE'S NOT ANSWERING!
DANG! WHAT SHOULD WE DO?
50
25
WE NEED TO GET A FIGHTING FORCE OF PLANTS UP ON THAT ROOFTOP!
"THEY NEED TO STOP ZOMBOSS!"
BUT WE CAN'T ALL GO, BECAUSE SOME OF US NEED TO STAY BEHIND AND PROTECT NEIGHBORVILLE'S CITIZENS!
THESE PEOPLE CAN'T GET INTO THEIR HOUSES ANYMORE! WE CAN'T JUST ABANDON THEM!
50

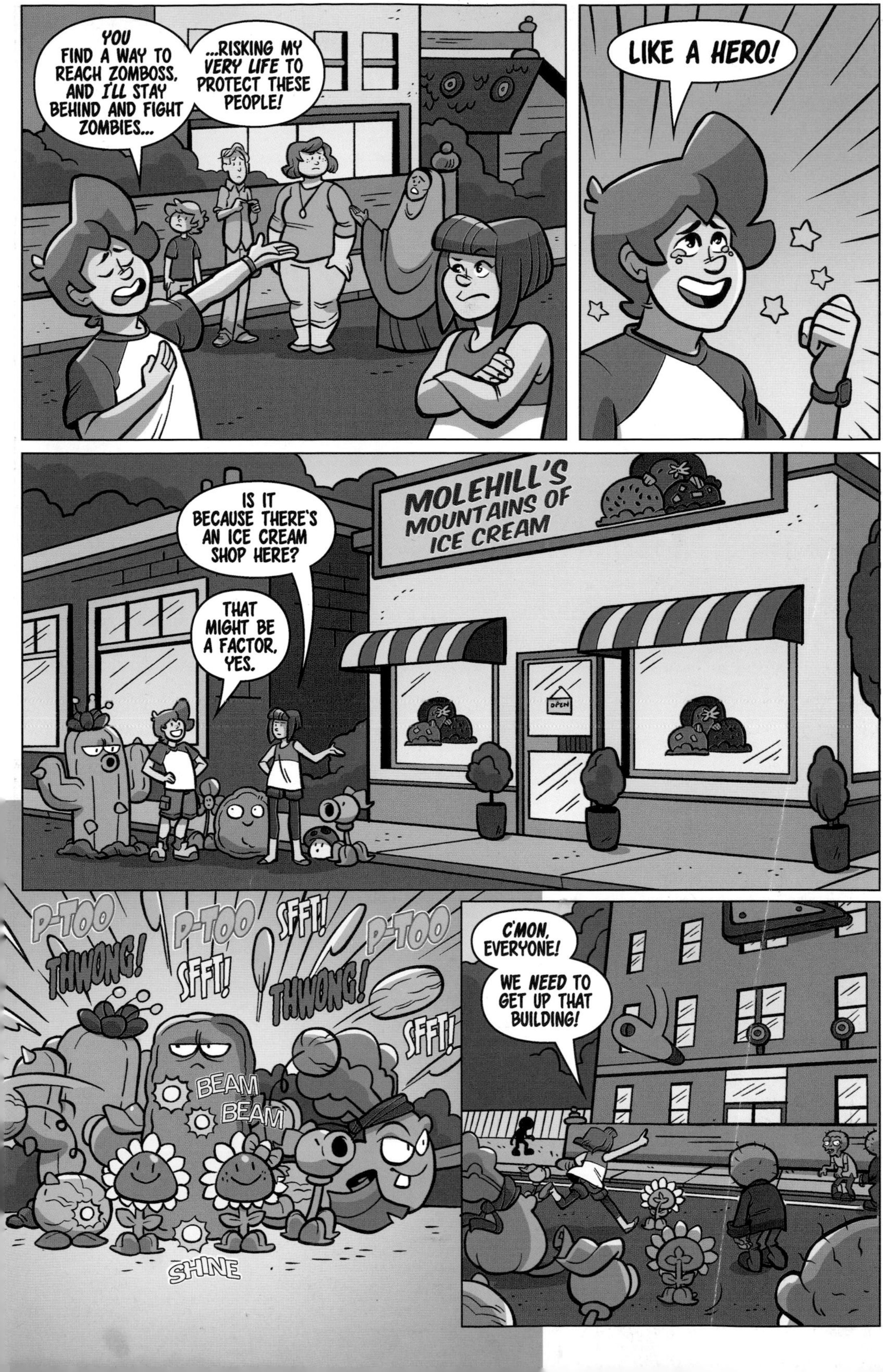
YOU FIND A WAY TO REACH ZOMBOSS, AND I'LL STAY BEHIND AND FIGHT ZOMBIES...
...RISKING MY VERY LIFE TO PROTECT THESE PEOPLE!
LIKE A HERO!
MOLEHILL'S MOUNTAINS OF ICE CREAM
IS IT BECAUSE THERE'S AN ICE CREAM SHOP HERE?
THAT MIGHT BE A FACTOR, YES.
OPEN
P-TOO
THWONG!
P-TOO
SFFT!
SFFT!
P-TOO
THWONG!
SFFT!
BEAM
BEAM
SHINE
C'MON, EVERYONE!
WE NEED TO GET UP THAT BUILDING!

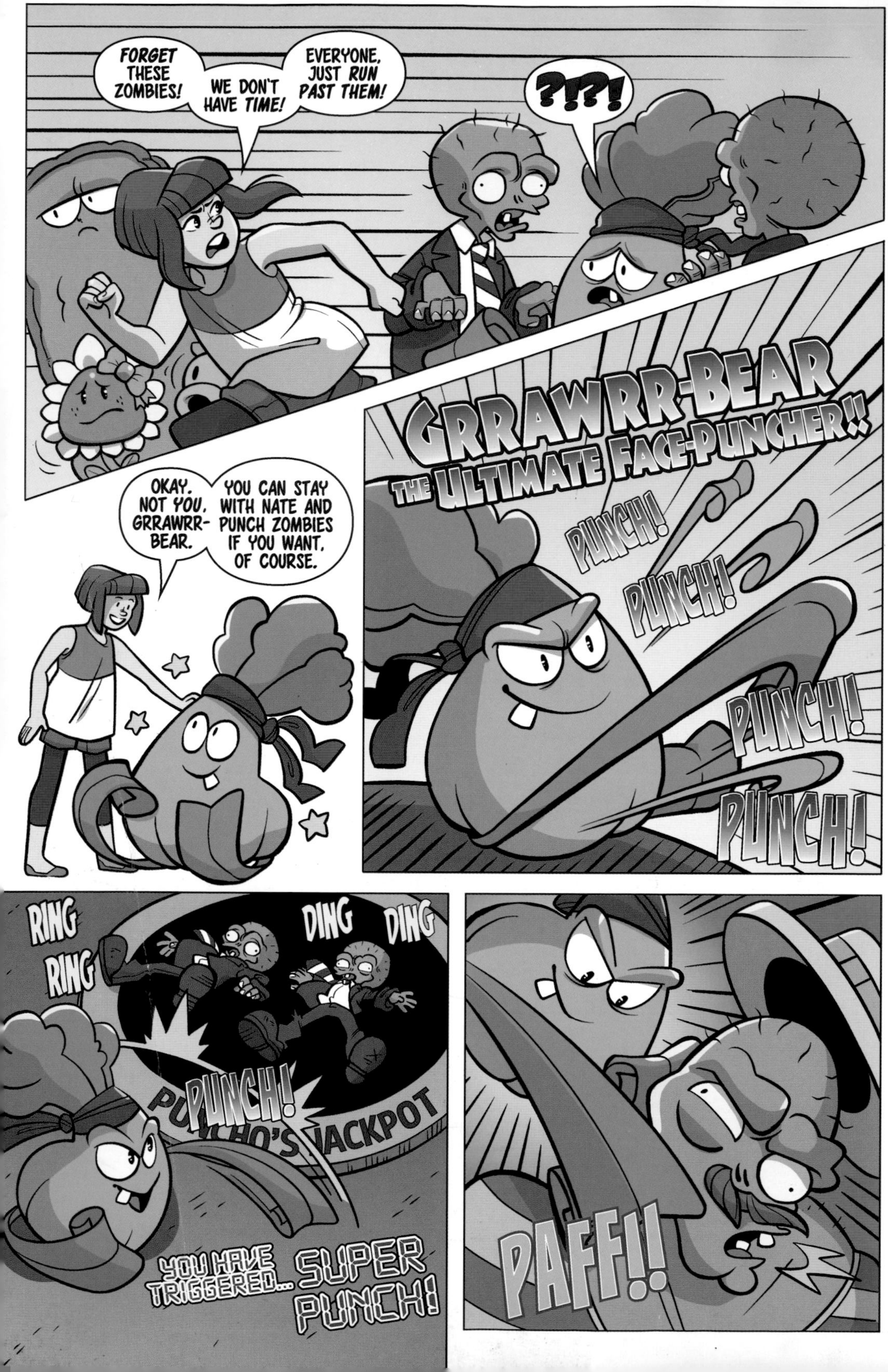
FORGET THESE ZOMBIES!
WE DON'T HAVE TIME!
EVERYONE, JUST RUN PAST THEM!
???!
OKAY. NOT YOU, GRRAWRR-BEAR.
YOU CAN STAY WITH NATE AND PUNCH ZOMBIES IF YOU WANT, OF COURSE.
GRRAWRR-BEAR THE ULTIMATE FACE-PUNCHER!!
PUNCH!
PUNCH!
PUNCH!
PUNCH!
RING RING
DING DING
PUNCH!
PUNCHO'S JACKPOT
YOU HAVE TRIGGERED... SUPER PUNCH!
PAFF!!

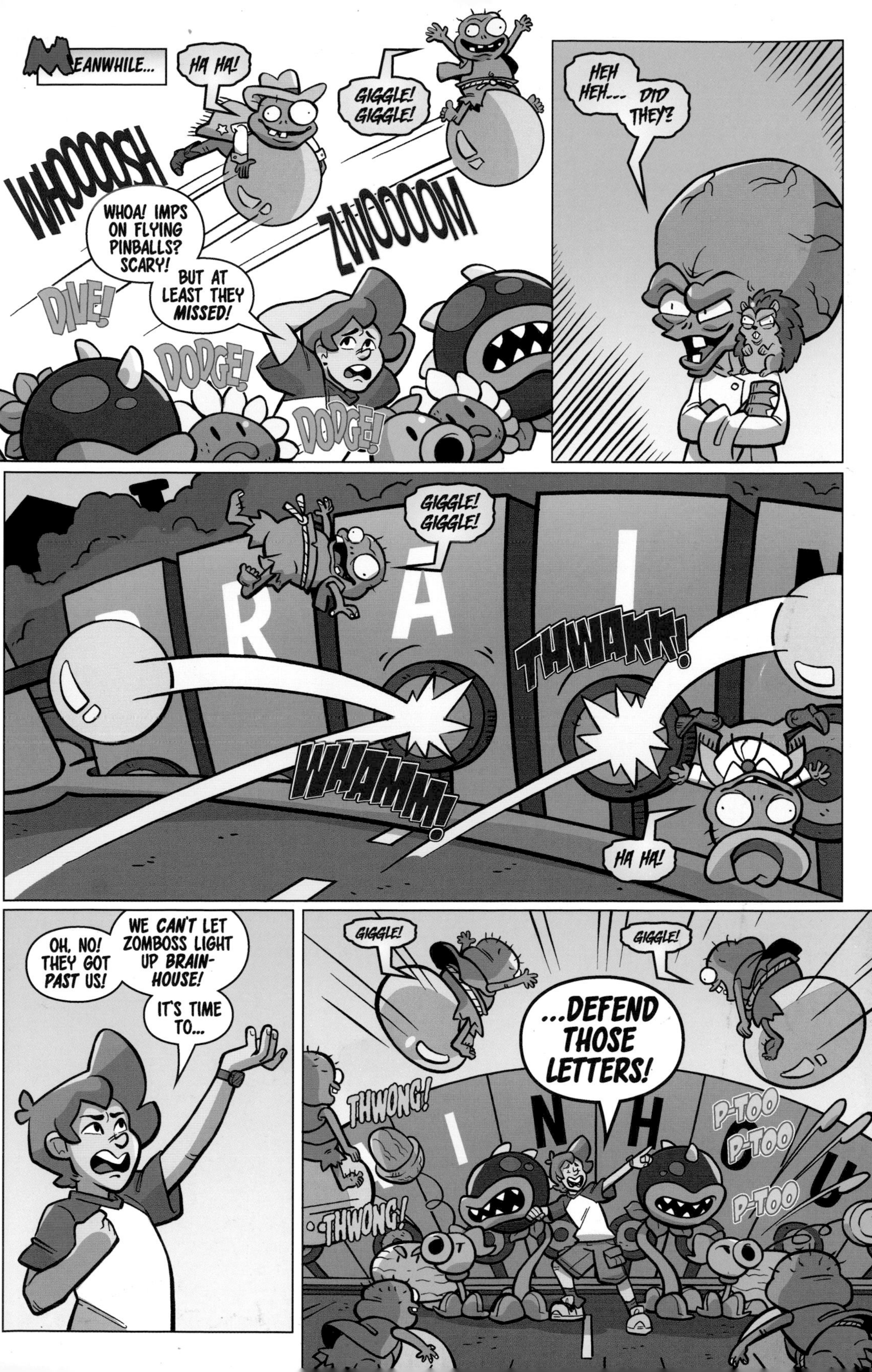
MEANWHILE...
HA HA!
GIGGLE! GIGGLE!
WHOOOOSH
ZWOOOOM
WHOA! IMPS ON FLYING PINBALLS? SCARY!
BUT AT LEAST THEY MISSED!
DIVE!
DODGE!
DODGE!
HEH HEH... DID THEY?
GIGGLE! GIGGLE!
THWAKK!
WHAMM!
HA HA!
OH, NO! THEY GOT PAST US!
WE CAN'T LET ZOMBOSS LIGHT UP BRAIN-HOUSE!
IT'S TIME TO...
GIGGLE!
GIGGLE!
...DEFEND THOSE LETTERS!
THWONG!
THWONG!
P-TOO
P-TOO
P-TOO

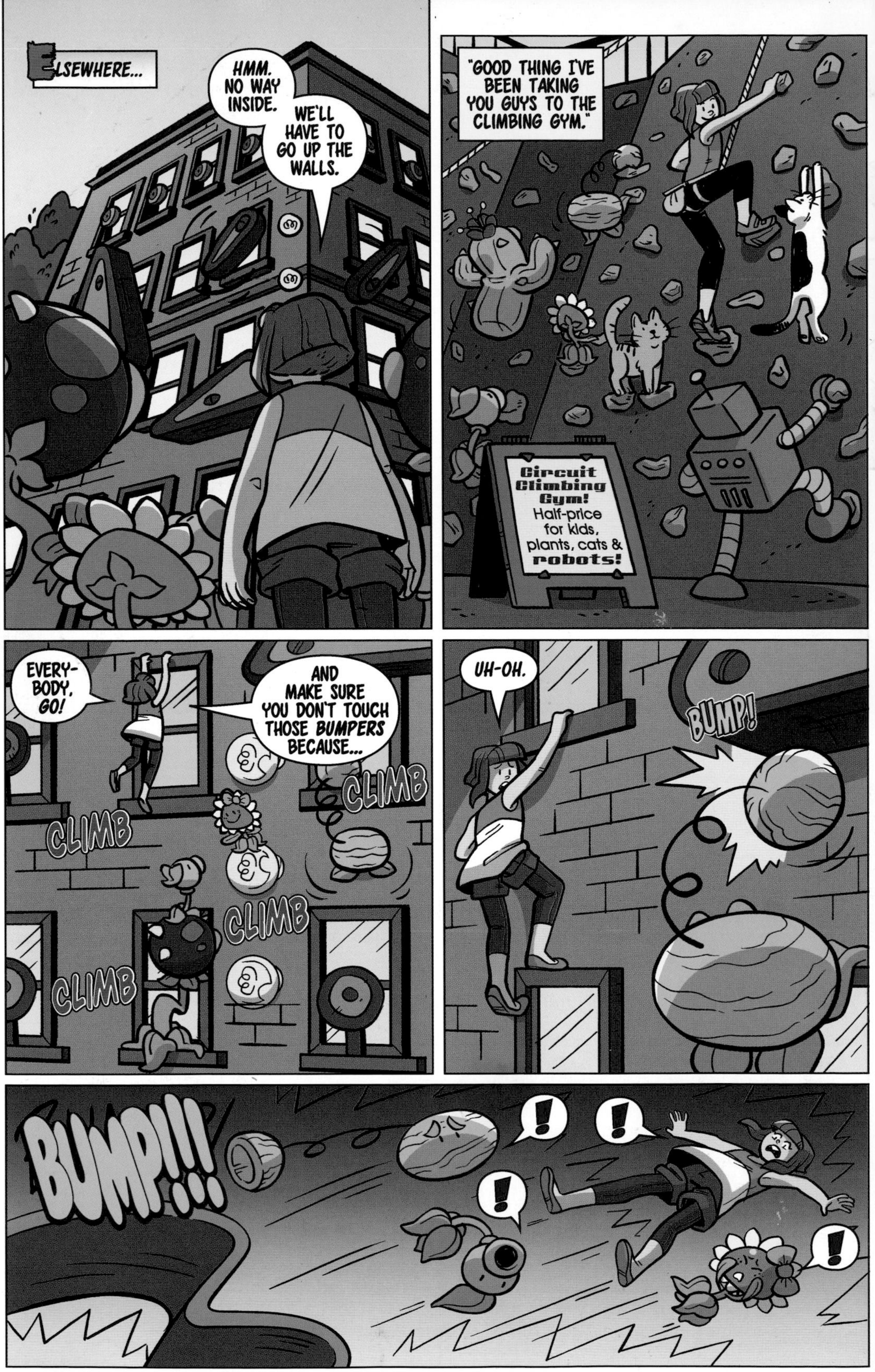
ELSEWHERE...
HMM. NO WAY INSIDE.
WE'LL HAVE TO GO UP THE WALLS.
"GOOD THING I'VE BEEN TAKING YOU GUYS TO THE CLIMBING GYM."
Circuit Climbing Gym! Half-price for kids, plants, cats & robots!
EVERY-BODY, GO!
AND MAKE SURE YOU DON'T TOUCH THOSE BUMPERS BECAUSE...
CLIMB
CLIMB
CLIMB
CLIMB
UH-OH.
BUMP!
BUMP!!!
!
!
!
!

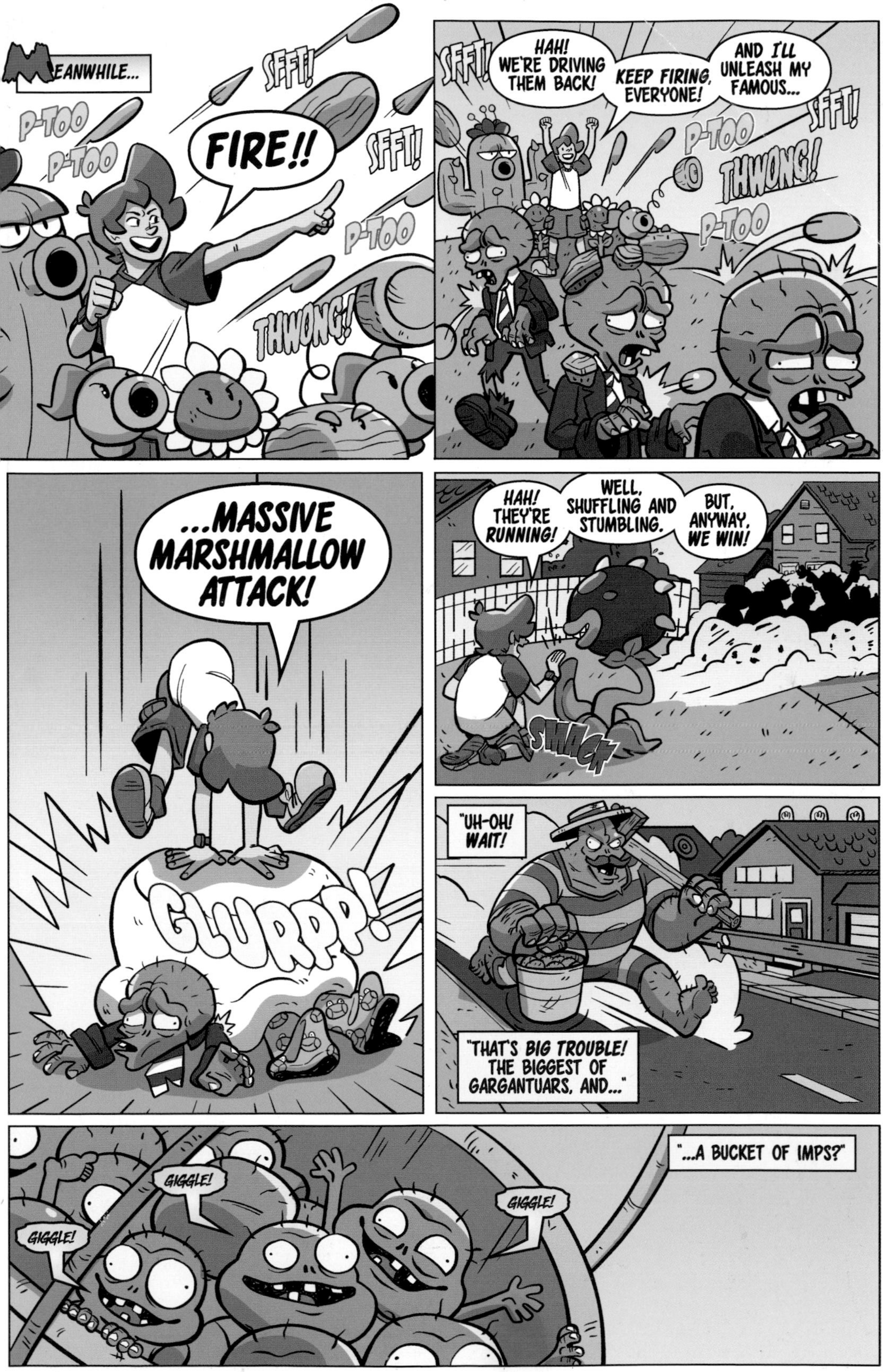
MEANWHILE...
P-TOO
P-TOO
SFFT!
FIRE!!
SFFT!
P-TOO
THWONG!
SFFT!
HAH! WE'RE DRIVING THEM BACK!
KEEP FIRING, EVERYONE!
AND I'LL UNLEASH MY FAMOUS...
P-TOO
SFFT!
THWONG!
P-TOO
...MASSIVE MARSHMALLOW ATTACK!
GLURPP!
HAH! THEY'RE RUNNING!
WELL, SHUFFLING AND STUMBLING.
BUT, ANYWAY, WE WIN!
SMACK
"UH-OH! WAIT!
"THAT'S BIG TROUBLE! THE BIGGEST OF GARGANTUARS, AND..."
"...A BUCKET OF IMPS?"
GIGGLE!
GIGGLE!
GIGGLE!

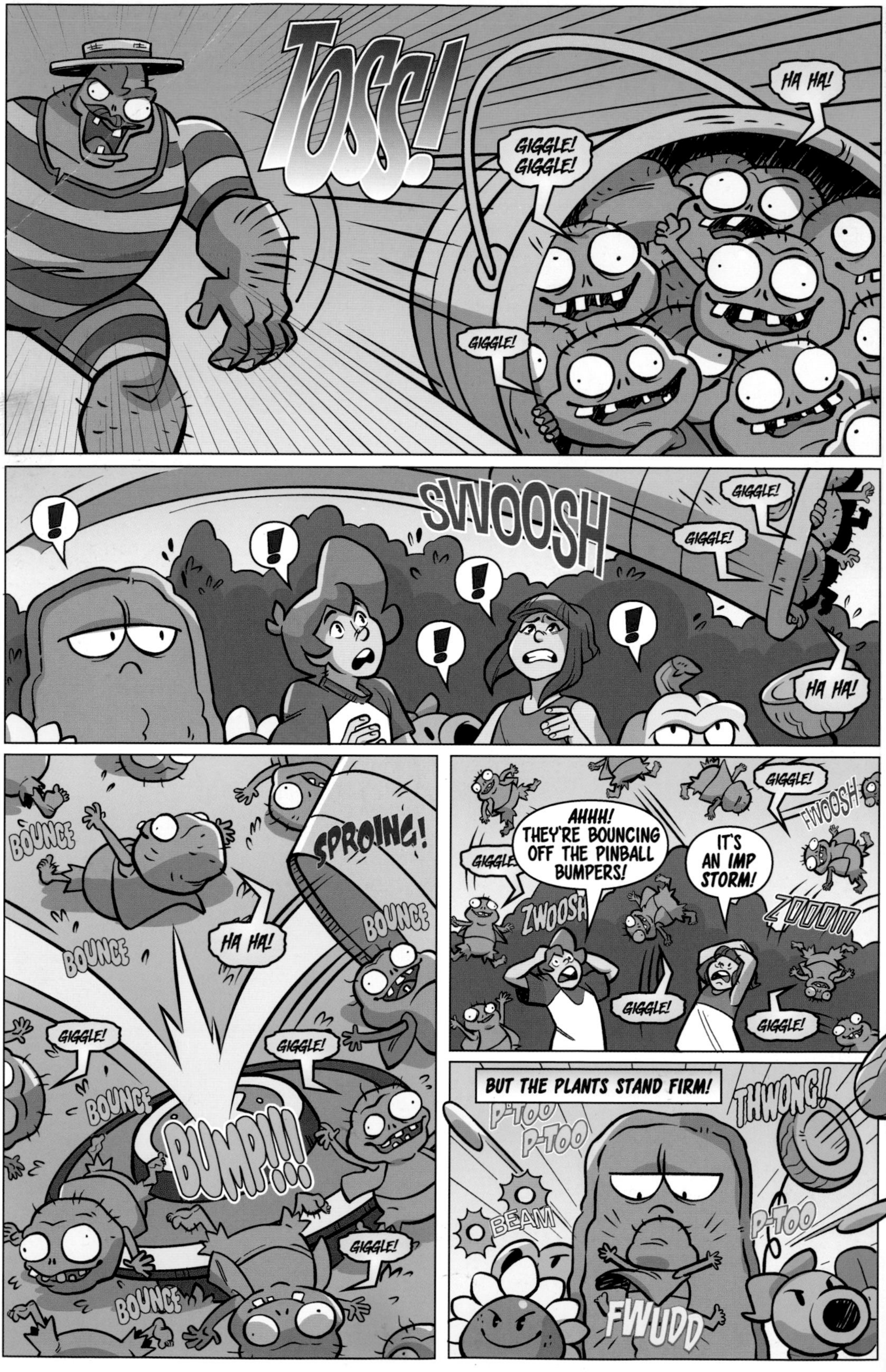
TOSS!
HA HA!
GIGGLE! GIGGLE!
GIGGLE!
SWOOSH
GIGGLE!
GIGGLE!
!
!
!
!
!
HA HA!
BOUNCE
SPROING!
BOUNCE
BOUNCE
HA HA!
GIGGLE!
GIGGLE!
BOUNCE
BUMP!!!
GIGGLE!
BOUNCE
GIGGLE!
AHHH! THEY'RE BOUNCING OFF THE PINBALL BUMPERS!
IT'S AN IMP STORM!
FWOOSH
ZWOOSH
ZOOOM
GIGGLE!
GIGGLE!
BUT THE PLANTS STAND FIRM!
THWONG!
P-TOO
P-TOO
BEAM
P-TOO
FWUDD

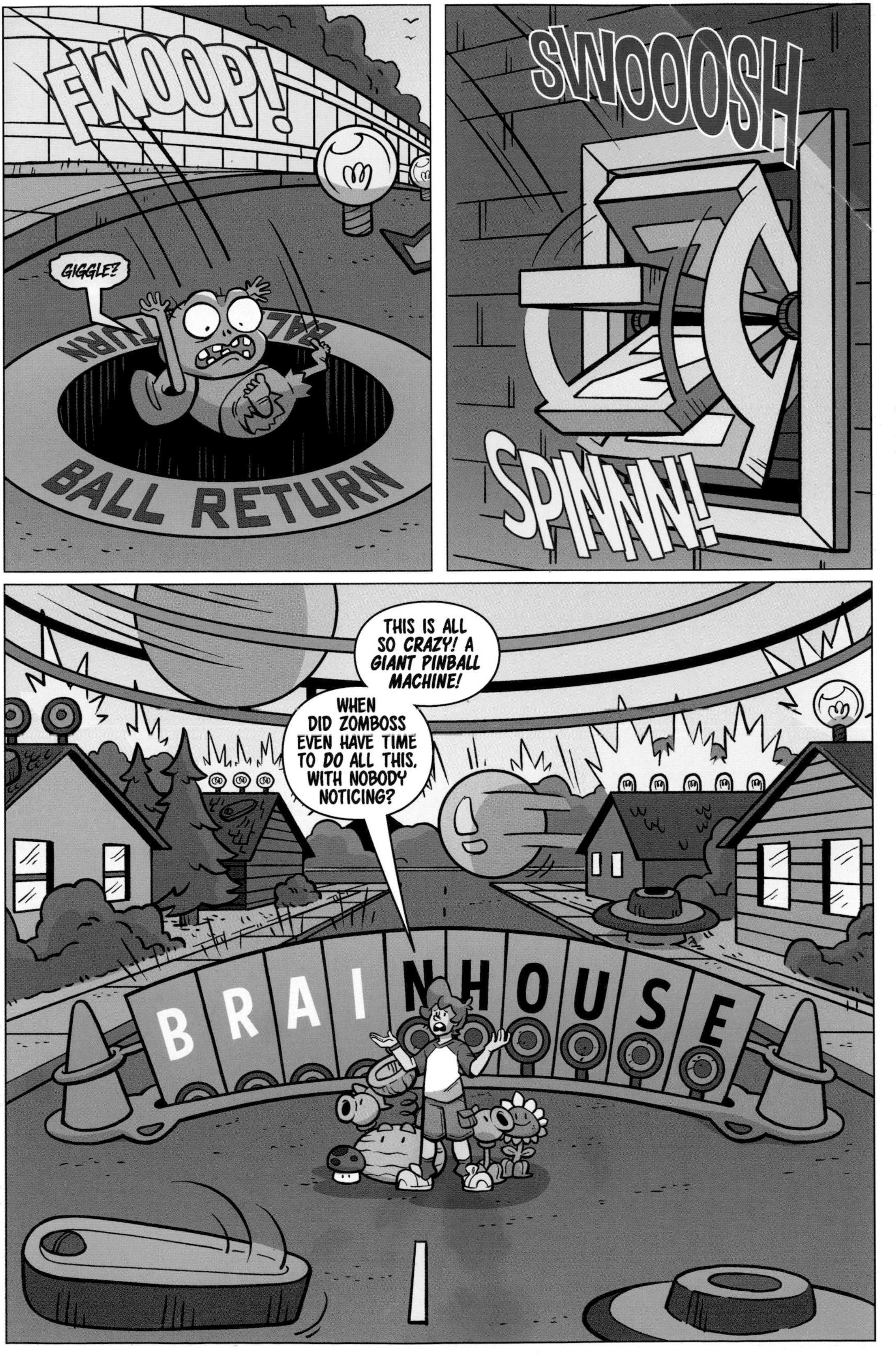

FWOOP!
GIGGLE?
BALL RETURN
BALL RETURN
SWOOOSH
SPINNNN!
THIS IS ALL SO CRAZY! A GIANT PINBALL MACHINE!
WHEN DID ZOMBOSS EVEN HAVE TIME TO DO ALL THIS, WITH NOBODY NOTICING?
BRAINHOUSE

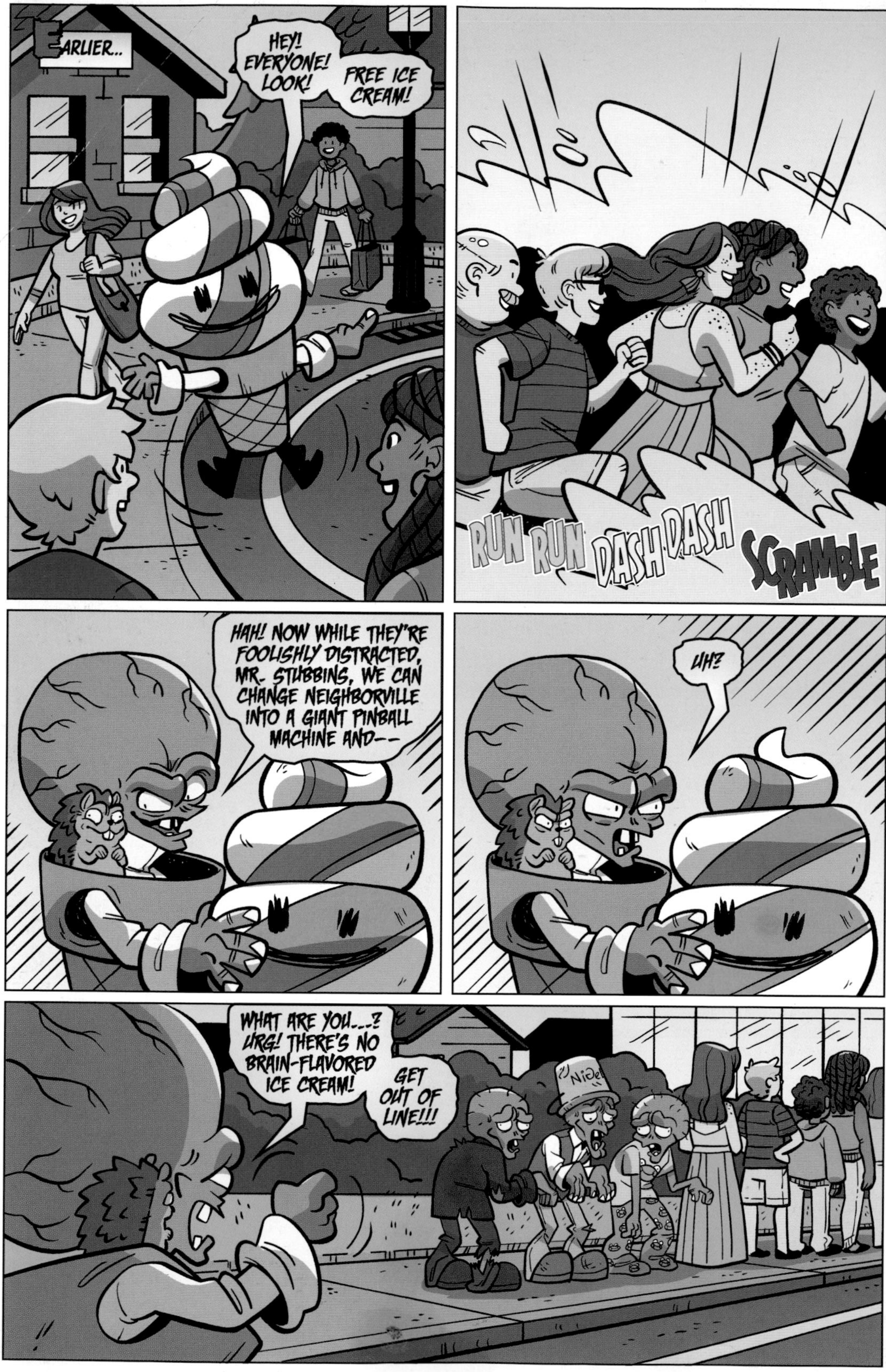
EARLIER...
HEY! EVERYONE! LOOK!
FREE ICE CREAM!
RUN RUN DASH DASH SCRAMBLE
HAH! NOW WHILE THEY'RE FOOLISHLY DISTRACTED, MR. STUBBINS, WE CAN CHANGE NEIGHBORVILLE INTO A GIANT PINBALL MACHINE AND--
UH?
WHAT ARE YOU...? URG! THERE'S NO BRAIN-FLAVORED ICE CREAM!
GET OUT OF LINE!!!

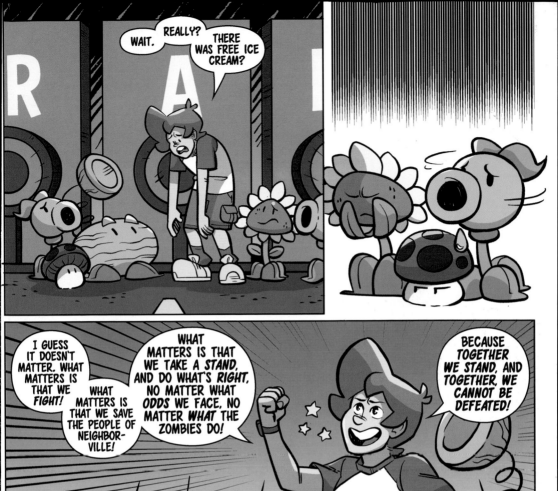

WAIT. REALLY? THERE WAS FREE ICE CREAM?

I GUESS IT DOESN'T MATTER. WHAT MATTERS IS THAT WE FIGHT!

WHAT MATTERS IS THAT WE SAVE THE PEOPLE OF NEIGHBORVILLE!

WHAT MATTERS IS THAT WE TAKE A STAND, AND DO WHAT'S RIGHT, NO MATTER WHAT ODDS WE FACE, NO MATTER WHAT THE ZOMBIES DO!

BECAUSE TOGETHER WE STAND, AND TOGETHER, WE CANNOT BE DEFEATED!

OH, NO!

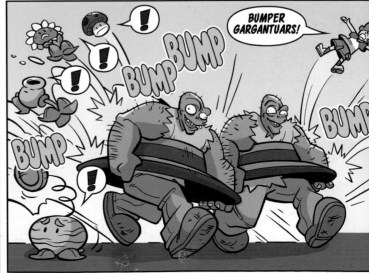

BUMPER GARGANTUARS!

BUMP BUMP BUMP BUMP

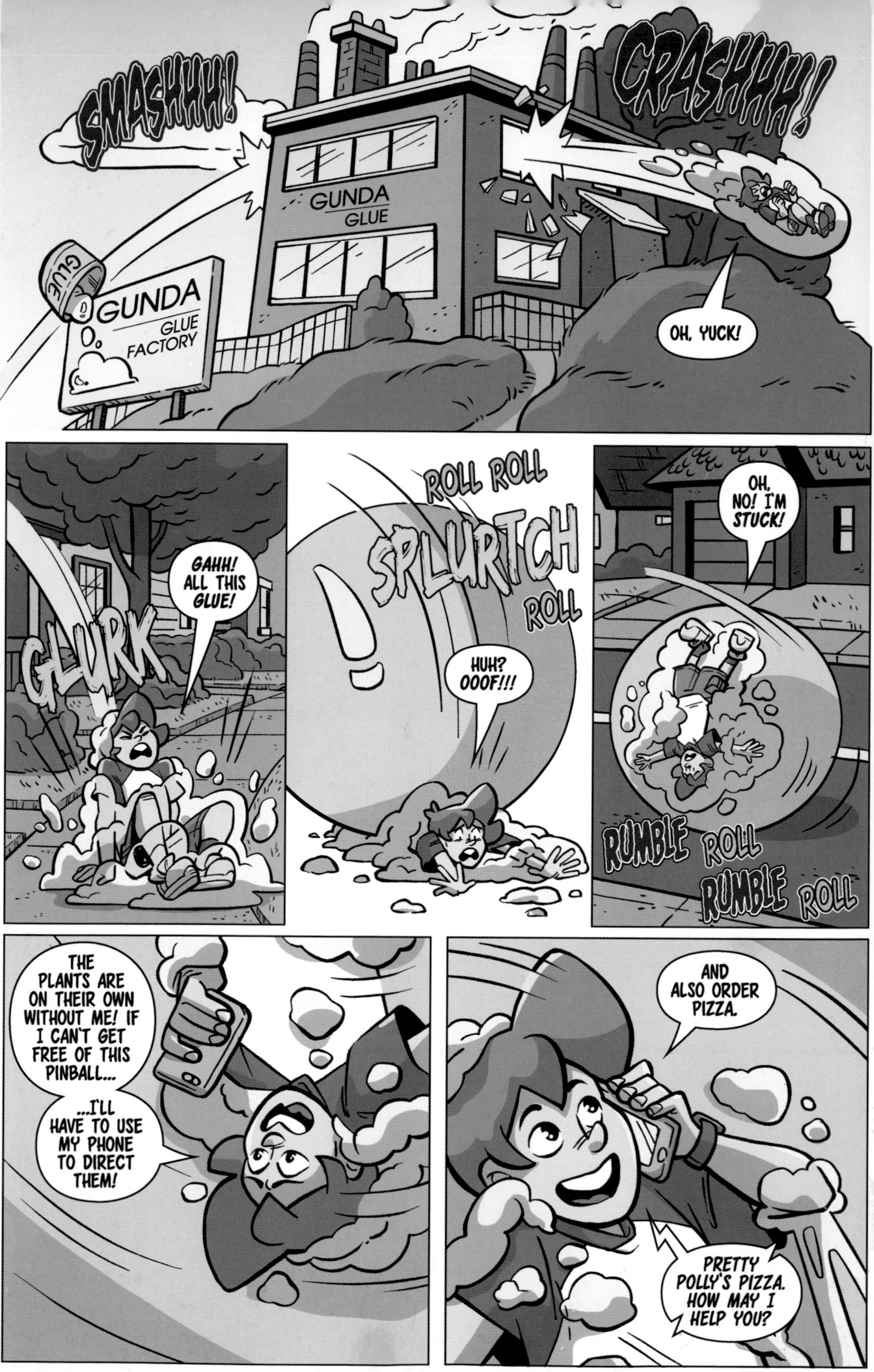
SMASHHH!
GLUE
GUNDA GLUE FACTORY
GUNDA GLUE
CRASHHH!
OH, YUCK!
GAHH! ALL THIS GLUE!
GLURK
ROLL ROLL
SPLURTCH
ROLL
HUH? OOOF!!!
OH, NO! I'M STUCK!
RUMBLE ROLL
RUMBLE ROLL
THE PLANTS ARE ON THEIR OWN WITHOUT ME! IF I CAN'T GET FREE OF THIS PINBALL...
...I'LL HAVE TO USE MY PHONE TO DIRECT THEM!
AND ALSO ORDER PIZZA.
PRETTY POLLY'S PIZZA. HOW MAY I HELP YOU?

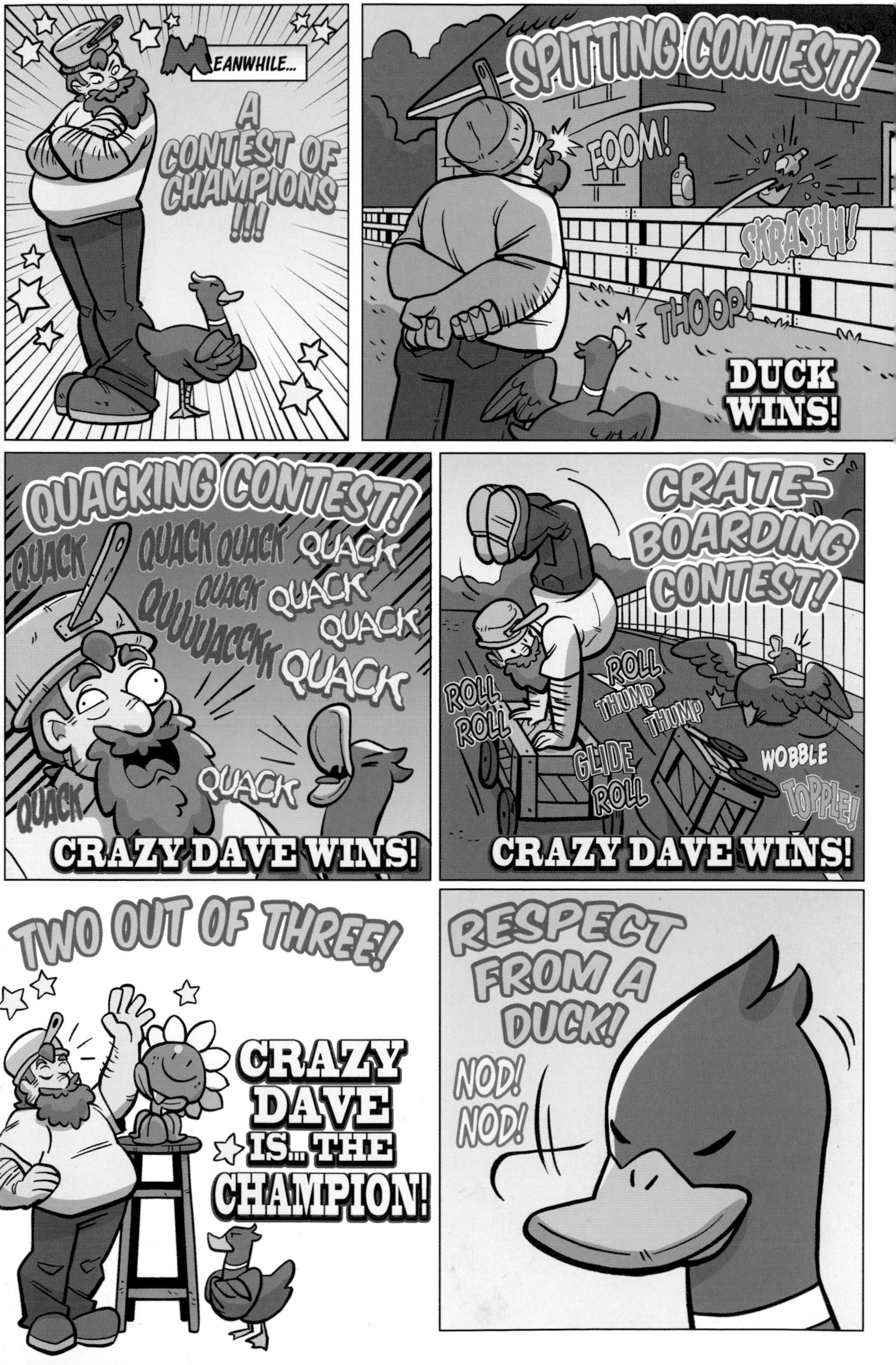

MEANWHILE...
A CONTEST OF CHAMPIONS !!!
SPITTING CONTEST!
FOOM!
SKRASHH!
THOOP!
DUCK WINS!
QUACKING CONTEST!
QUACK QUACK QUACK QUACK
QUACK QUACK
QUUUUACCKK QUACK
QUACK
QUACK
QUACK
CRAZY DAVE WINS!
CRATE-BOARDING CONTEST!
ROLL ROLL
ROLL
THUMP THUMP
GLIDE ROLL
WOBBLE
TOPPLE!
CRAZY DAVE WINS!
TWO OUT OF THREE!
CRAZY DAVE IS... THE CHAMPION!
RESPECT FROM A DUCK!
NOD! NOD!

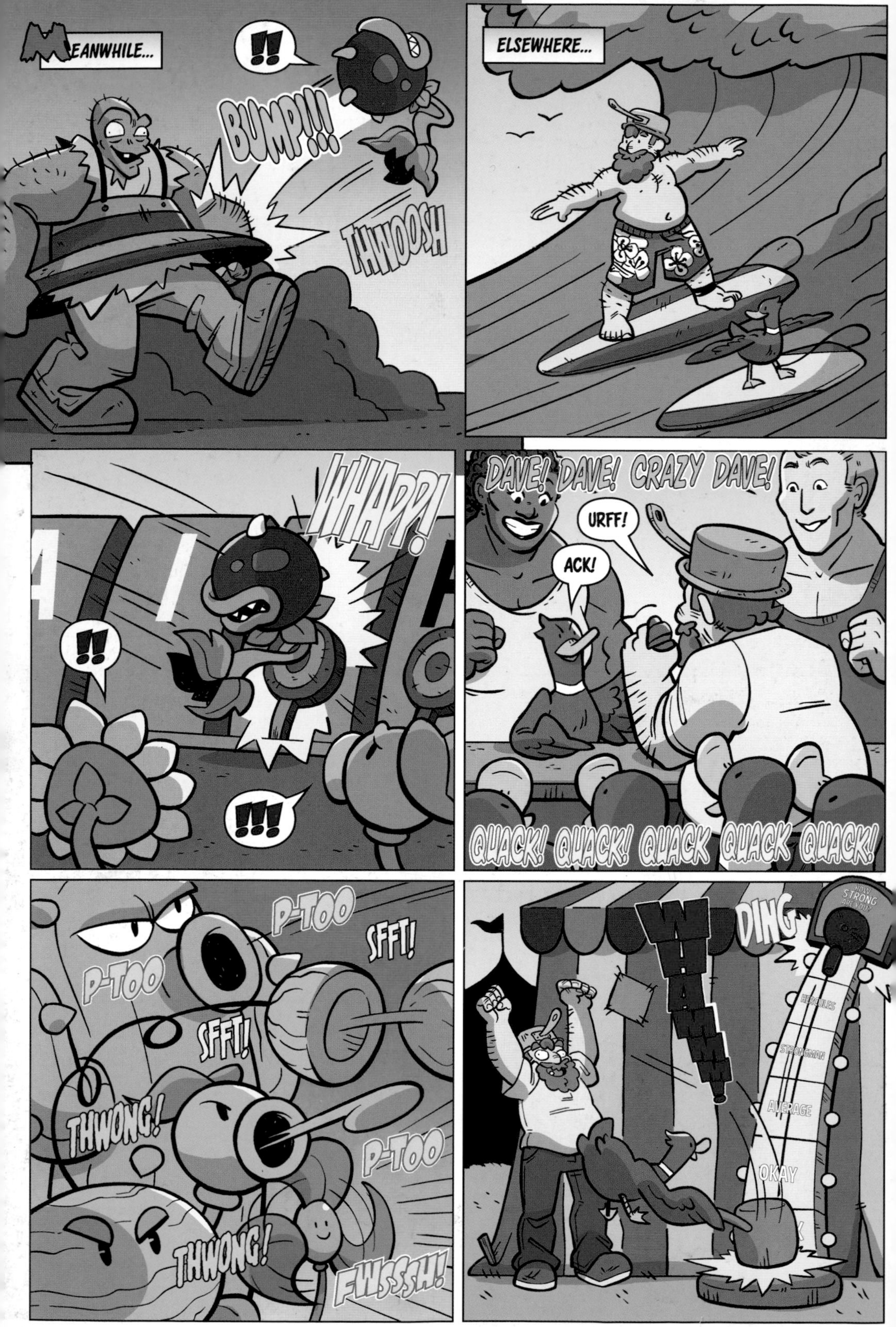
MEANWHILE...
!!
BUMP!!!
THWOOSH
ELSEWHERE...
WHAPP!
!!
!!!
DAVE! DAVE! CRAZY DAVE!
URFF!
ACK!
QUACK! QUACK! QUACK QUACK QUACK!
P-TOO
SFFT!
P-TOO
SFFT!
THWONG!
P-TOO
THWONG!
FWSSSH!
WHAMM
DING
HOW STRONG ARE YOU?
HERCULES
STRONGMAN
AVERAGE
OKAY

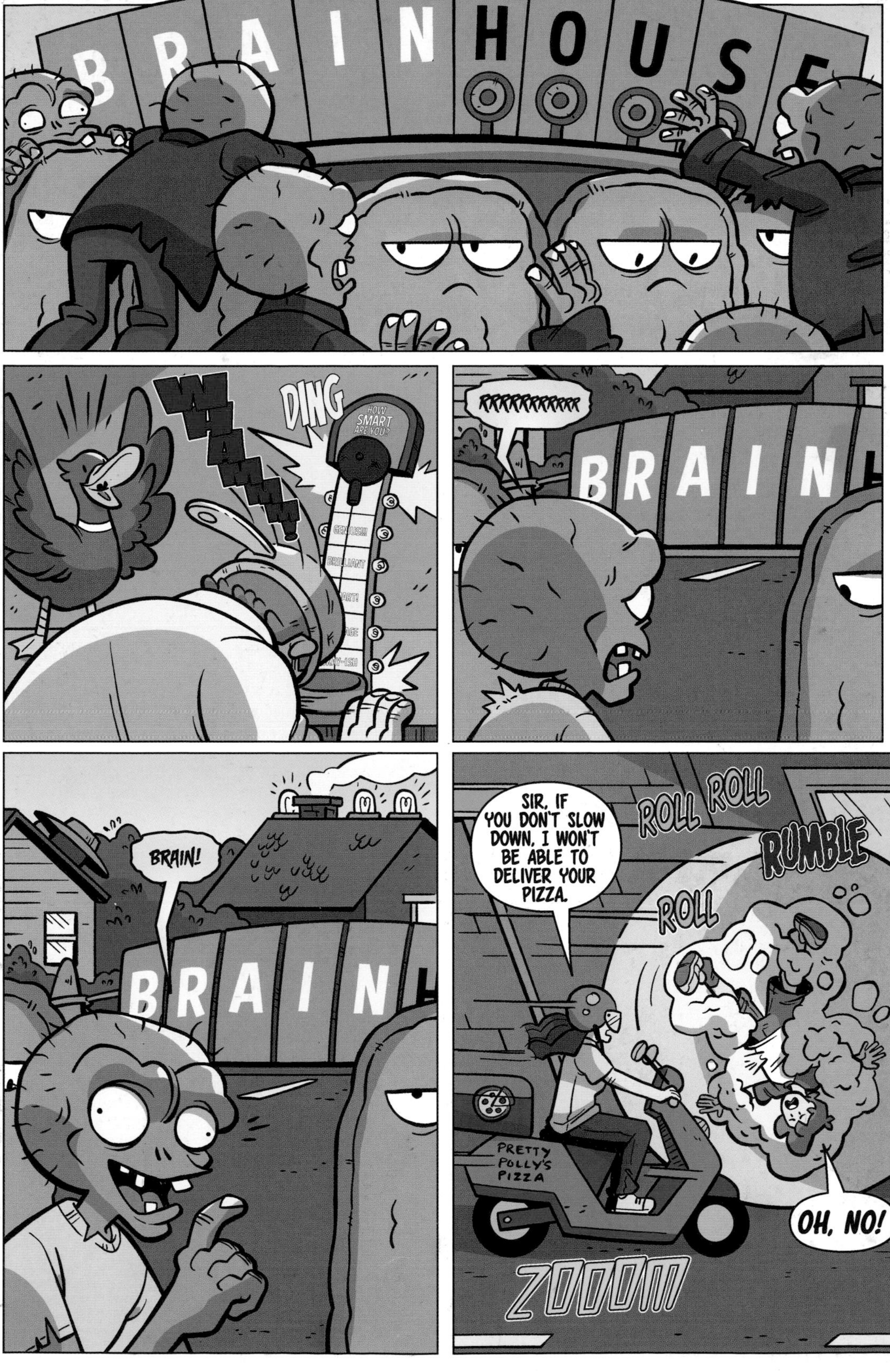
BRAIN HOUSE
WHAMMM!
DING
HOW SMART ARE YOU?
GENIUS!!
BRILLIANT
RRRRRRRRRRR
BRAIN
BRAIN!
BRAIN
SIR, IF YOU DON'T SLOW DOWN, I WON'T BE ABLE TO DELIVER YOUR PIZZA.
ROLL ROLL
RUMBLE
ROLL
PRETTY POLLY'S PIZZA
OH, NO!
ZOOOM

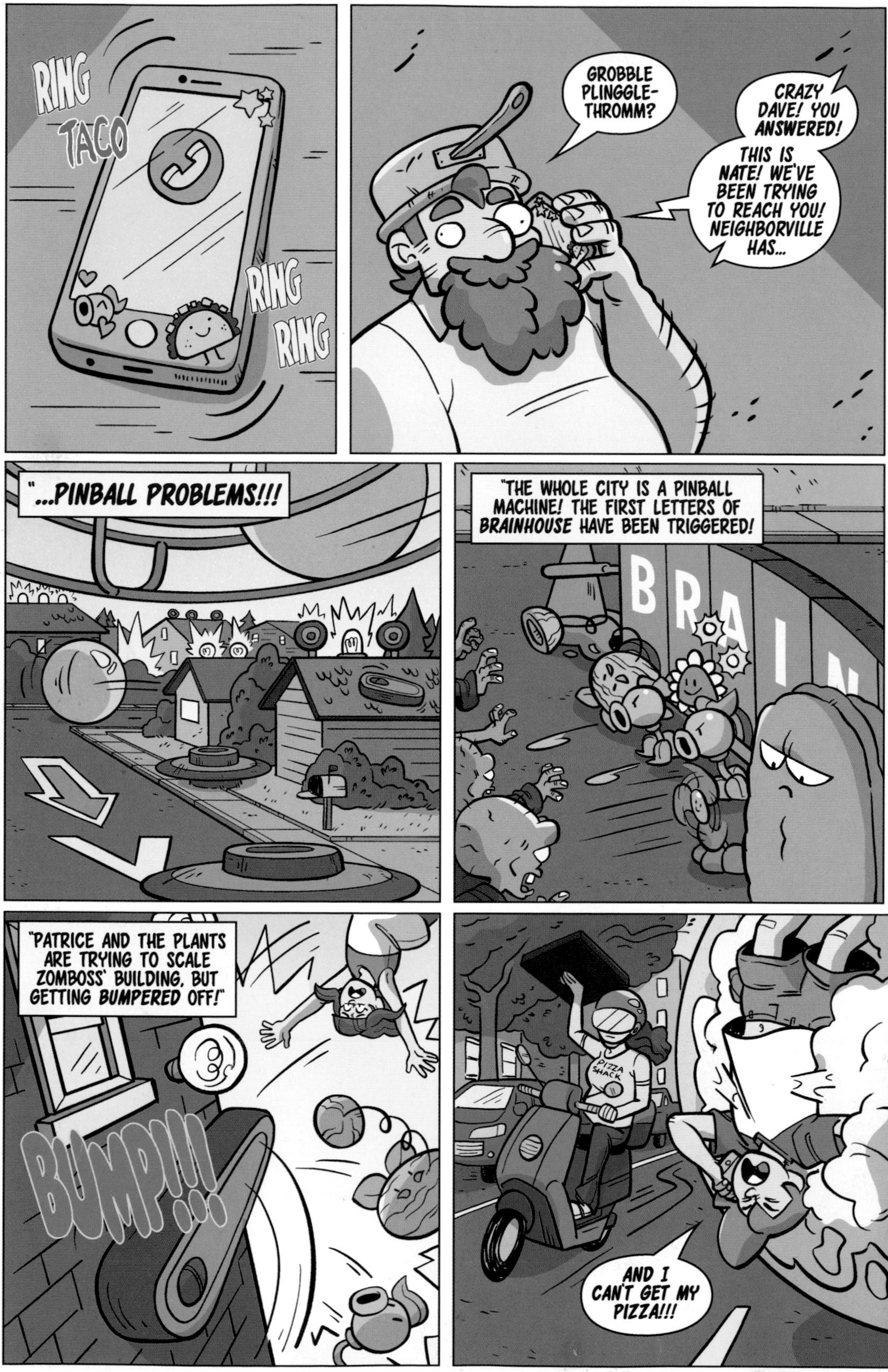
RING
TACO
RING
RING
GROBBLE PLINGGLE-THROMM?
CRAZY DAVE! YOU ANSWERED!
THIS IS NATE! WE'VE BEEN TRYING TO REACH YOU! NEIGHBORVILLE HAS...
"...PINBALL PROBLEMS!!!
"THE WHOLE CITY IS A PINBALL MACHINE! THE FIRST LETTERS OF BRAINHOUSE HAVE BEEN TRIGGERED!
BRAIN
"PATRICE AND THE PLANTS ARE TRYING TO SCALE ZOMBOSS' BUILDING, BUT GETTING BUMPERED OFF!"
BUMP!!!
PIZZA SHACK
AND I CAN'T GET MY PIZZA!!!

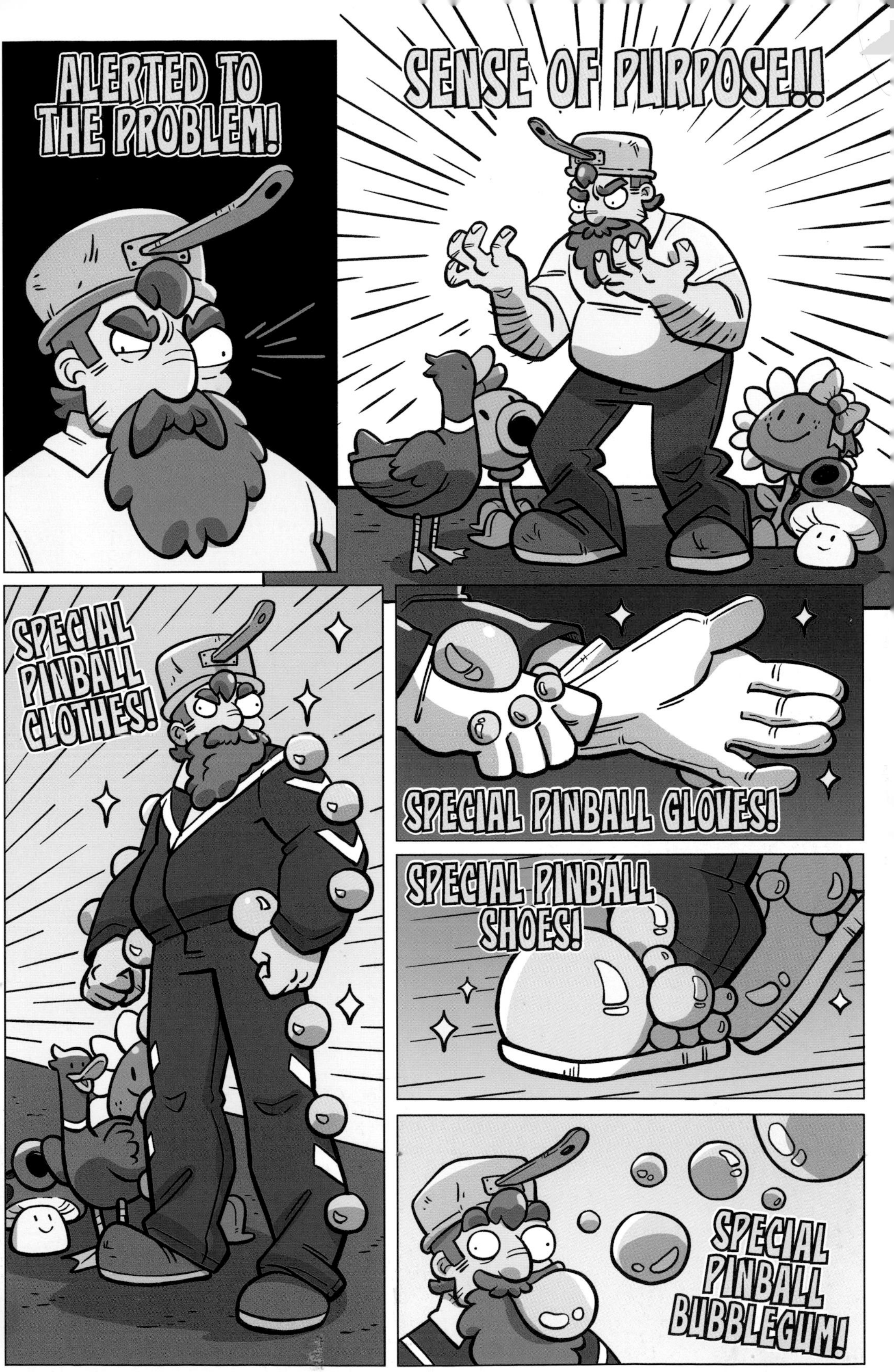
ALERTED TO THE PROBLEM!
SENSE OF PURPOSE!!
SPECIAL PINBALL CLOTHES!
SPECIAL PINBALL GLOVES!
SPECIAL PINBALL SHOES!
SPECIAL PINBALL BUBBLEGUM!

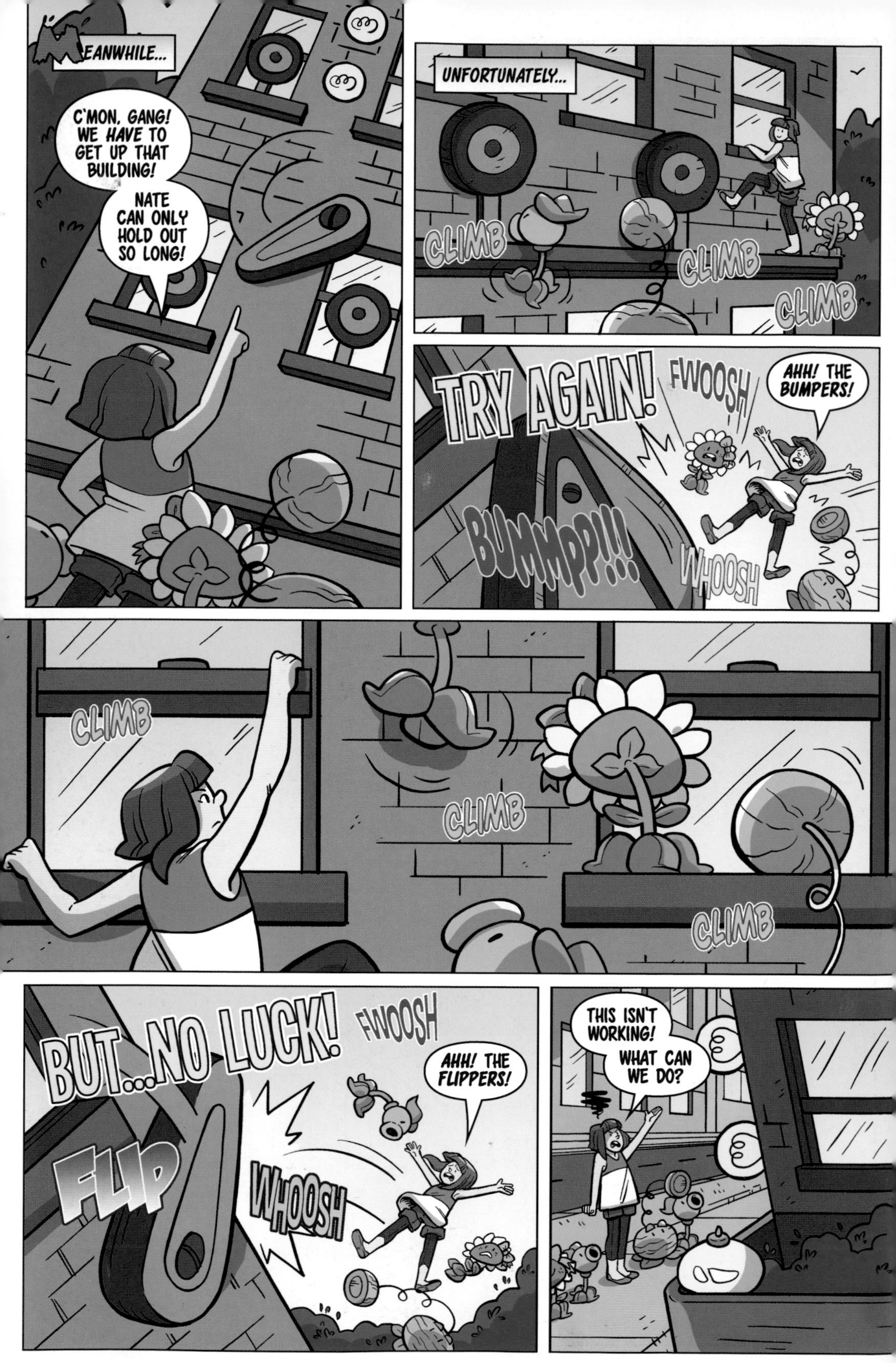
MEANWHILE...
C'MON, GANG! WE HAVE TO GET UP THAT BUILDING!
NATE CAN ONLY HOLD OUT SO LONG!
UNFORTUNATELY...
CLIMB
CLIMB
CLIMB
TRY AGAIN!
FWOOSH
AHH! THE BUMPERS!
BUMMPP!!!
WHOOSH
CLIMB
CLIMB
CLIMB
BUT...NO LUCK!
FWOOSH
AHH! THE FLIPPERS!
FLIP
WHOOSH
THIS ISN'T WORKING!
WHAT CAN WE DO?

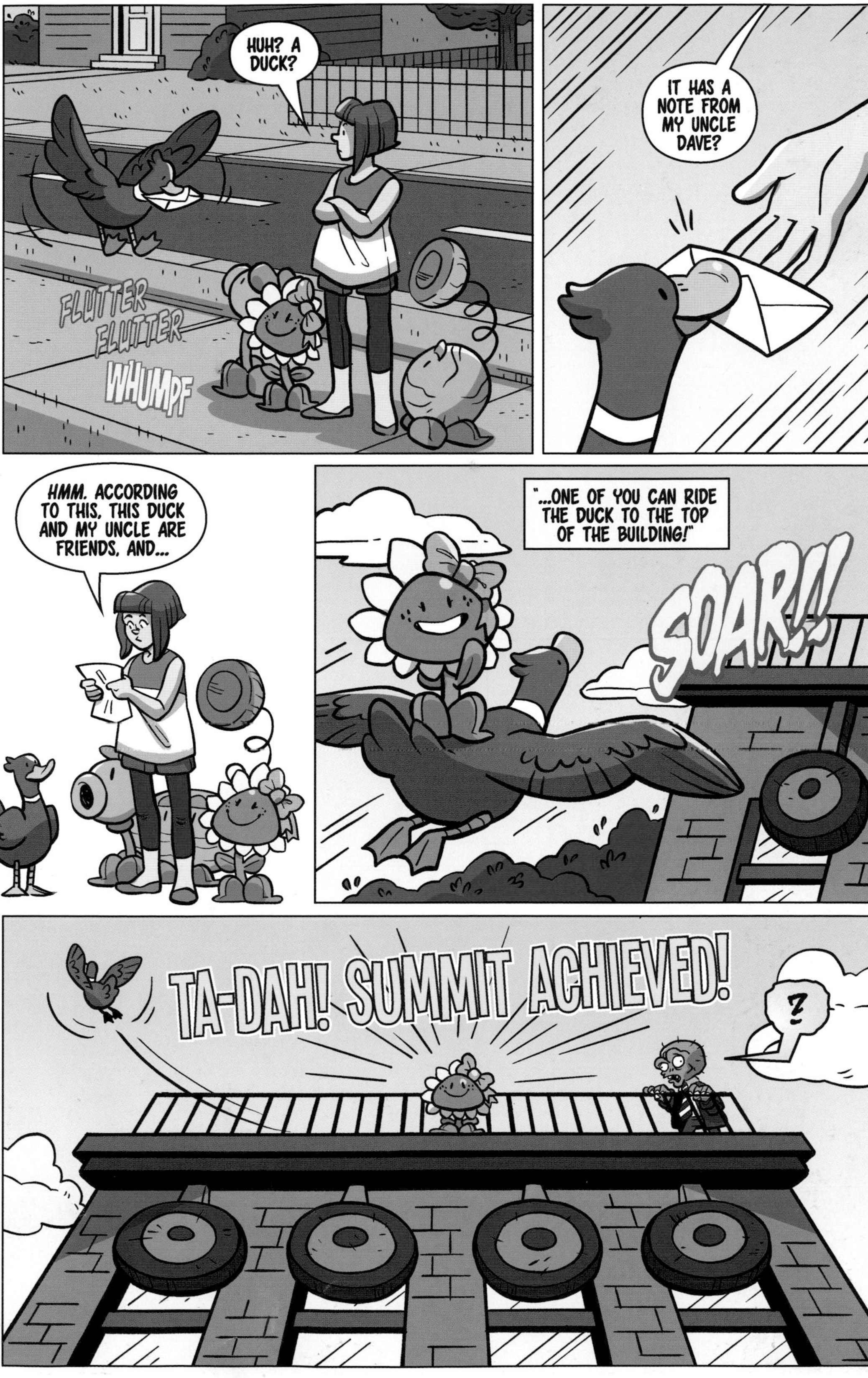
HUH? A DUCK?
FLUTTER FLUTTER
WHUMPF
IT HAS A NOTE FROM MY UNCLE DAVE?
HMM. ACCORDING TO THIS, THIS DUCK AND MY UNCLE ARE FRIENDS, AND...
"...ONE OF YOU CAN RIDE THE DUCK TO THE TOP OF THE BUILDING!"
SOAR!!
TA-DAH! SUMMIT ACHIEVED!
?

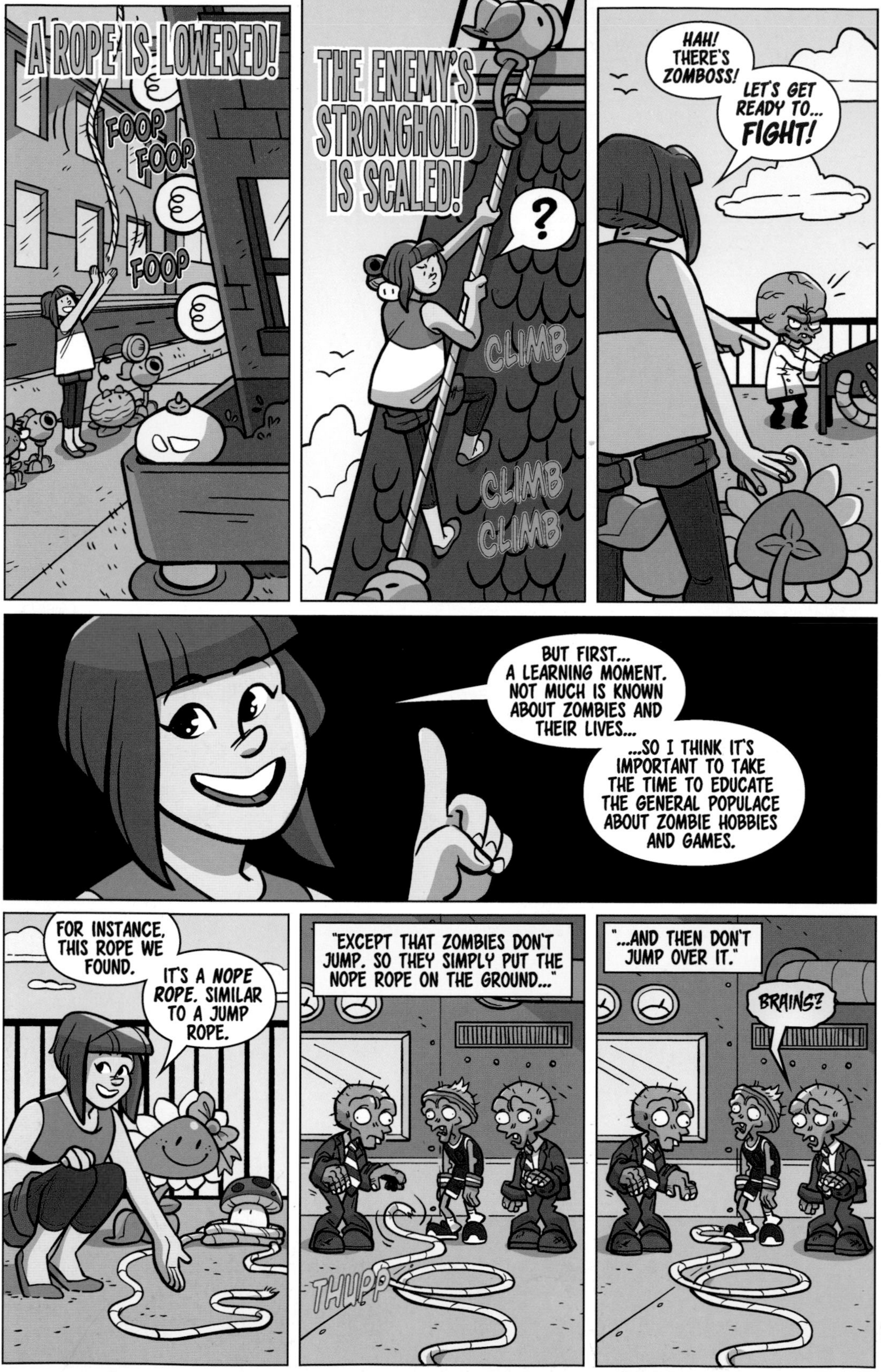
A ROPE IS LOWERED!
FOOP FOOP
FOOP
THE ENEMY'S STRONGHOLD IS SCALED!
?
CLIMB
CLIMB
CLIMB
HAH! THERE'S ZOMBOSS!
LET'S GET READY TO... FIGHT!
BUT FIRST... A LEARNING MOMENT. NOT MUCH IS KNOWN ABOUT ZOMBIES AND THEIR LIVES...
...SO I THINK IT'S IMPORTANT TO TAKE THE TIME TO EDUCATE THE GENERAL POPULACE ABOUT ZOMBIE HOBBIES AND GAMES.
FOR INSTANCE, THIS ROPE WE FOUND.
IT'S A NOPE ROPE. SIMILAR TO A JUMP ROPE.
"EXCEPT THAT ZOMBIES DON'T JUMP. SO THEY SIMPLY PUT THE NOPE ROPE ON THE GROUND..."
THUPP
"...AND THEN DON'T JUMP OVER IT."
BRAINS?

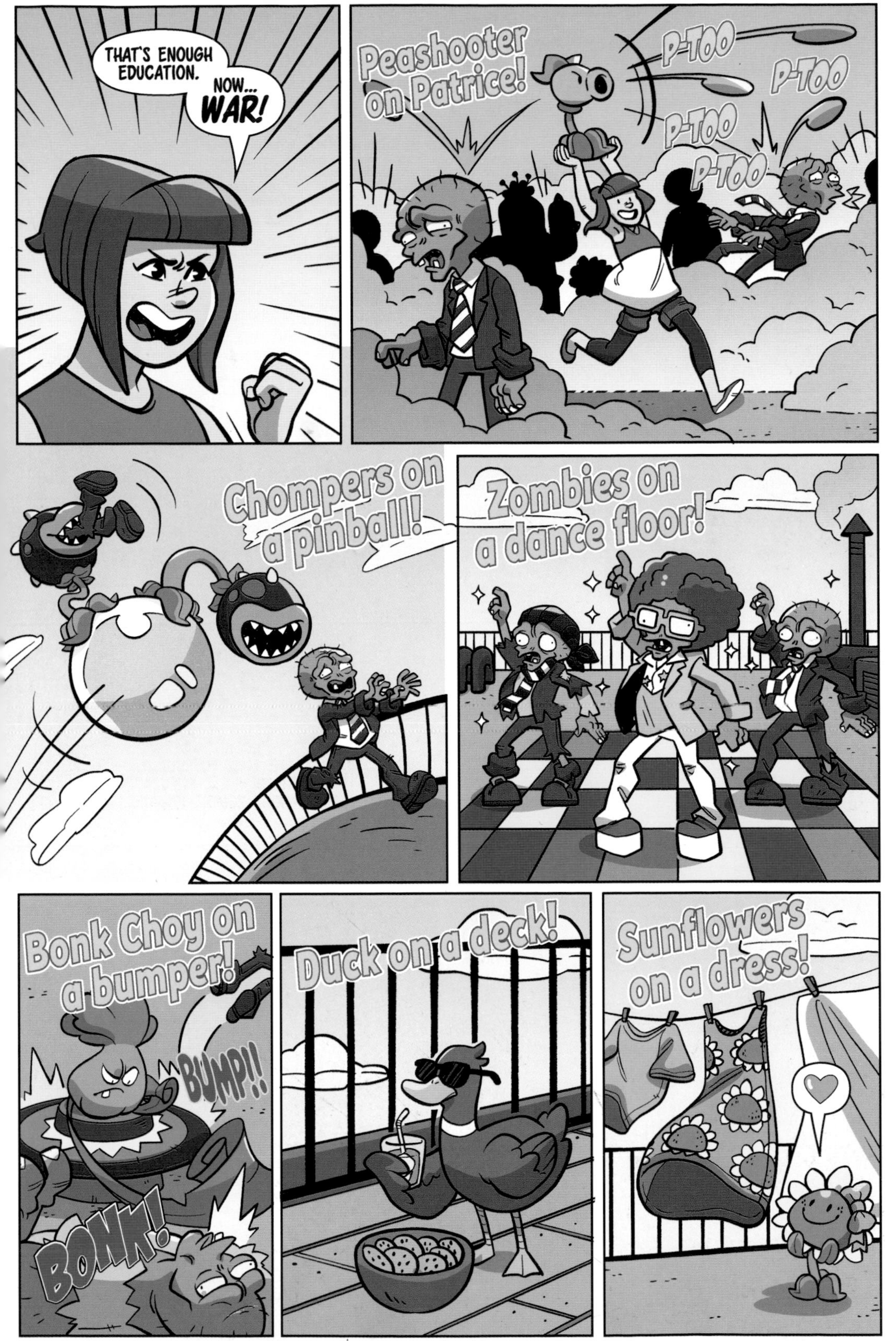
THAT'S ENOUGH EDUCATION.
NOW... WAR!
Peashooter on Patrice!
P-TOO
P-TOO
P-TOO
P-TOO
Chompers on a pinball!
Zombies on a dance floor!
Bonk Choy on a bumper!
BUMP!!
BONK!
Duck on a deck!
Sunflowers on a dress!

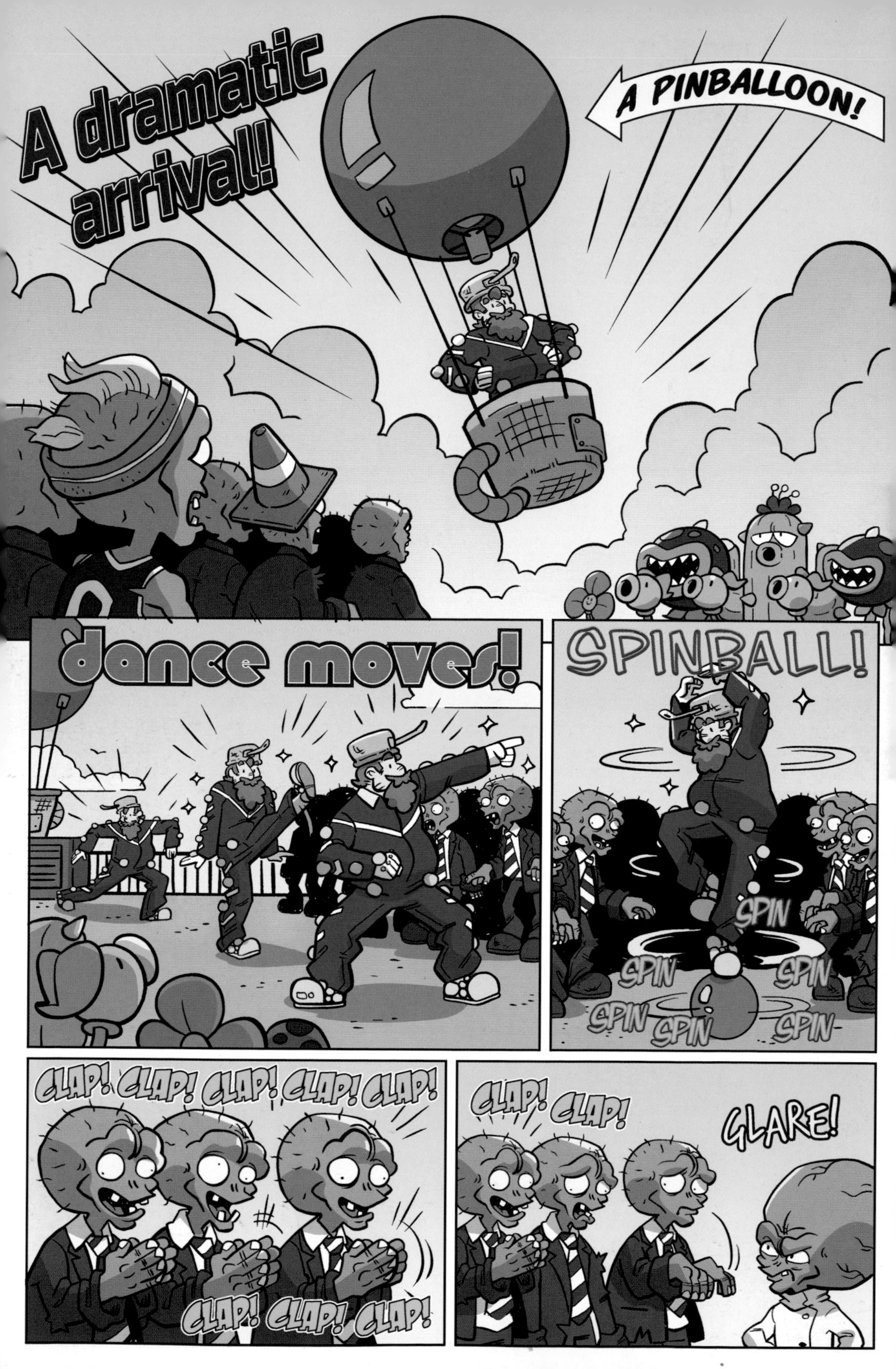
A dramatic arrival!
A PINBALLOON!
dance moves!
SPINBALL!
SPIN
SPIN
SPIN
SPIN
SPIN
SPIN
CLAP! CLAP! CLAP! CLAP! CLAP!
CLAP! CLAP! CLAP!
CLAP! CLAP!
GLARE!

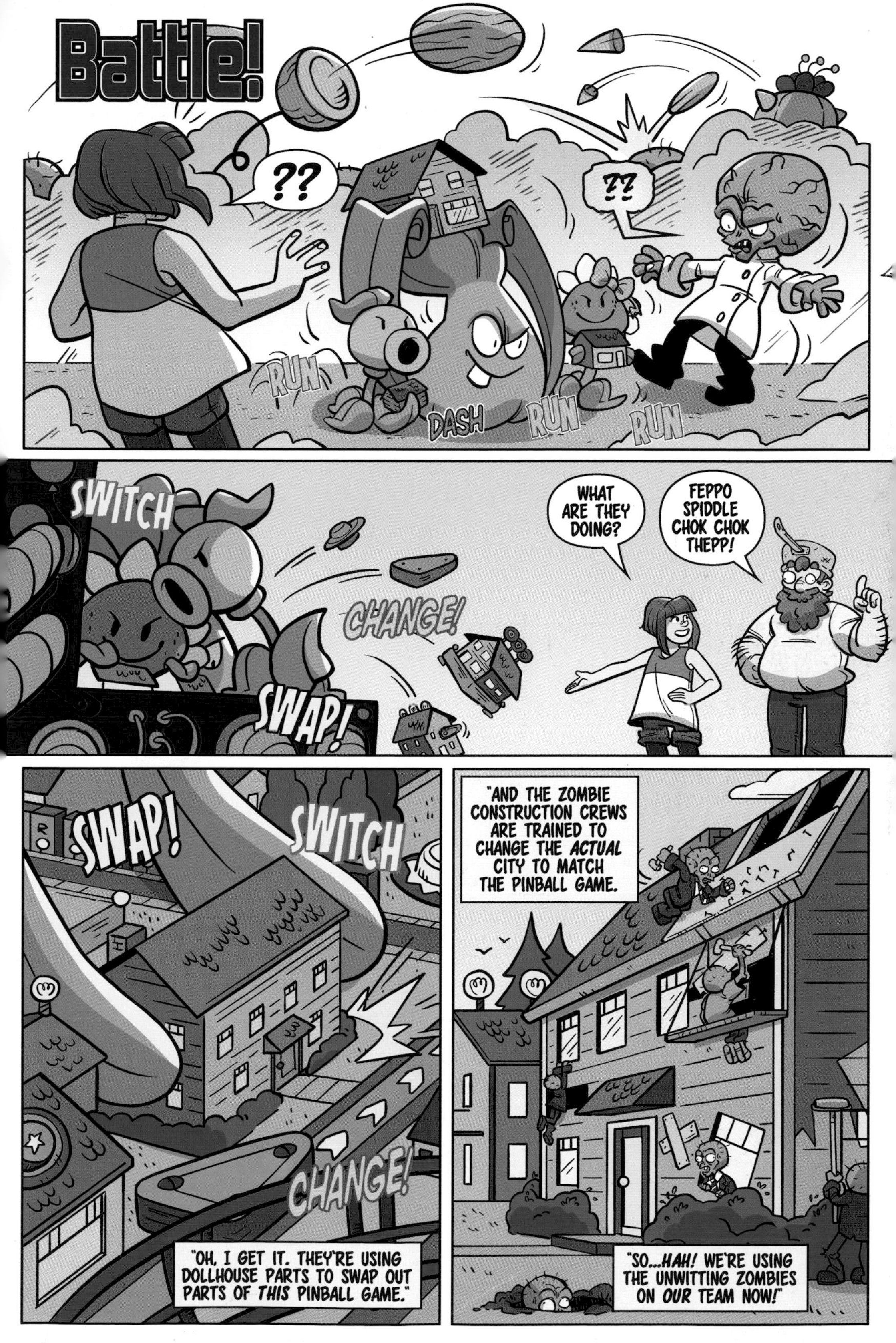
Battle!
??
??
RUN
DASH
RUN
RUN
SWITCH
CHANGE!
SWAP!
WHAT ARE THEY DOING?
FEPPO SPIDDLE CHOK CHOK THEPP!
SWAP!
SWITCH
CHANGE!
"OH, I GET IT. THEY'RE USING DOLLHOUSE PARTS TO SWAP OUT PARTS OF *THIS* PINBALL GAME."
"AND THE ZOMBIE CONSTRUCTION CREWS ARE TRAINED TO CHANGE THE *ACTUAL* CITY TO MATCH THE PINBALL GAME.
"SO...*HAH!* WE'RE USING THE UNWITTING ZOMBIES ON *OUR* TEAM NOW!"

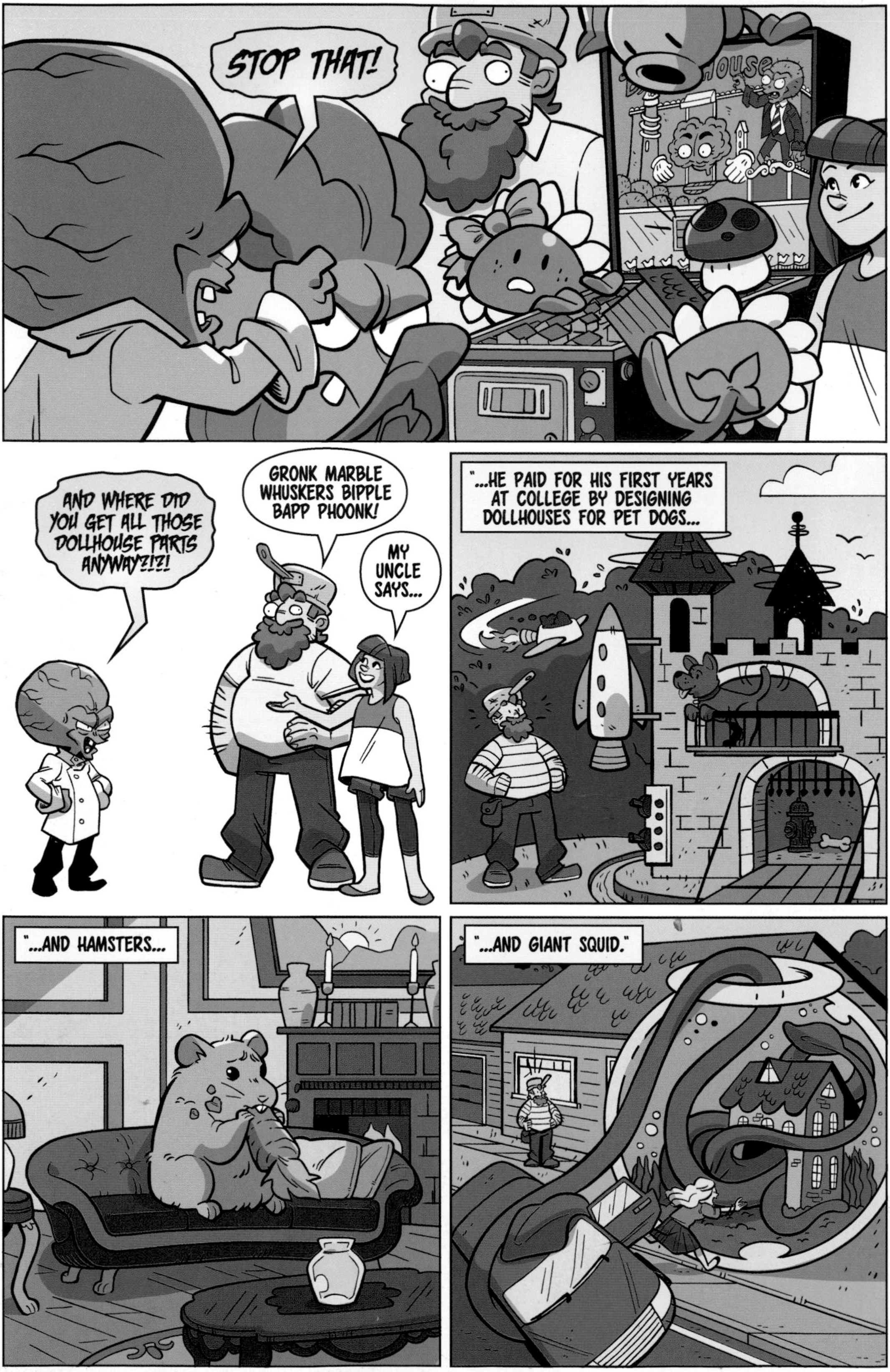
STOP THAT!
AND WHERE DID YOU GET ALL THOSE DOLLHOUSE PARTS ANYWAY?!?!?!
GRONK MARBLE WHUSKERS BIPPLE BAPP PHOONK!
MY UNCLE SAYS...
"...HE PAID FOR HIS FIRST YEARS AT COLLEGE BY DESIGNING DOLLHOUSES FOR PET DOGS...
"...AND HAMSTERS...
"...AND GIANT SQUID."

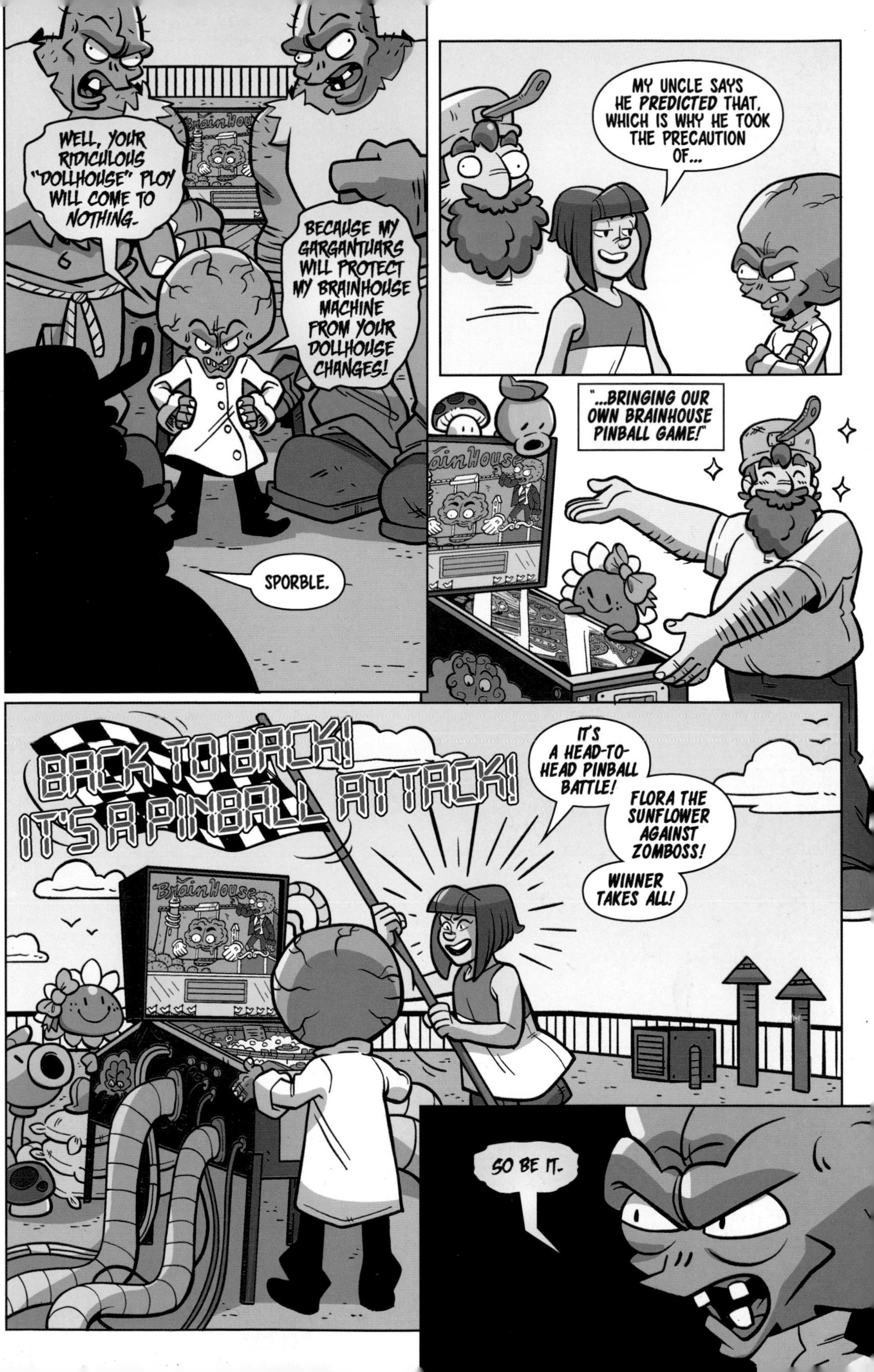
WELL, YOUR RIDICULOUS "DOLLHOUSE" PLOY WILL COME TO NOTHING.
BECAUSE MY GARGANTUARS WILL PROTECT MY BRAINHOUSE MACHINE FROM YOUR DOLLHOUSE CHANGES!
SPORBLE.
MY UNCLE SAYS HE PREDICTED THAT, WHICH IS WHY HE TOOK THE PRECAUTION OF...
"...BRINGING OUR OWN BRAINHOUSE PINBALL GAME!"
BACK TO BACK! IT'S A PINBALL ATTACK!
IT'S A HEAD-TO-HEAD PINBALL BATTLE!
FLORA THE SUNFLOWER AGAINST ZOMBOSS!
WINNER TAKES ALL!
SO BE IT.

MEANWHILE, AT STREET LEVEL...

WHOOSH

AHH!

Dodge!

OH, NO!

BONK!

BLINK

OKAY! BUT THAT'S THE LAST LETTER YOU ZOMBIES WILL EVER HIT! I SWEAR ON THIS SANDWICH!

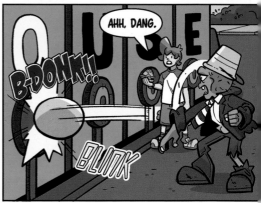

AHH, DANG.

B-DONK!!

BLINK

OKAY! NEW PRONOUNCEMENT. I SPOKE TOO SOON BEFORE. WHAT I MEANT WAS, THAT WILL BE THE LAST LETTER YOU ZOMBIES EVER--

PITCH!

SPANK!

!

BLINK

AWW, COME ON! I'M TRYING TO EAT A SANDWICH HERE!

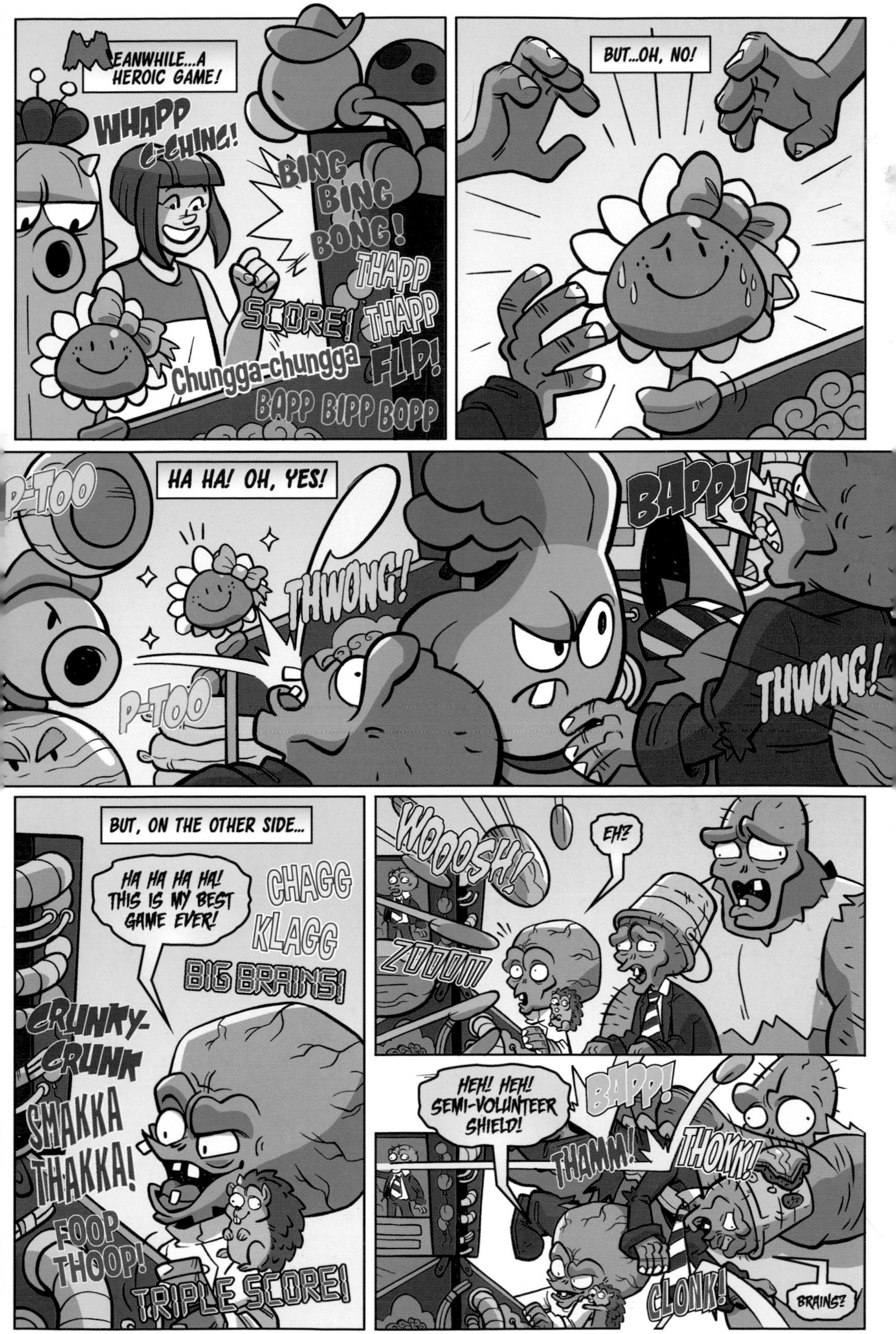
MEANWHILE...A HEROIC GAME!
WHAPP
C-CHING!
BING BING BONG!
THAPP THAPP
SCORE!
FLIP!
Chungga-chungga
BAPP BIPP BOPP
BUT...OH, NO!
P-TOO
HA HA! OH, YES!
BAPP!
THWONG!
P-TOO
THWONG!
BUT, ON THE OTHER SIDE...
HA HA HA HA! THIS IS MY BEST GAME EVER!
CHAGG
KLAGG
BIG BRAINS!
CRUNKY-CRUNK
SMAKKA THAKKA!
FOOP THOOP!
TRIPLE SCORE!
WOOOSH!
EH?
ZOOOM
HEH! HEH! SEMI-VOLUNTEER SHIELD!
BAPP!
THAMM!
THOKK!
CLONK!
BRAINS?

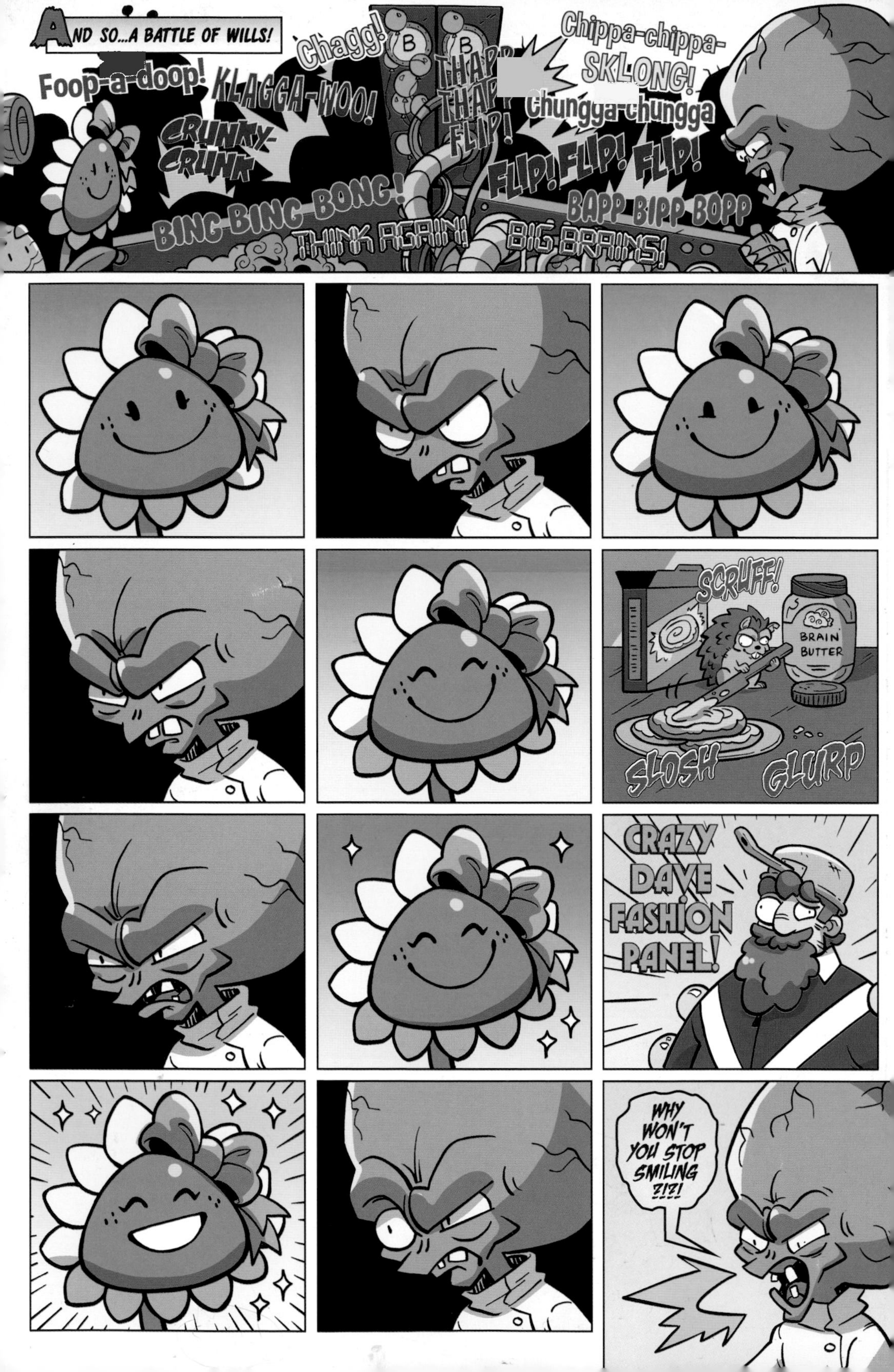

AND SO...A BATTLE OF WILLS!
[redacted]
Foop-a-doop!
KLAGGA-WOO!
Chagg!
THAPP THAPP FLIP!
Chippa-chippa-SKLONG!
Chungga-chungga
CRUNKY-CRUNK
FLIP! FLIP! FLIP!
BING BING BONG!
BAPP BIPP BOPP
THINK AGAIN!
BIG BRAINS!
SCRUFF!
BRAIN BUTTER
SLOSH
GLURP
CRAZY DAVE FASHION PANEL!
WHY WON'T YOU STOP SMILING ?!?!

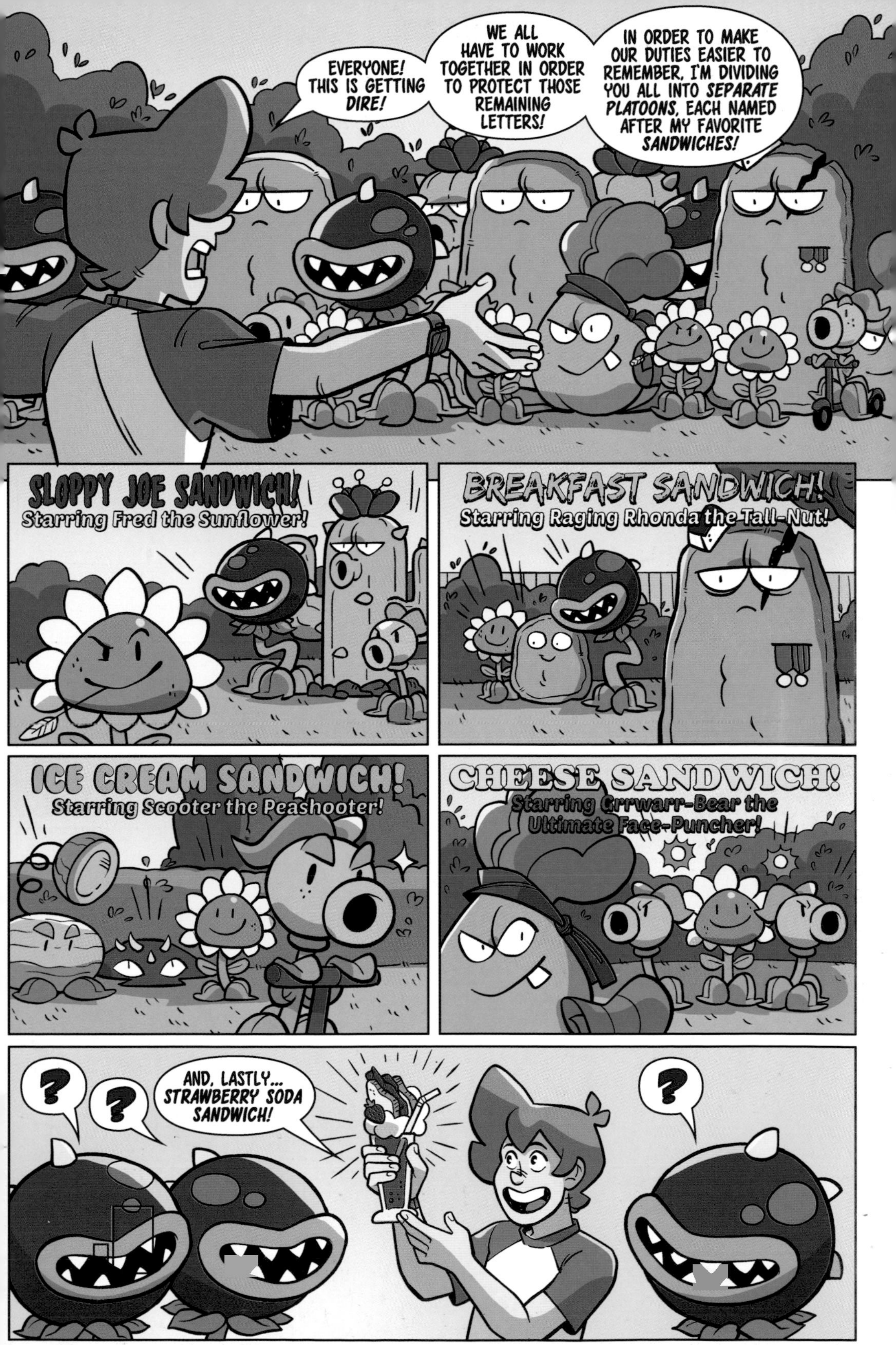
EVERYONE! THIS IS GETTING DIRE!
WE ALL HAVE TO WORK TOGETHER IN ORDER TO PROTECT THOSE REMAINING LETTERS!
IN ORDER TO MAKE OUR DUTIES EASIER TO REMEMBER, I'M DIVIDING YOU ALL INTO SEPARATE PLATOONS, EACH NAMED AFTER MY FAVORITE SANDWICHES!
SLOPPY JOE SANDWICH!
Starring Fred the Sunflower!
BREAKFAST SANDWICH!
Starring Raging Rhonda the Tall-Nut!
ICE CREAM SANDWICH!
Starring Scooter the Peashooter!
CHEESE SANDWICH!
Starring Grrwarr-Bear the Ultimate Face-Puncher!
?
?
AND, LASTLY... STRAWBERRY SODA SANDWICH!
?

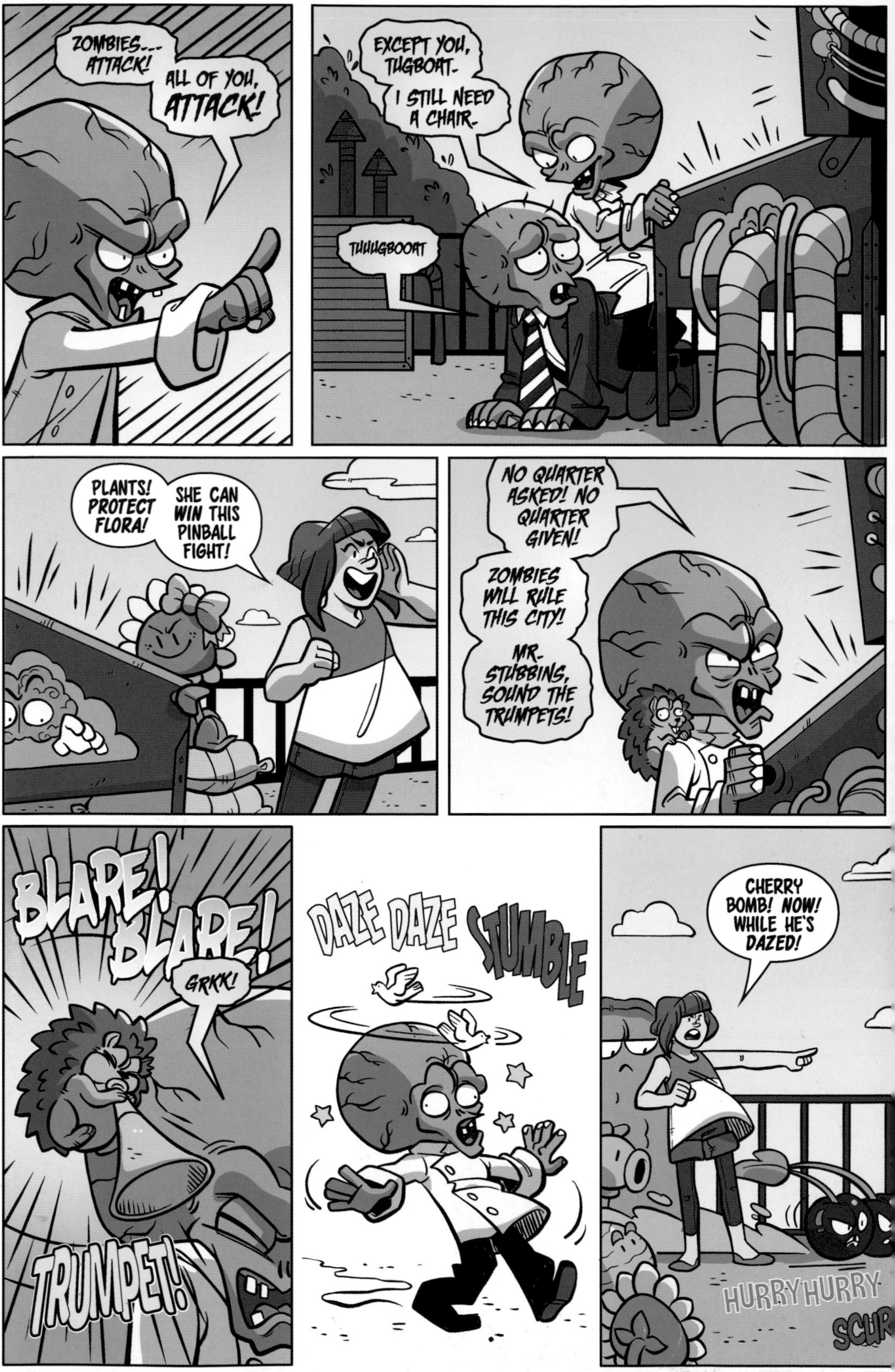
ZOMBIES... ATTACK!
ALL OF YOU, ATTACK!
EXCEPT YOU, TUGBOAT.
I STILL NEED A CHAIR.
TUUUGBOOAT
PLANTS! PROTECT FLORA!
SHE CAN WIN THIS PINBALL FIGHT!
NO QUARTER ASKED! NO QUARTER GIVEN!
ZOMBIES WILL RULE THIS CITY!
MR. STUBBINS, SOUND THE TRUMPETS!
BLARE! BLARE!
GRKK!
TRUMPET!
DAZE DAZE STUMBLE
CHERRY BOMB! NOW! WHILE HE'S DAZED!
HURRY HURRY

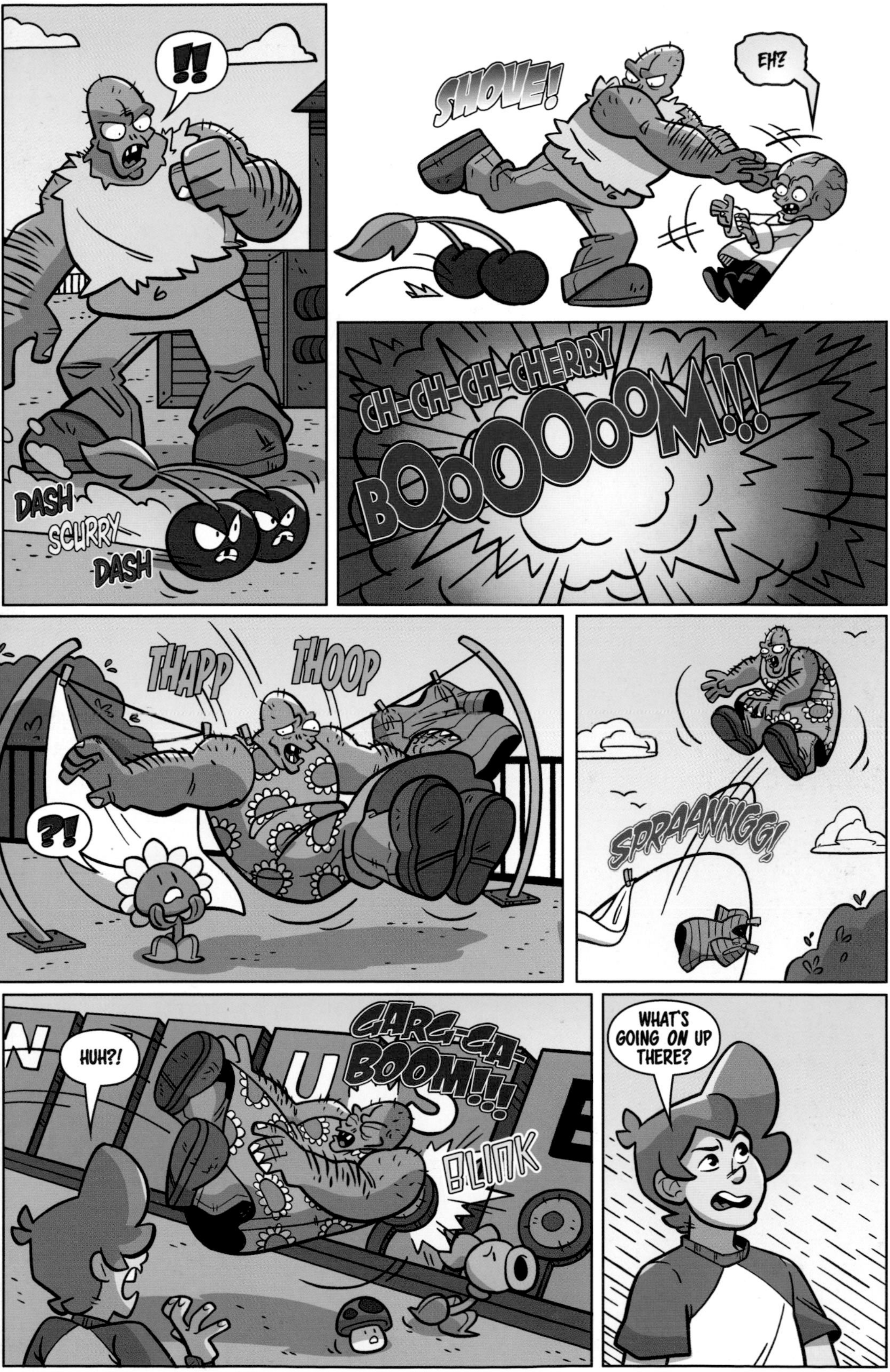
!!
DASH
SCURRY
DASH
SHOVE!
EH?
CH-CH-CH-CHERRY
BOOOOOOOM!!!
THAPP
THOOP
?!
SPRAANNGG!
HUH?!
GARG-GA-BOOM!!!
BLINK
WHAT'S GOING ON UP THERE?

FLIPPERS BLAZING!

FLIP FLIP FLIPPITY FLIP FLIP

POWER BOOST

PINBALLS RACING!

BONUS

THE TEAMS CHEERING

SHAKE! SHAKE!

LEAP! giggle

ADVICE FROM THE MASTERS!

TRY TO LOOK MORE INTENSE. MORE INTIMIDATING.

NARROW YOUR EYES. GRIT YOUR TEETH.

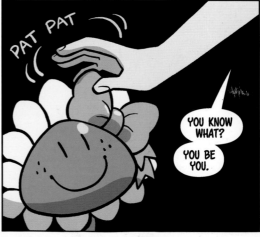

PAT PAT

YOU KNOW WHAT?

YOU BE YOU.

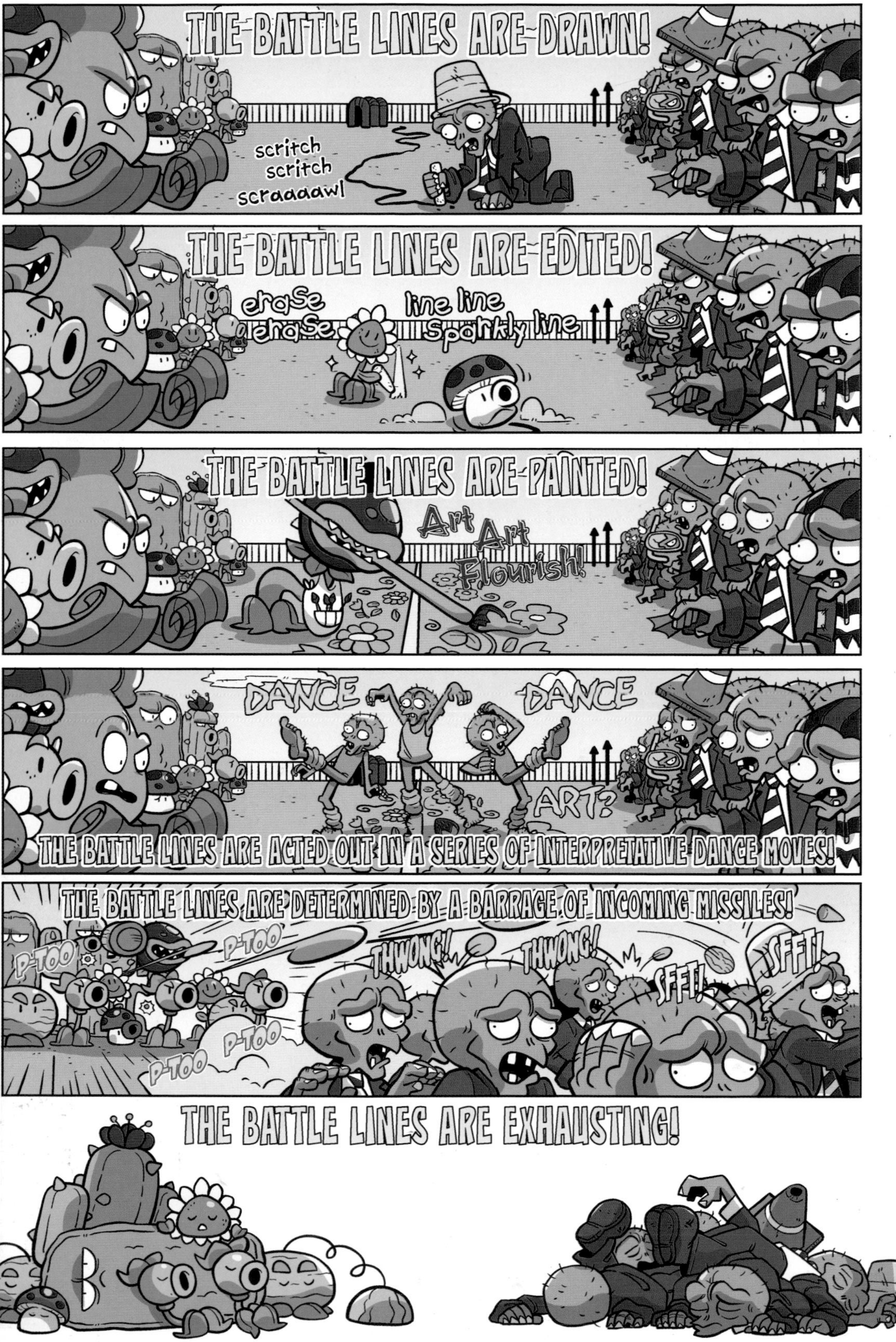
THE BATTLE LINES ARE DRAWN!
scritch
scritch
scraaaawl
THE BATTLE LINES ARE EDITED!
erase
erase
line line
sparkly line
THE BATTLE LINES ARE PAINTED!
Art Art
Flourish!
DANCE
DANCE
ART?
THE BATTLE LINES ARE ACTED OUT IN A SERIES OF INTERPRETATIVE DANCE MOVES!
THE BATTLE LINES ARE DETERMINED BY A BARRAGE OF INCOMING MISSILES!
P-TOO
P-TOO
THWONG!
THWONG!
SFFT!
SFFT!
P-TOO
P-TOO
THE BATTLE LINES ARE EXHAUSTING!

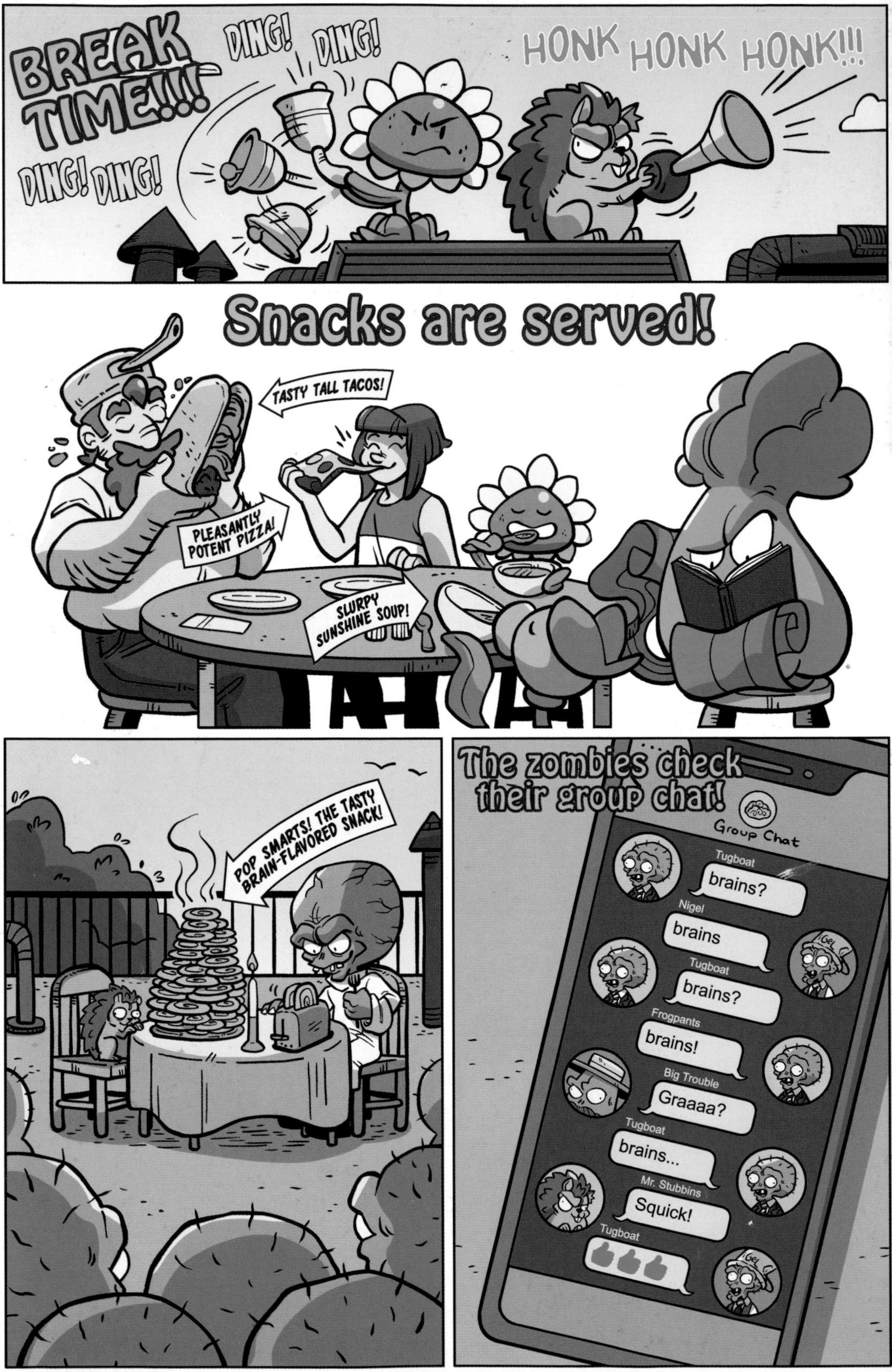
BREAK TIME!!!
DING! DING!
DING! DING!
HONK HONK HONK!!!
Snacks are served!
TASTY TALL TACOS!
PLEASANTLY POTENT PIZZA!
SLURPY SUNSHINE SOUP!
POP SMARTS! THE TASTY BRAIN-FLAVORED SNACK!
The zombies check their group chat!
Group Chat
Tugboat
brains?
Nigel
brains
Tugboat
brains?
Frogpants
brains!
Big Trouble
Graaaa?
Tugboat
brains...
Mr. Stubbins
Squick!
Tugboat

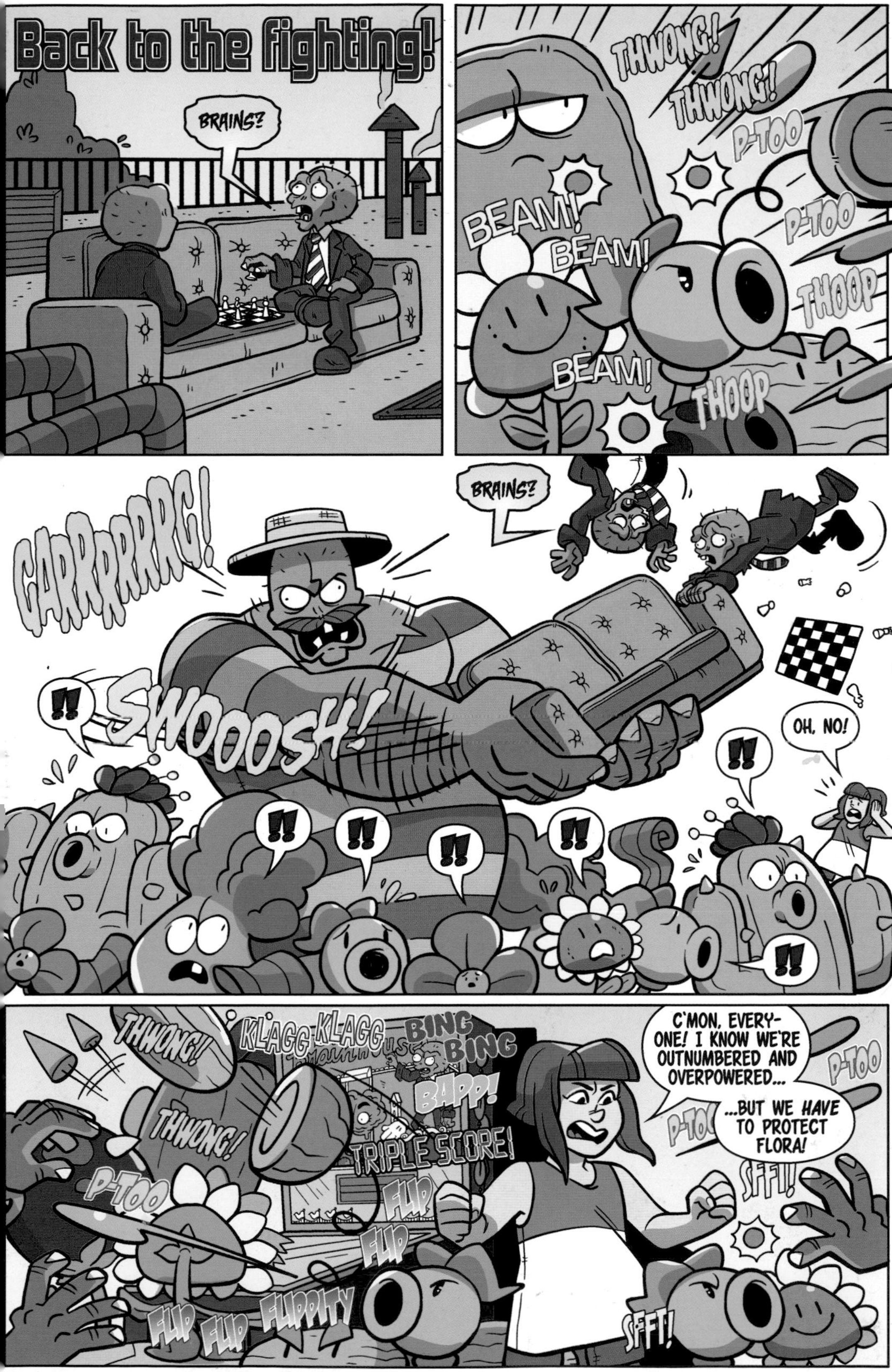
Back to the fighting!
BRAINS?
THWONG!
THWONG!
P-TOO
P-TOO
BEAM!
BEAM!
BEAM!
THOOP
THOOP
GARRRRRRG!
BRAINS?
SWOOOSH!
!!
OH, NO!
!!
!!
!!
!!
!!
!!
THWONG!
KLAGG KLAGG
BING
BING
BAPP!
THWONG!
TRIPLE SCORE!
P-TOO
FLIP
FLIP
FLIP FLIP FLIPPITY
C'MON, EVERY-ONE! I KNOW WE'RE OUTNUMBERED AND OVERPOWERED...
...BUT WE HAVE TO PROTECT FLORA!
P-TOO
P-TOO
SFFT!
SFFT!

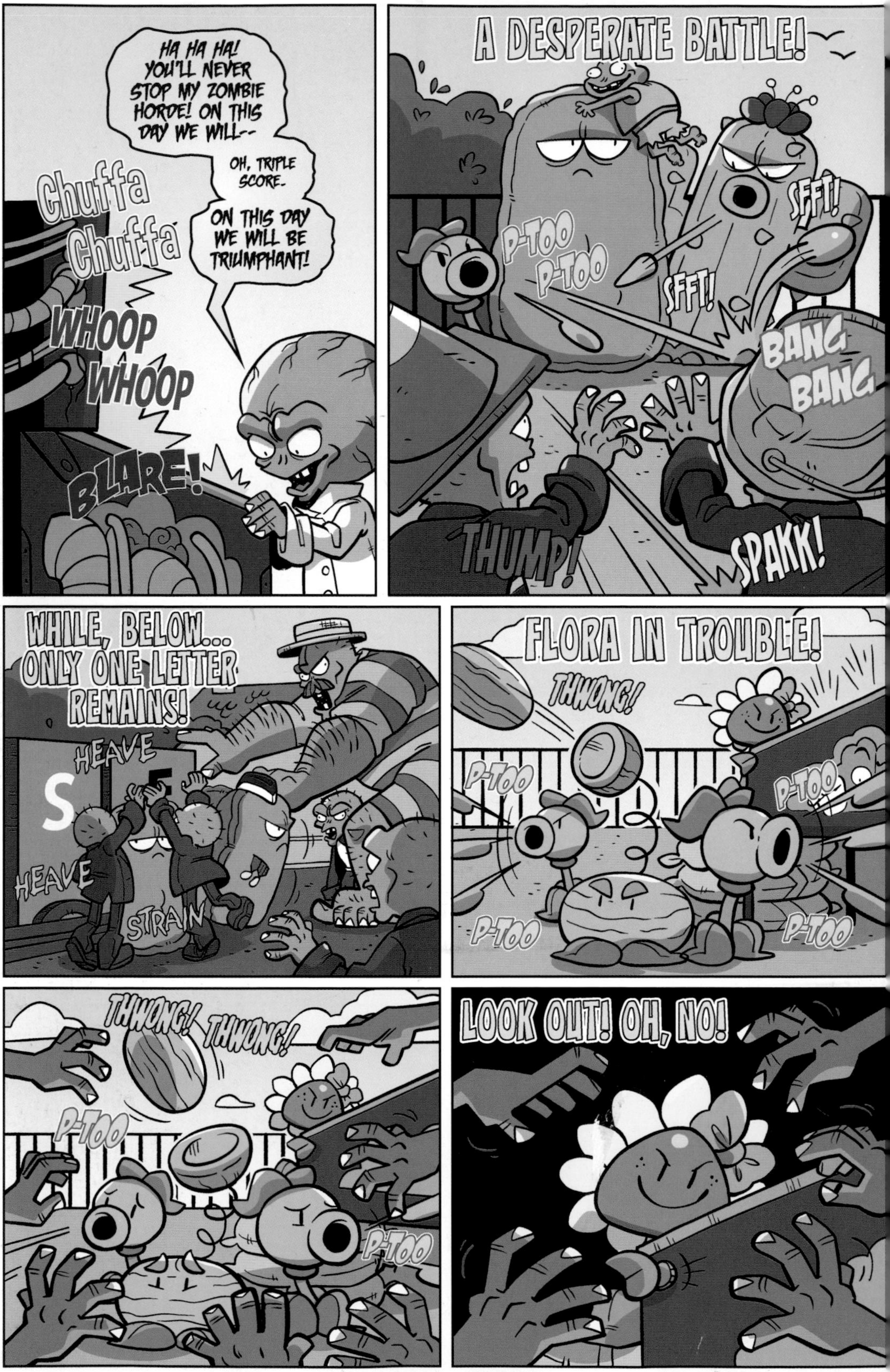
HA HA HA! YOU'LL NEVER STOP MY ZOMBIE HORDE! ON THIS DAY WE WILL--
OH, TRIPLE SCORE.
ON THIS DAY WE WILL BE TRIUMPHANT!
Chuffa Chuffa
WHOOP WHOOP
BLARE!
A DESPERATE BATTLE!
P-TOO P-TOO
SFFT!
SFFT!
BANG BANG
THUMP!
SPAKK!
WHILE, BELOW... ONLY ONE LETTER REMAINS!
HEAVE
HEAVE
STRAIN
FLORA IN TROUBLE!
THWONG!
P-TOO
P-TOO
P-TOO
P-TOO
THWONG! THWONG!
P-TOO
P-TOO
LOOK OUT! OH, NO!

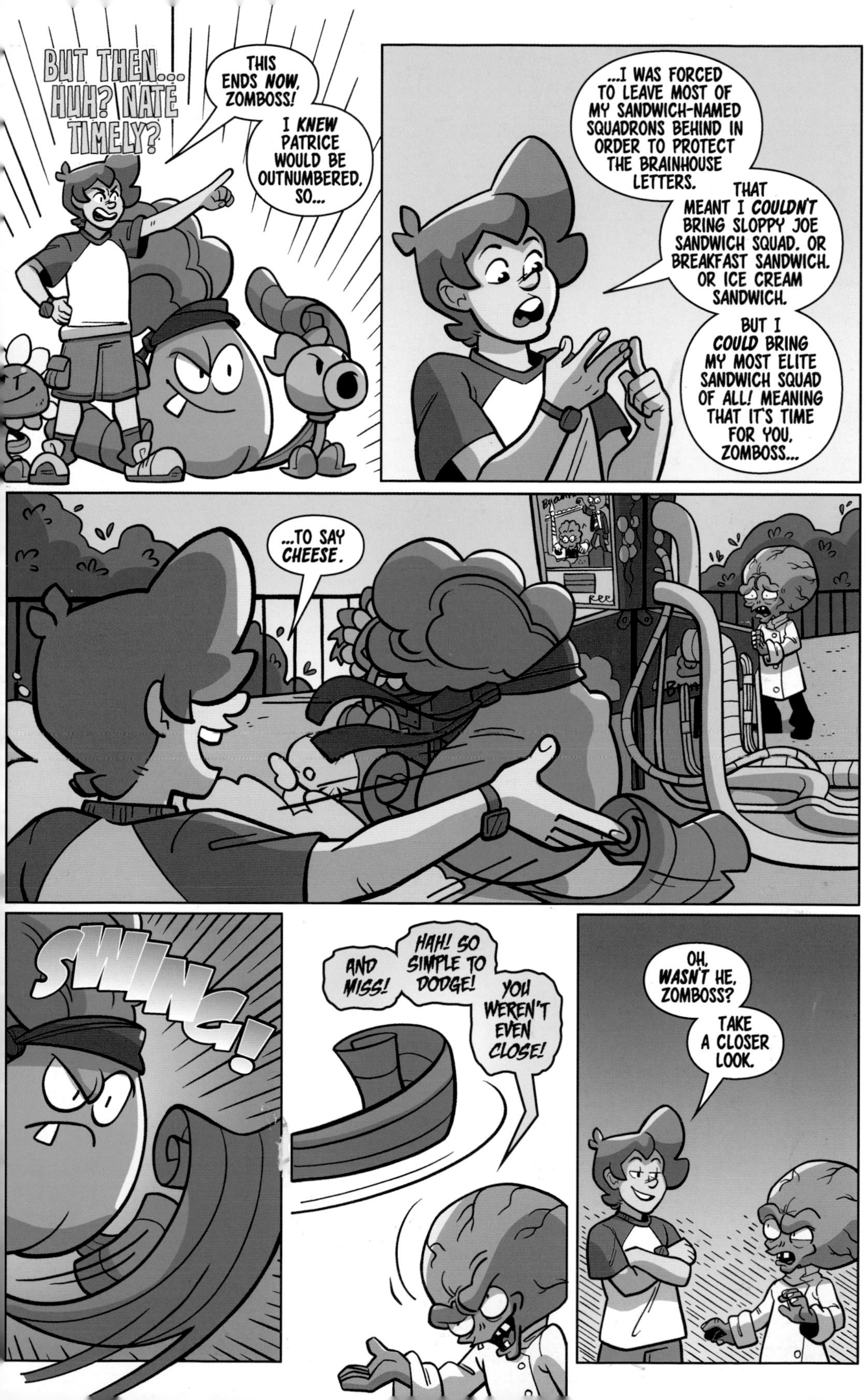
BUT THEN... HUH? NATE TIMELY?
THIS ENDS NOW, ZOMBOSS!
I KNEW PATRICE WOULD BE OUTNUMBERED, SO...
...I WAS FORCED TO LEAVE MOST OF MY SANDWICH-NAMED SQUADRONS BEHIND IN ORDER TO PROTECT THE BRAINHOUSE LETTERS.
THAT MEANT I COULDN'T BRING SLOPPY JOE SANDWICH SQUAD. OR BREAKFAST SANDWICH. OR ICE CREAM SANDWICH.
BUT I COULD BRING MY MOST ELITE SANDWICH SQUAD OF ALL! MEANING THAT IT'S TIME FOR YOU, ZOMBOSS...
...TO SAY CHEESE.
SWING!
AND MISS!
HAH! SO SIMPLE TO DODGE!
YOU WEREN'T EVEN CLOSE!
OH, WASN'T HE, ZOMBOSS?
TAKE A CLOSER LOOK.

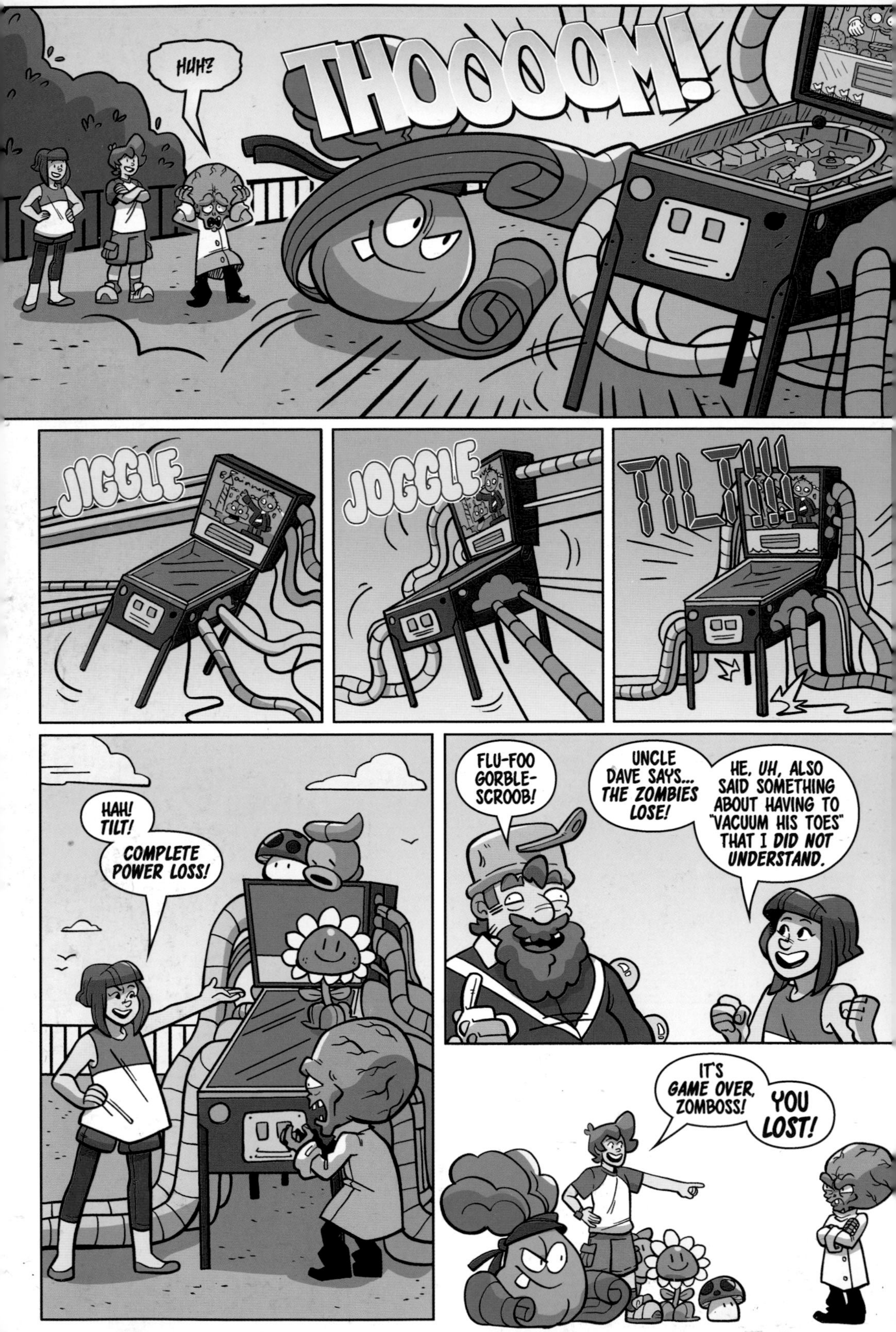
HUH?
THOOOOM!
JIGGLE
JOGGLE
TILT!!!
HAH! TILT!
COMPLETE POWER LOSS!
FLU-FOO GORBLE-SCROOB!
UNCLE DAVE SAYS... THE ZOMBIES LOSE!
HE, UH, ALSO SAID SOMETHING ABOUT HAVING TO "VACUUM HIS TOES" THAT I DID NOT UNDERSTAND.
IT'S GAME OVER, ZOMBOSS!
YOU LOST!

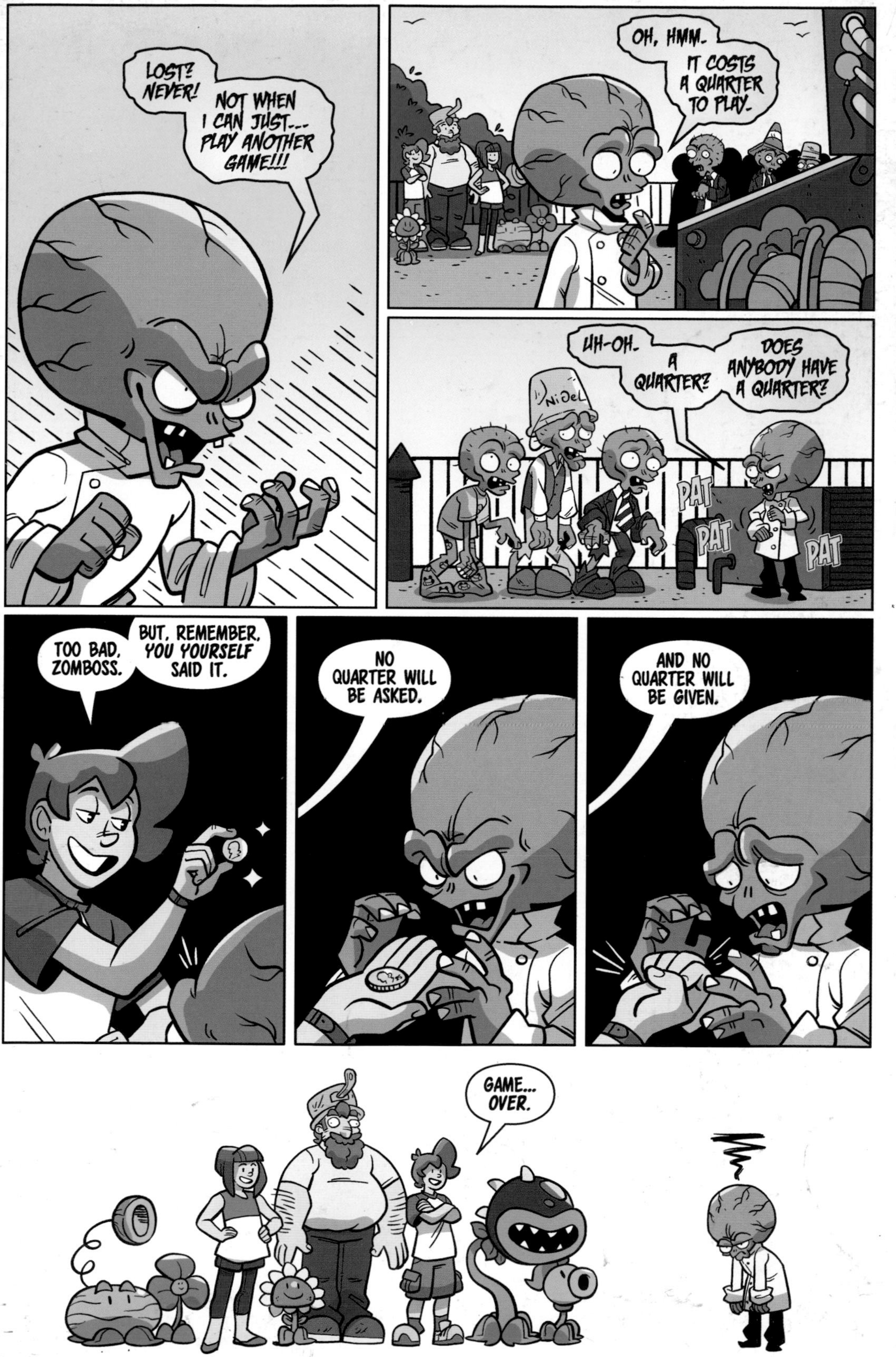
LOST? NEVER!
NOT WHEN I CAN JUST... PLAY ANOTHER GAME!!!
OH, HMM.
IT COSTS A QUARTER TO PLAY.
UH-OH.
A QUARTER?
DOES ANYBODY HAVE A QUARTER?
PAT
PAT
PAT
TOO BAD, ZOMBOSS.
BUT, REMEMBER, YOU YOURSELF SAID IT.
NO QUARTER WILL BE ASKED.
AND NO QUARTER WILL BE GIVEN.
GAME... OVER.

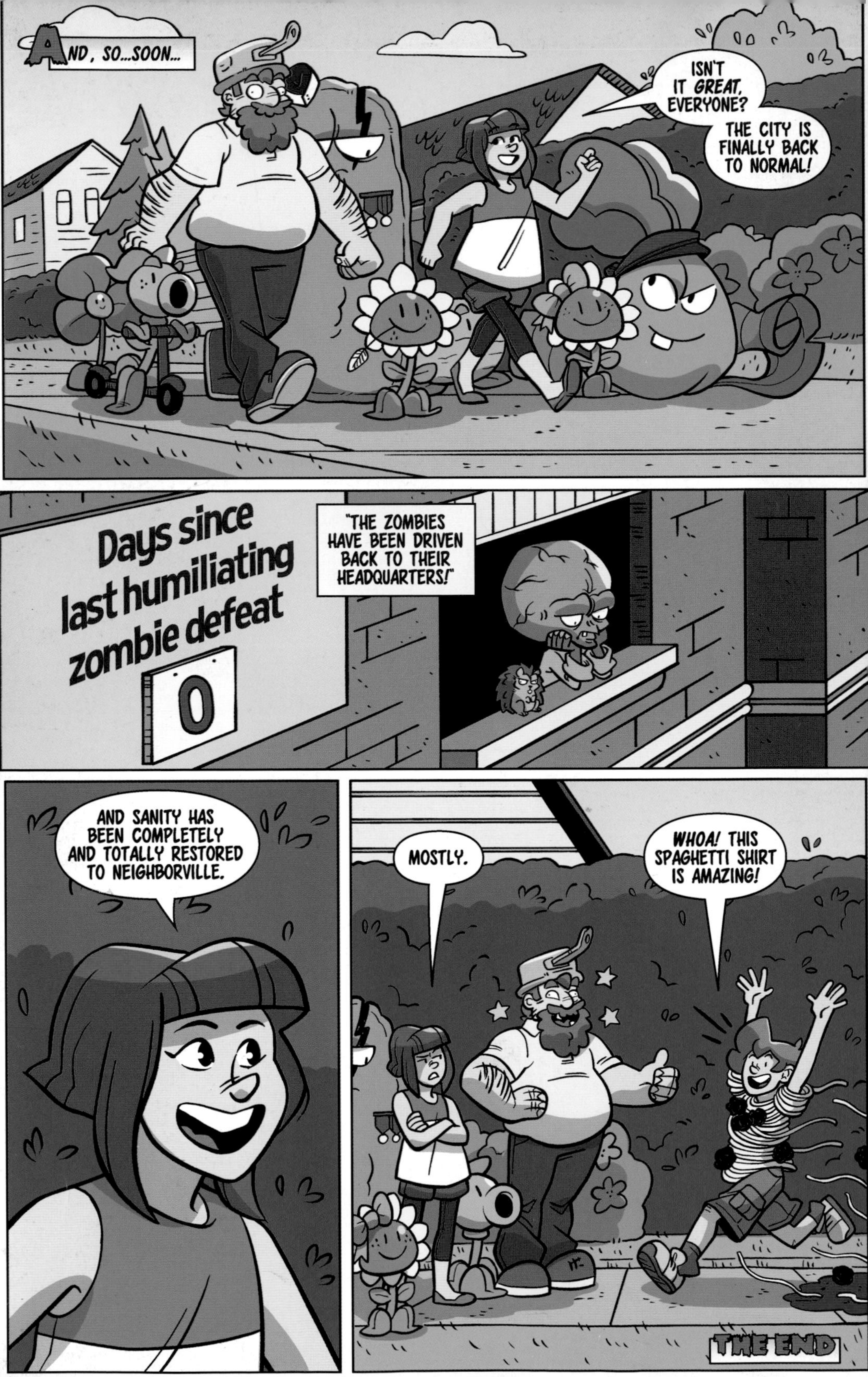
AND, SO...SOON...
ISN'T IT GREAT, EVERYONE?
THE CITY IS FINALLY BACK TO NORMAL!
Days since last humiliating zombie defeat
0
"THE ZOMBIES HAVE BEEN DRIVEN BACK TO THEIR HEADQUARTERS!"
AND SANITY HAS BEEN COMPLETELY AND TOTALLY RESTORED TO NEIGHBORVILLE.
MOSTLY.
WHOA! THIS SPAGHETTI SHIRT IS AMAZING!
THE END

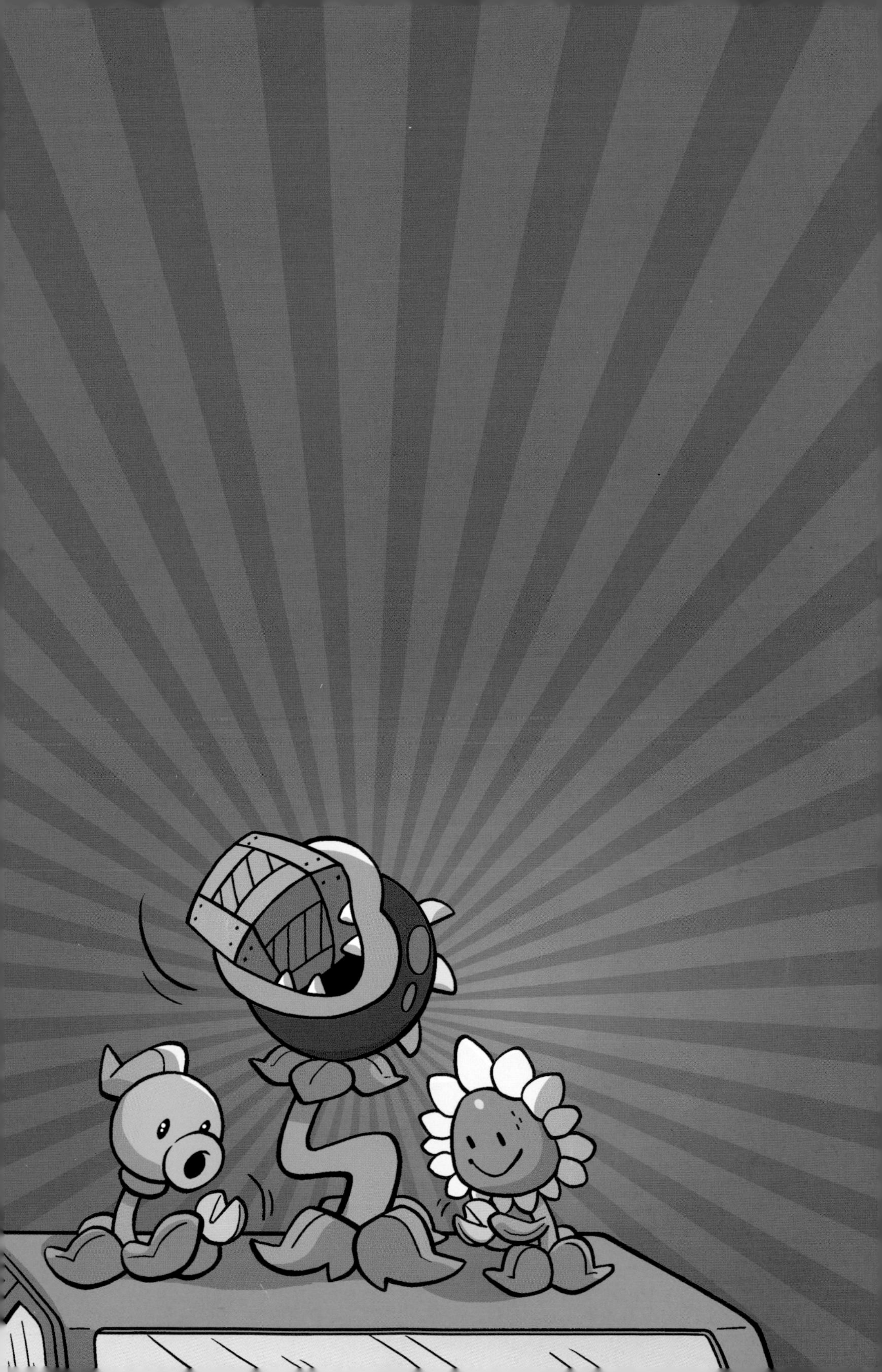

PLANTS VS. ZOMBIES: MULTI-BALL-ISTIC
COVER PENCILS BY CHRISTIANNE GILLENARDO-GOUDREAU

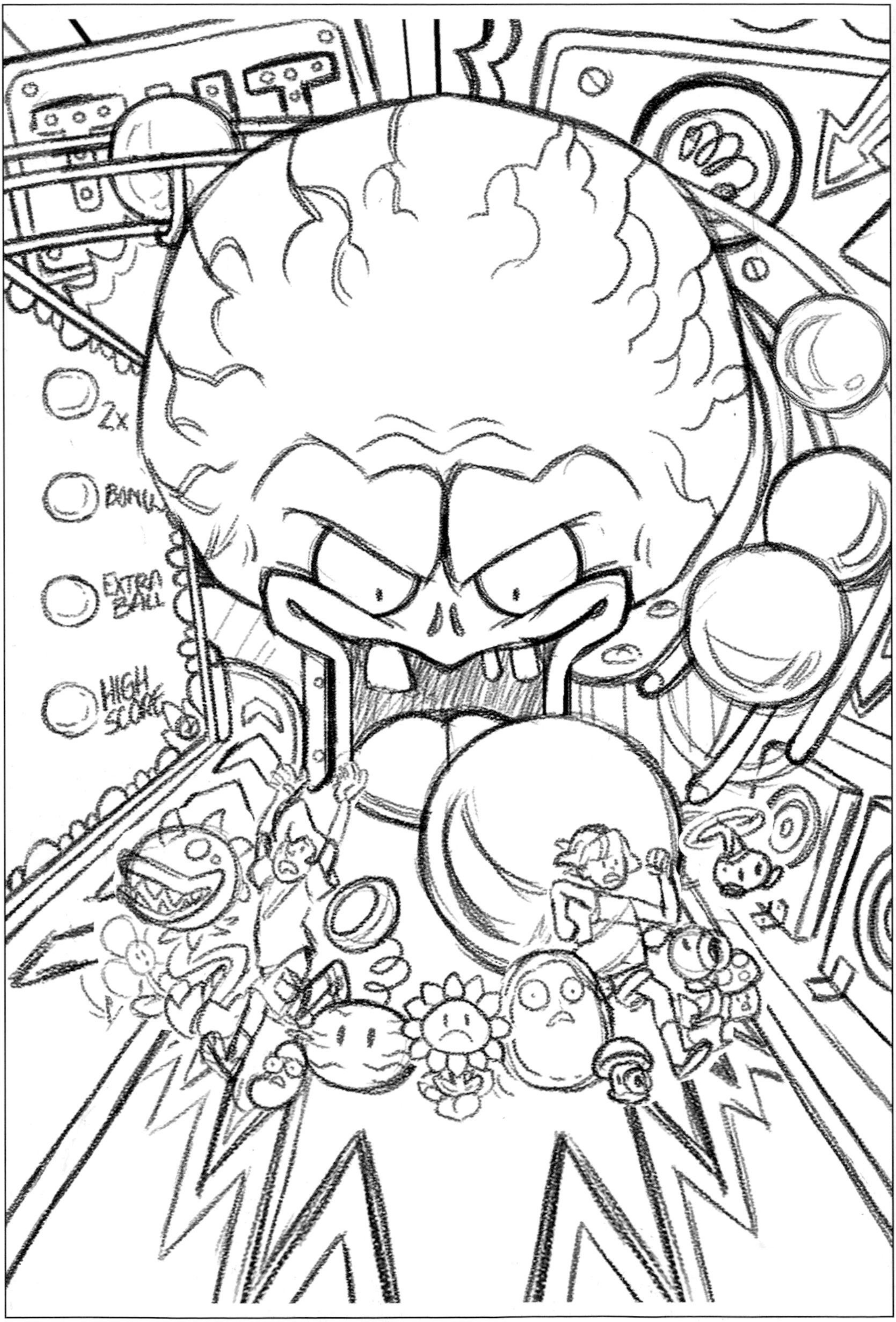
2x
BONUS
EXTRA BALL
HIGH SCORE

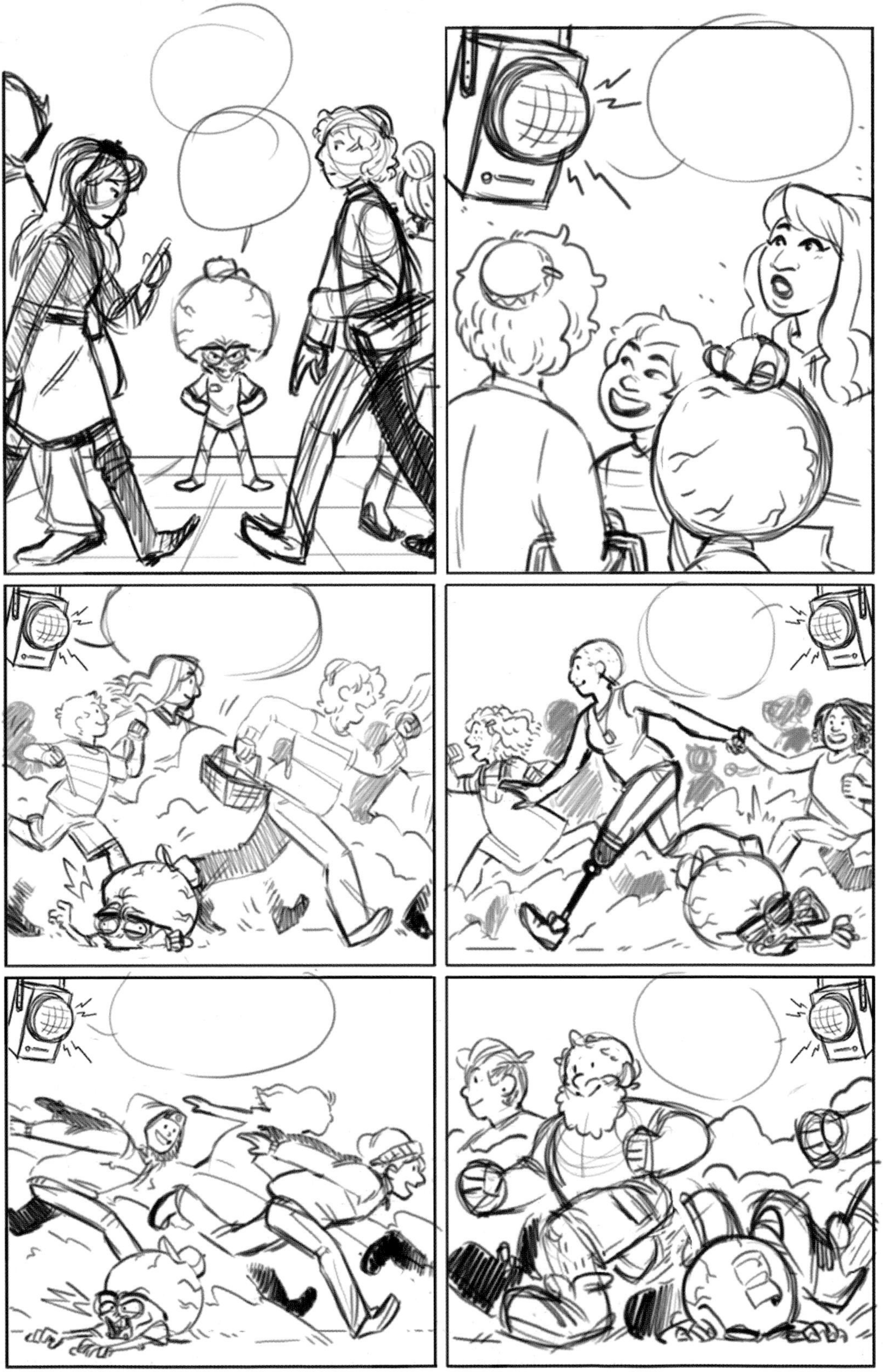

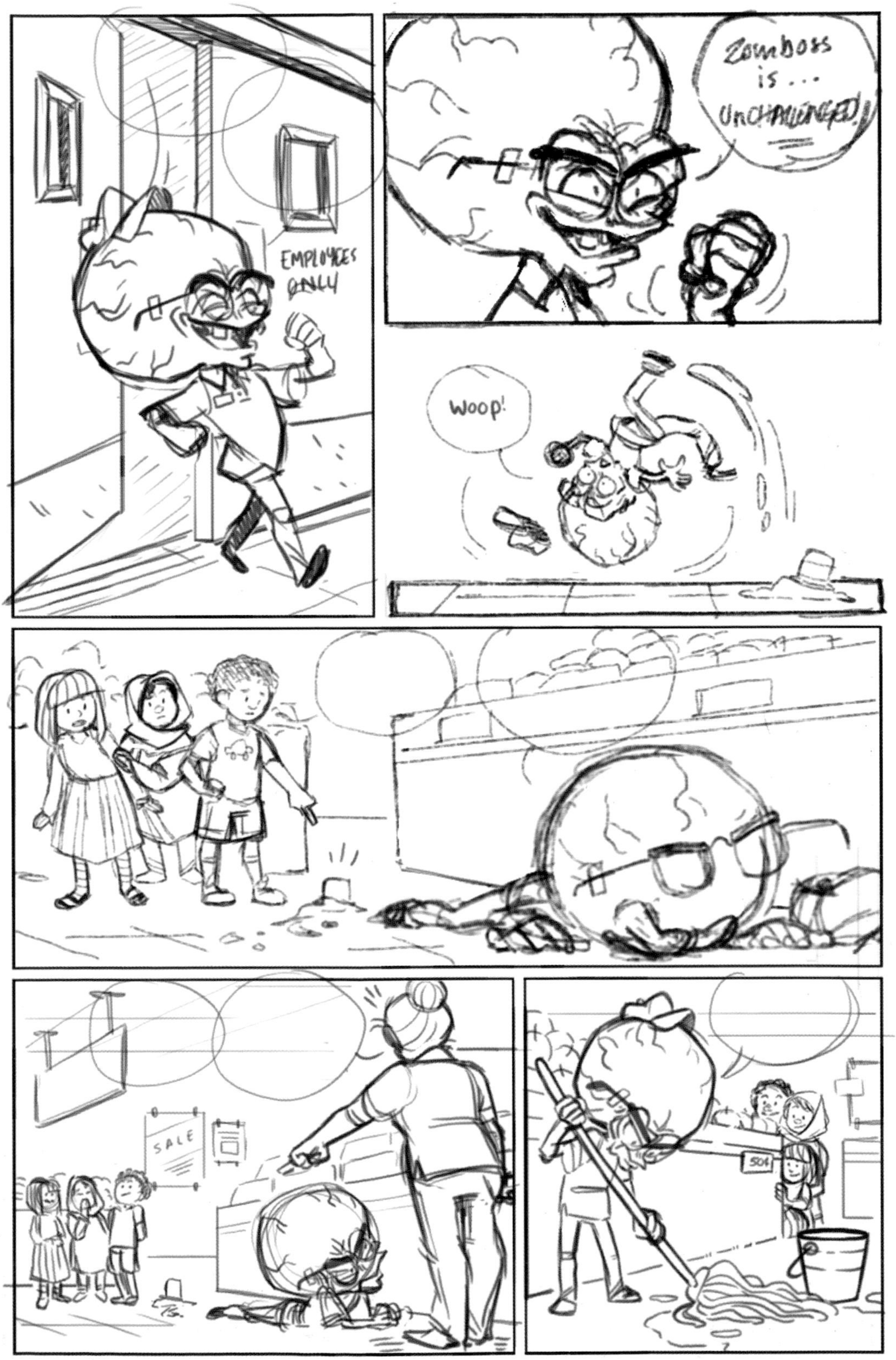
EMPLOYEES ONLY
Zomboss is... UNCHALLENGED!
Woop!
SALE
50¢

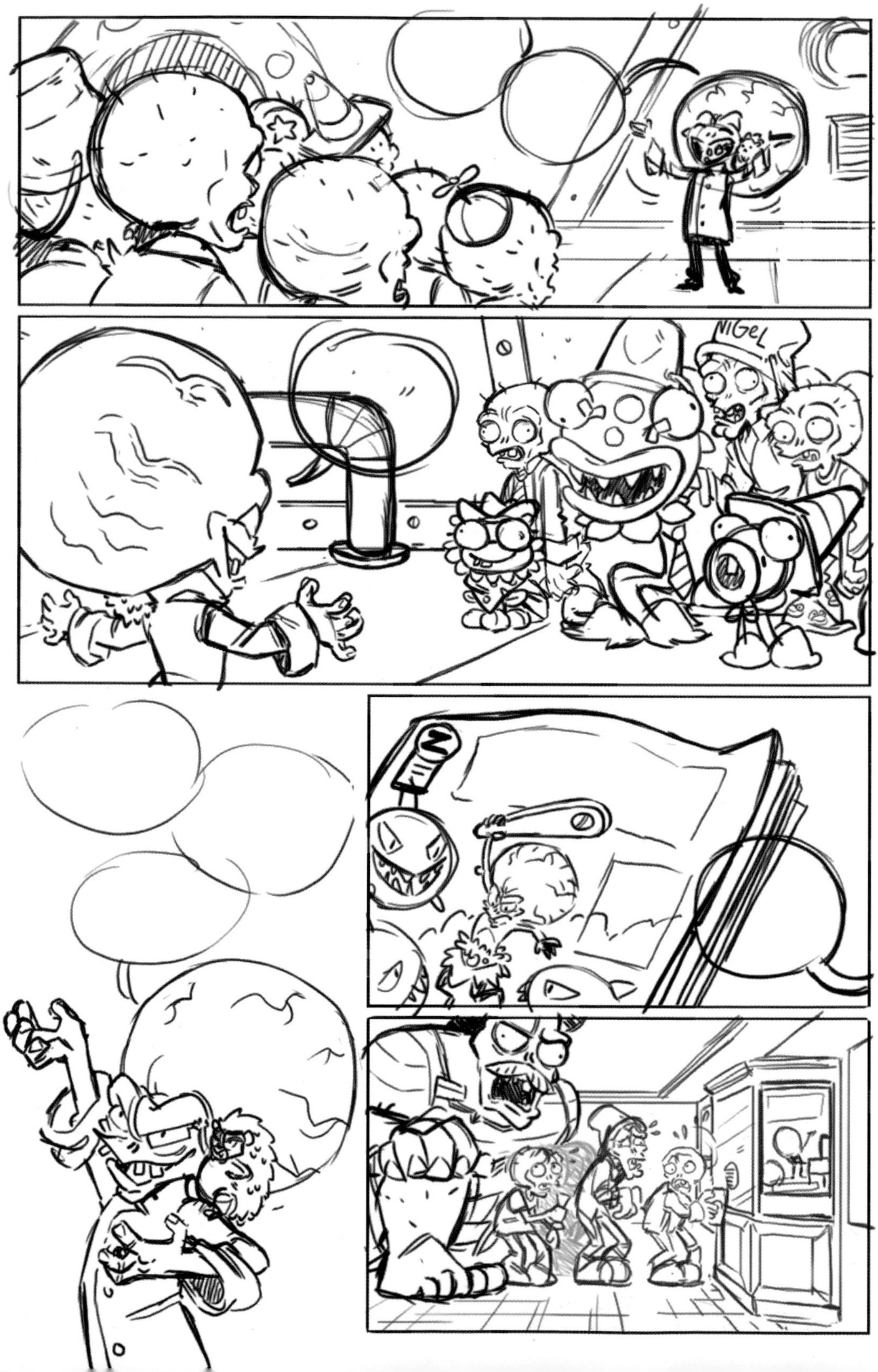
NIGEL

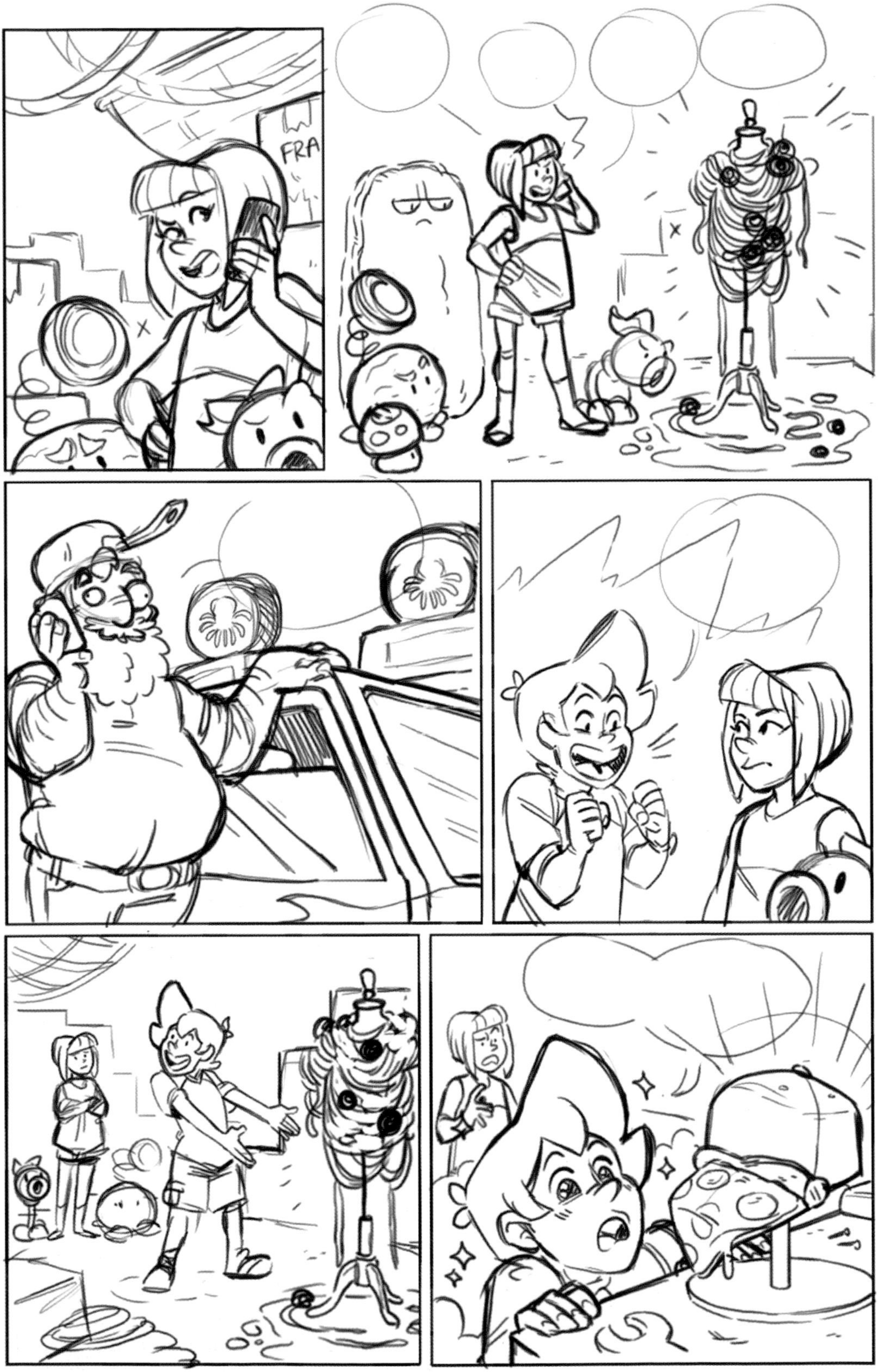
FRA

CREATOR BIOS

PAUL TOBIN is a 12th level writer and a 15th level cookie eater. He begins each morning in the manner we all do, by battling those zombies that have strayed too close to his pillow fort. Between writing all the *Plants vs. Zombies* comics and taking four naps a day, he's also found time to write the *Genius Factor* series of novels, the ape-filled *Banana Sunday* graphic novel, the award-winning *Bandette* series, the upcoming *Wrassle Castle* and *Earth Boy* graphic novels, and many other works. He has ridden a giant turtle and an elephant on purpose, and a tornado by accident.

Paul Tobin

CHRISTIANNE GILLENARDO-GOUDREAU is a comic artist and illustrator from Portland, Oregon. Her work has been featured in various anthologies and comics, including *Beyond: A Queer Sci-Fi And Fantasy Anthology*, *Plants vs. Zombies*, *Harrow County*, and *Dept. H*. She is currently the interior artist for the series *I am Hexed*, by Kirsten Thompson. She lives with her wife, Donna, and their dumb cats, Hot Dog and Pancake.

Christianne
Gillenardo-Goudreau

Heather Breckel

HEATHER BRECKEL went to the Columbus College of Art and Design for animation. She decided animation wasn't for her, so she switched to comics. She's been working as a colorist for nearly ten years and has worked for nearly every major comics publisher out there. When she's not burning the midnight oil in a deadline crunch, she's either dying a bunch in videogames or telling her cats to stop running around at two in the morning.

Steve Dutro

STEVE DUTRO is a pinball fan and an Eisner Award-nominated comic book letterer from Redding, California, who can also drive a tractor. He graduated from the Kubert School and has been lettering comics since the days when foil-embossed covers were cool, working for Dark Horse (*The Fifth Beatle*, *I Am a Hero*, *StarCraft*, *Star Wars*, *Witcher*), Viz, Marvel, and DC Comics. He has submitted a request to the Department of Homeland Security that in the event of a zombie apocalypse he be put in charge of all digital freeway signs so citizens can be alerted to avoid nearby brain-eatings and the like. He finds the *Plants vs. Zombies* game to be a real stress-fest, but highly recommends the *Plants vs. Zombies* table on *Pinball FX2* for game-room hipsters.

ALSO AVAILABLE FROM DARK HORSE!

THE HIT VIDEO GAME CONTINUES ITS COMIC BOOK INVASION!

PLANTS VS. ZOMBIES: LAWNMAGEDDON
Crazy Dave—the babbling-yet-brilliant inventor and top-notch neighborhood defender—helps young adventurer Nate fend off a zombie invasion that threatens to overrun the peaceful town of Neighborville in *Plants vs. Zombies: Lawnmageddon*! Their only hope is a brave army of chomping, squashing, and pea-shooting plants! A wacky adventure for zombie zappers young and old!
ISBN 978-1-61655-192-6 | $10.99

THE ART OF PLANTS VS. ZOMBIES
Part zombie memoir, part celebration of zombie triumphs, and part anti-plant screed, *The Art of Plants vs. Zombies* is a treasure trove of never-before-seen concept art, character sketches, and surprises from PopCap's popular *Plants vs. Zombies* games!
ISBN 978-1-61655-331-9 | $9.99

PLANTS VS. ZOMBIES: TIMEPOCALYPSE
Crazy Dave helps Patrice and Nate Timely fend off Zomboss' latest attack in *Plants vs. Zombies: Timepocalypse*! This new standalone tale will tickle your funny bones and thrill your brains through any timeline!
ISBN 978-1-61655-621-1 | $10.99

PLANTS VS. ZOMBIES: BULLY FOR YOU
Patrice and Nate are ready to investigate a strange college campus to keep the streets safe from zombies!
ISBN 978-1-61655-889-5 | $10.99

PLANTS VS. ZOMBIES: GARDEN WARFARE VOLUME 1
Based on the hit video game, this comic tells the story leading up to the events in *Plants vs. Zombies: Garden Warfare 2*!
ISBN 978-1-61655-946-5 | $10.99

VOLUME 2
ISBN 978-1-50670-548-4 | $10.99

VOLUME 3
ISBN 978-1-50670-837-9 | $10.99

PLANTS VS. ZOMBIES: GROWN SWEET HOME
With newfound knowledge of humanity, Dr. Zomboss strikes at the heart of Neighborville . . . sparking a series of plant-versus-zombie brawls!
ISBN 978-1-61655-971-7 | $10.99

PLANTS VS. ZOMBIES: PETAL TO THE METAL
Crazy Dave takes on the tough *Don't Blink* video game—and challenges Dr. Zomboss to a race to determine the future of Neighborville!
ISBN 978-1-61655-999-1 | $9.99

PLANTS VS. ZOMBIES: BOOM BOOM MUSHROOM
The gang discover Zomboss' secret plan for swallowing the city of Neighborville whole! A rare mushroom must be found in order to save the humans aboveground!
ISBN 978-1-50670-037-3 | $10.99

PLANTS VS. ZOMBIES: BATTLE EXTRAVAGONZO
Zomboss is back, hoping to buy the same factory that Crazy Dave is eyeing! Will Crazy Dave and his intelligent plants beat Zomboss and his zombie army to the punch?
ISBN 978-1-50670-189-9 | $9.99

PLANTS VS. ZOMBIES: LAWN OF DOOM
With Zomboss filling everyone's yards with traps and special soldiers, will he and his zombie army turn Halloween into their zanier Lawn of Doom celebration?!
ISBN 978-1-50670-204-9 | $10.99

PLANTS VS. ZOMBIES: THE GREATEST SHOW UNEARTHED
Dr. Zomboss believes that all humans hold a secret desire to run away and join the circus, so he aims to use his "Big Z's Adequately Amazing Flytrap Circus" to lure Neighborville's citizens to their doom!
ISBN 978-1-50670-298-8 | $9.99

PLANTS VS. ZOMBIES: RUMBLE AT LAKE GUMBO
The battle for clean water begins! Nate, Patrice, and Crazy Dave spot trouble and grab all the Tangle Kelp and Party Crabs they can to quell another zombie attack!
ISBN 978-1-50670-497-5 | $9.99

PLANTS VS. ZOMBIES: WAR AND PEAS
When Dr. Zomboss and Crazy Dave find themselves members of the same book club, a literary war is inevitable! The position of leader of the book club opens up and Zomboss and Crazy Dave compete for the top spot in a scholarly scuffle for the ages!
ISBN 978-1-50670-677-1 | $9.99

PLANTS VS. ZOMBIES: DINO-MIGHT
Dr. Zomboss sets his sights on destroying the yards in town and rendering the plants homeless—and his plans include dogs, cats, rabbits, hammock sloths, and, somehow, dinosaurs . . . !
ISBN 978-1-50670-838-6 | $9.99

PLANTS VS. ZOMBIES: SNOW THANKS
Dr. Zomboss invents a Cold Crystal capable of freezing Neighborville, burying the town in snow and ice! It's up to the humans and the fieriest plants to save Neighborville—with the help of pirates!
ISBN 978-1-50670-839-3 | $10.99

PLANTS VS. ZOMBIES: A LITTLE PROBLEM
Will an invasion of teeny-tiny miniature zombies mean the party for Crazy Dave's two-hundred-year-old pants gets canceled?
ISBN 978-1-50670-840-9 | $10.99

PLANTS VS. ZOMBIES: BETTER HOMES AND GUARDENS
Nate and Patrice try thwarting zombie attacks by putting defending "Guardens" plants *inside* homes as well as in yards! But as soon as Dr. Zomboss finds out, he's determined to circumvent this plan with an epically evil one of his own . . .
ISBN 978-1-50671-305-2 | $9.99

PLANTS VS. ZOMBIES: MULTI-BALL-ISTIC
Dr. Zomboss turns the entirety of Neighborville into a giant, fully functional pinball machine! Nate, Patrice, and their plant posse must find a way to halt this uniquely horrifying zombie invasion. Will the battle go full-tilt zombies?!
ISBN 978-1-50671-307-6 | $10.99

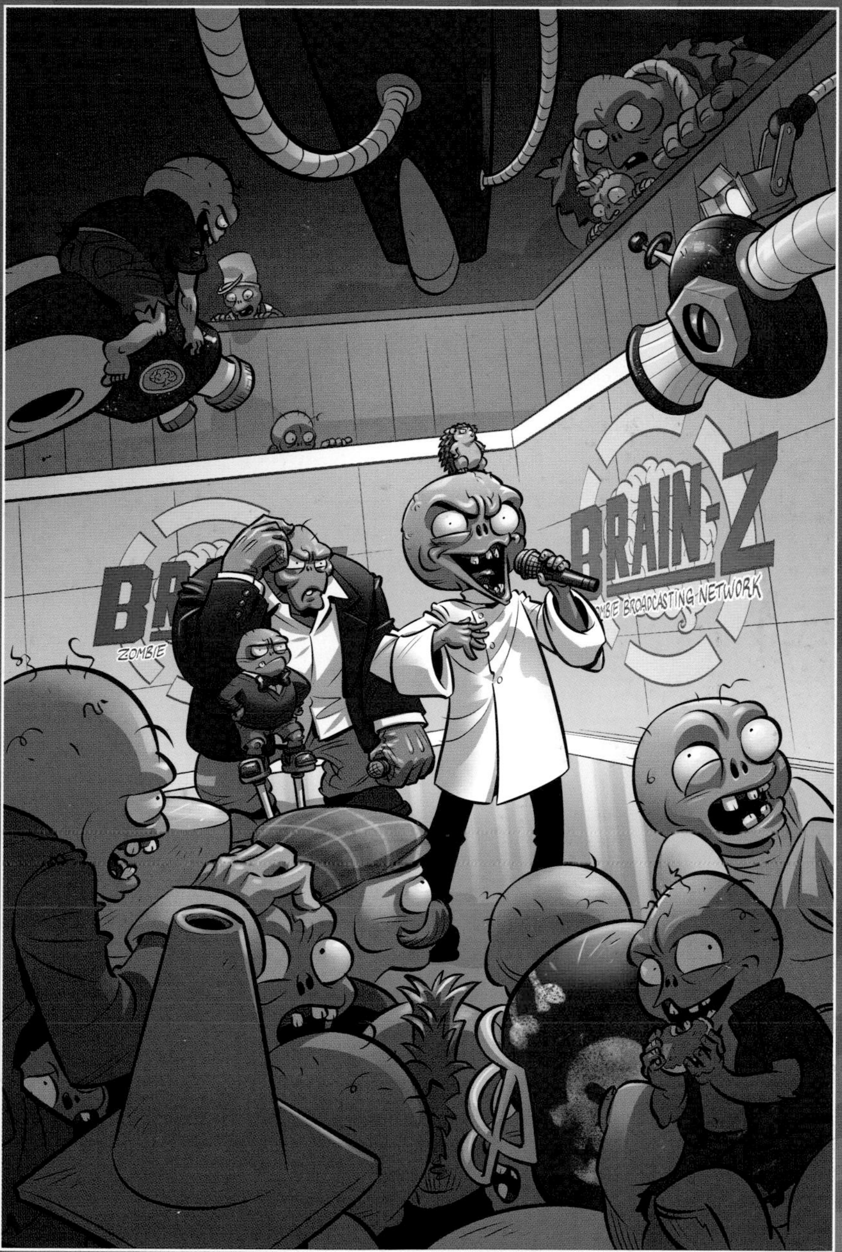
BRAIN-Z
BROADCASTING NETWORK
ZOMBIE

Our next exciting volume provides behind-the-scenes peeks at the secret schemes, ridiculous plans, and craziest contraptions concocted by the bizarre Dr. Zomboss, leader of the zombie army, as he proudly leads around a film crew from the Zombie Broadcasting Network. Crazy Dave has some silly schemes and convoluted contraptions of his own, though, to protect Neighborville's citizens and keep his plant friends healthy. With his niece Patrice, neighborhood hero Nate Timely, and his own army of powerful plants and strange inventions, Dave's ready to counter any frightening invasion that Zomboss can think up! Eisner Award-winning writer Paul Tobin (*Bandette*, *Genius Factor*) collaborates with artist Jesse Hamm (*Batman 66*, *Hawkeye*) for a brand-new *Plants vs. Zombies* graphic novel adventure—with beaming colors by Heather Breckel and lavish lettering by Steve Dutro!

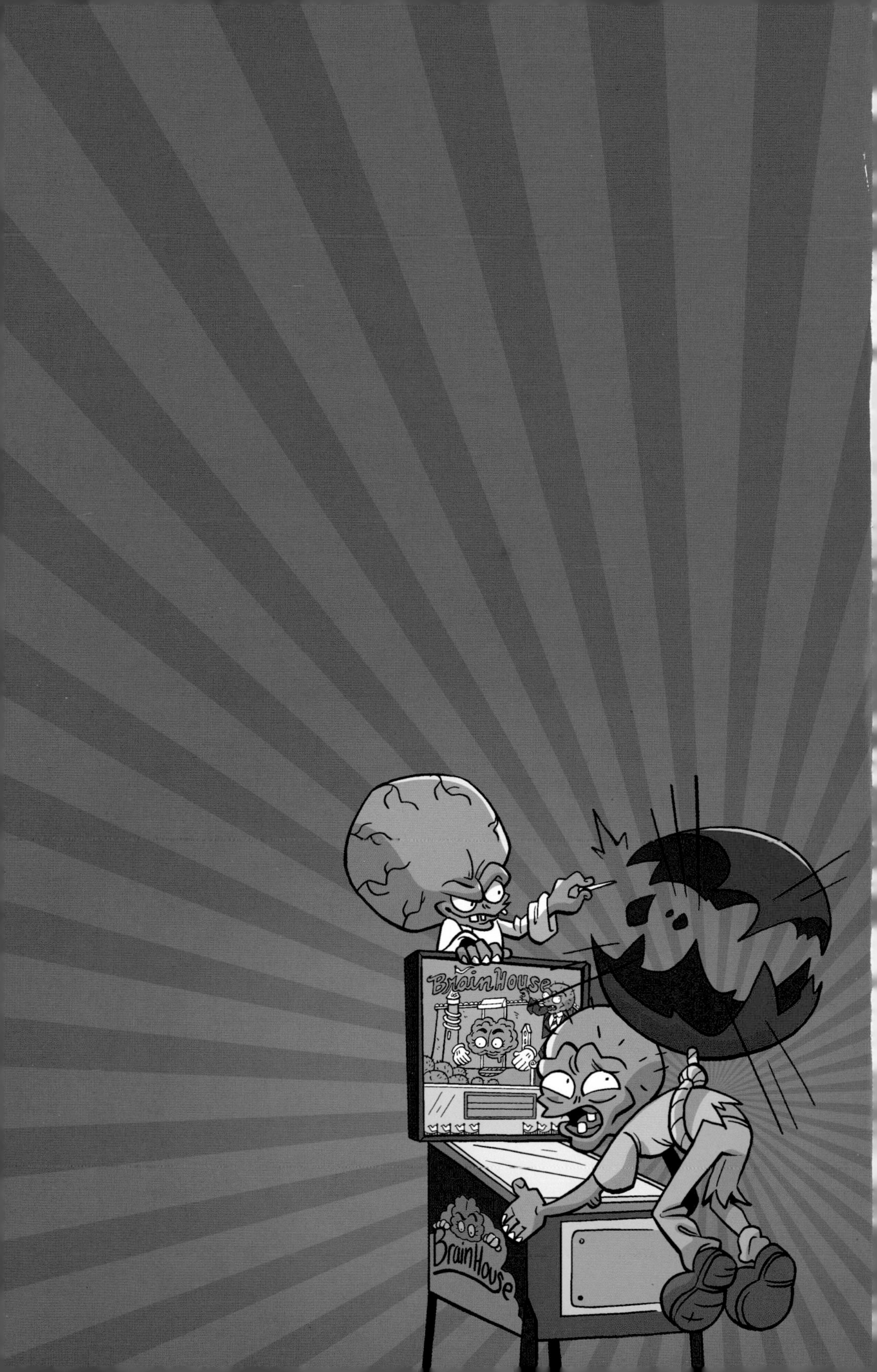
BrainHouse
BrainHouse

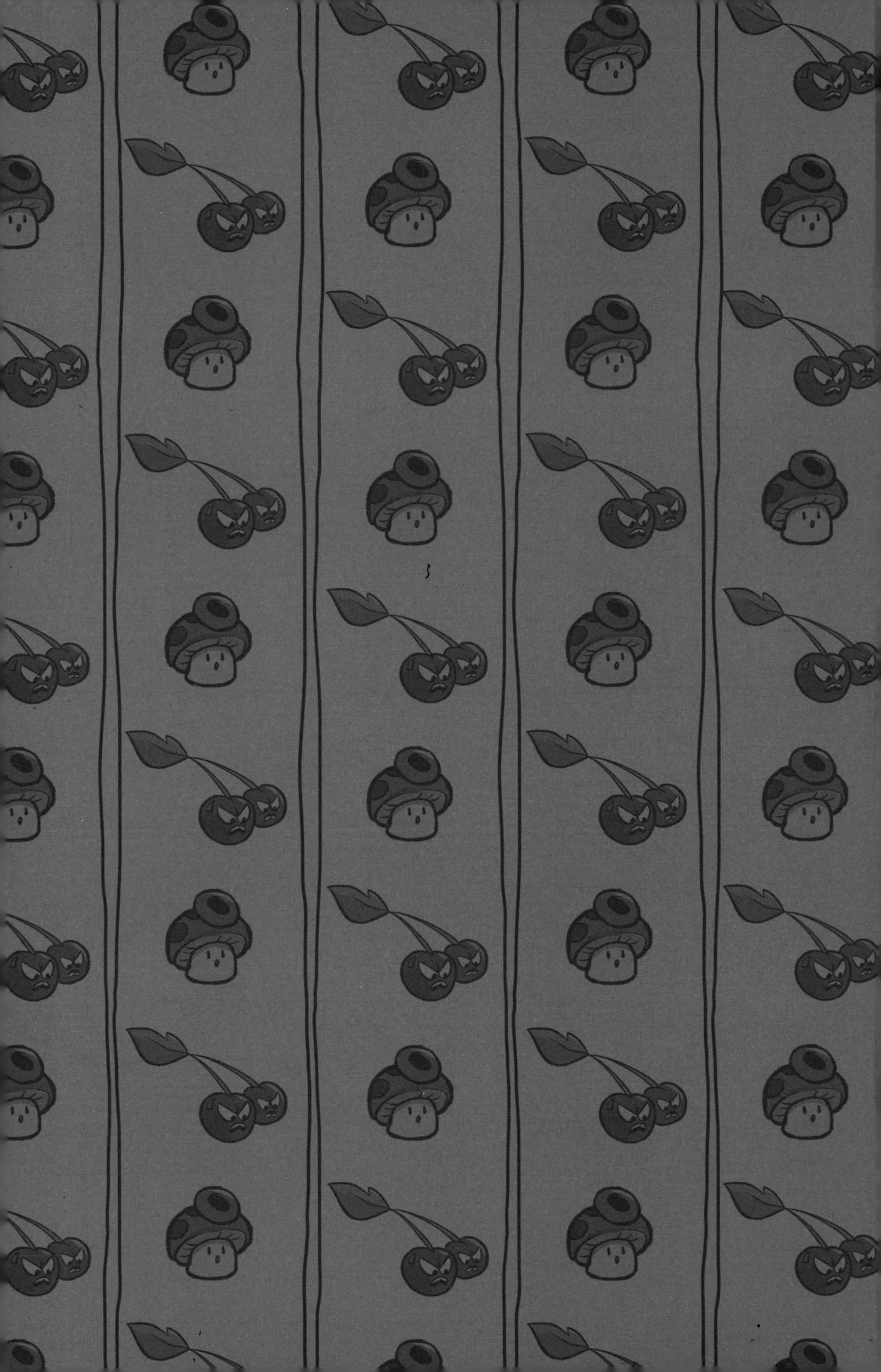